HEALING
THE FAE

HEALING THE FAE

DEEDRA MEADEN
AND
TRISHA HORNER

To order additional copies of this book, contact:
Xlibris
844-714-8691
www.Xlibris.com
Orders@Xlibris.com
819792

DEDICATION

To our families who supported us while we were writing this book.
The late nights and time away from you all did not go unnoticed.
This book would not be possible without you.

We love you.

PROLOGUE

Fae Realm, Summer 1457

Evilyn has entered the Fae Council room made up of black-with-white marble stone, the huge circular chandelier with layers of candles at the center of the room shining off the floor and walls being the only source of light. High-backed chairs made of the same marble line three of the four walls, and they are placed high so those who sit on the council are looking down to where she now stands at the center while waiting, unsure as to why they have called for her. The council is made up of blood-born mated Fae; each species has its own seat. Her parents are the last soul-mated vampire couple, meaning their hearts beat. This only happens when a vampire finds their soul mate, which has not happened to anyone in Evie's lifetime, making her the last blood-born from a mated vampire couple, which is another reason why her parents sit on the council for the vampire species. Her life has been full of love, happiness, and joy.

Stories have been told by humans about vampires and all Fae in general. Vampires are made to look like soulless, bloodsucking fiends who kill for sport. This can be true if a vampire is not born as Evie was from a mated couple, but a turned vampire. That usually happens when a vampire hits the lowest point in life. Loneliness, lack of love and soul mates in the Fae realm have caused the vampires to seek humans that they might just like, and try turning them in hopes that the bond created between them is strong enough. Humans who have either seen or remember being fed upon by a vampire have spread fear with the tales of their encounters, and this is where the stories come from. Because of the lack of soul mates, vampires are not coming before the council, but turning the humans without the council's approval. Humans are not supposed to be turned without the permission of the Fae Council. The vampire who turns them has to prove the reason why the human is to be turned, by showing he or she is pure of heart and a soul mate with good deeds done in their lifetime, who must agree to the transformation. This is not easily done, and as of Evie's birth 122 years ago, she has never heard of it happening. She is still young, only in her late teens by human standards, so the hope for her soul mate is still strong, and it could happen.

Evie, by all accounts, is beautiful. She is five feet ten inches tall; her eyes are the color of jade, wide and tilted up at the ends, giving her a catlike look, her nose is slim and tilted slightly at the tip, with full lips that are a natural pink, all set perfectly in her heart-shaped face. Her mahogany hair falls past her waist in waves. Her skin is pale and flawless, not a blemish to be seen. She is slender, ample breasts rounded and full, with hips meant for bearing children, long legs that any woman would envy and any man would long to feel wrapped around him. She is her father's kitten and her mother's greatest joy.

Evie is standing with her shoulders back and head up, hiding her fear, all the while wondering what she could have done to warrant the attention of the entire Fae Council. She looks at her parents as if to ask them what's going on; they are looking at her with love and utter devotion. Alfred, her father, whose green eyes sparkle with love for his family, hair the same color as her own, with no gray to show even at his 467 years of age. He stands six feet four inches tall; her mother says he is still as handsome as the day she met him. Amelia, her mother, also has green eyes, though her hair is a beautiful chocolate brown and falls clear to the floor in wave after wave, and shines slightly from the low light of the candles. Standing at five feet eleven inches, she is obviously where Evie gets her fair skin, when one looks upon the woman. Amelia was Evie's age when she married Alfred; they will be celebrating 339 years together come the Yule, and they are more in love than they were all those years ago. "Mama, Papa?"

"Do not worry, my love," her mother says, as if trying to calm her.

"Everything is fine, you are fine, kitten," says her father, using the nickname he has had for her as long as Evie can remember.

"But what have I done?" Fear is in Evie's voice. "Why am I here?"

"You have done nothing. It is us who need you," her father says matter-of-factly.

"Yes, dearling," her mother confirms.

"Me? Why would the entire Fae Council need me?" So many thoughts are running through her mind. She is the last blood-born vampire—could that have anything to do with why she is here, and if so, why would it?

"Just hang on. We are going to explain it all. Do not be frightened." Evie visibly relaxes, knowing she isn't in any trouble. But what could the council want?

"Evilyn?" says the booming voice of Edward, the mage council member.

"Yes?" Evie confirms.

"You are the last blood-born from soul-mated vampires?"

"Of course—what does that have to do with anything?" she answers, looking at her parents who have an apologetic look on their faces, because the mage is being an arrogant ass and questioning Evie as if she were a child. She looks back at Edward, who is tall, with dark hair, blue eyes, defined cheekbones, and square jaw and always seems to be frowning, she notices while he was awaiting her answer.

"The Fae Council needs a job done. You are the only one who can do as we ask because of you being a pure blood-born. This is not something we would normally ask, but with the Fae lines disappearing and no soul mates being produced, we do not have any choice," he states.

Evie is standing there, waiting for him to continue; he looks down at her with superiority, as if knowing he has the upper hand. Her mind is trying to think, what job could she be needed for that only she can do? Evie slowly looks around the room, waiting for any one of the other species to say something. Her eyes fall to her parents, who look as concerned as Evie did when she arrived. *Mama, Papa, what job are they going to ask me to do?* She sends the message using the mind link she and her parents share.

They don't answer right away, and Evie feels panic rise in her chest. *It is okay. Give him time to tell you.*

This is not something that has ever been asked of any Fae because it goes against everything we are and believe in.

Evie hears his reply in her head and sees a mental picture of her mother nodding in agreement and feels the reassuring energy as if Amelia is hugging her. Evie turns her attention back to Edward, and the council is still waiting for them to continue. Edward looks around the room to see if anyone else stands in an attempt to take this satisfaction from him, but knowing none of the Fae would dare to overstep his authority, he looks back at Evie, more than delighted to be the one giving this order. Her eyes meet his with a look of fear that has Edward smiling. Evie can't help but think he may be insane. "The council has come to the conclusion that with all our races dying out, we needed to consult with the seer. She has revealed that in order to save the Fae races, a blood-born vampire must search out the Finder. We know this Finder is of the human race. Evilyn, your job is to search for this human, turn them, and bring them to us."

Evie looks at him in shock and contempt. "Wh-what? Are you serious? But this goes against our laws! How am I going to turn a human who isn't my soul mate? Why would the council even ask this of me? What if the human goes rogue? The bloodlust alone could cost them their life. Mama, Papa, why does this fall to me? NO! I won't do it, I can't. You raised me to never do this, and now I'm being asked to do it?" Evie's surprise is clear to see on her face. She stands her ground and will say no, refusing to do it. Every council member is watching her, daring her to refuse.

"You are not getting a choice, Evilyn, because we are not asking you, we are telling you that you will do it, whether you like it or not. The Fae are dying out. We have already lost the unicorns, dragons, and the leprechauns will soon fade as well. I know we are asking a lot of you,

Evilyn, but you truly are the last vampire blood-born and the only one who can do this." Edward tries sounding as if he cares.

"What do you mean I don't have a choice? Are you forcing me to do this? I cannot say no?" Evie is close to tears.

"That is precisely what we are telling you. This will not count against you or your family in any way. It's the only option we have to save us all. If you do not do it, the Fae will die out and the magic does as well. The stories will end, and both our realm and the human realm will be impacted. The council has decided that this is our only hope. Do you understand what I am saying, Evilyn? We can't let that happen."

"And you all think I can do this? Make the right choice, find the Finder, and save us all?"

"This is a lot to ask of you but yes, Evilyn. You were born of love, raised with kindness, and your heart, though it doesn't beat, is pure. These are traits you are going to need, and these make you perfect for the job. The Fae are counting on you to help save us all."

Evie looks around the room; she can see all the Fae are worried and watching her. "Well, since I don't have a say in any of this, I will go and prepare for my journey."

With that and an enormous amount of anger, Evie turns to leave, without even looking back at her parents.

CHAPTER 1

Winter Cody, Wyoming

Aniya Filmore is almost finished with her twelve-hour shift at the hospital in the small town she grew up in. She could have had a job at any hospital she wanted, but she decided to stay close to her dad and Uncle Mike. At twenty-five years old, she is one of the youngest doctors in the United States; graduating high school at sixteen, she went straight to college before going to the University of Washington for med school, here in the good ole state of Wyoming. Aniya can remember the day she had decided to become a doctor.

Aniya and her family had come out of a restaurant, walking to their car, when a man that was taller than her father's six feet, dressed all in black with a leather jacket and face mask, pointed a gun at them and demanded her dad's wallet and mom's purse. Her father, Peter, fought the attacker, and the gun went off, the bullet hitting her mom in the chest. Someone in the parking lot must have seen or heard the commotion and called the police because they were there before the mugger could run off. Uncle Mike showed up right after the gunshot and caught Marriam before she hit the ground. He was a stranger at that point. Aniya had never seen him before. He pressed his hand to her mom's chest to try and stop the bleeding. Aniya, scared and crying, knelt down next to her mother. "Mommy, what's wrong? Mommy, please!" Aniya didn't understand what was happening, and her mother's last words still echo in her mind today. "Protect her."

Uncle Mike had replied with a simple "I promise."

Marriam went still, and Aniya watched as her mother took her last breath. From that day on, the stranger was known as Uncle Mike and was never far away; her father and he had become best friends, raising Aniya together. That was when she decided she wanted to be a doctor and save lives.

She was eight years old.

"Doctor?" The nurse named Jean slightly shook Aniya from her memories.

"Jean, please call me Aniya, and do you have something for me?" she asks, smiling.

"Yes, bed 3, her name is Rachel. She says she is having some pain in her ribs and stomach. Her boyfriend is with her." Jean tells her with a *be careful* look on her face. Aniya heads over, slowly opening the privacy curtain to give the occupants warning that she is coming in.

"Hello, Rachel, I'm Dr. Filmore. I hear you are having some abdominal pain?" she says, approaching the hospital bed.

"Yes, I . . . I fell," Rachel says, giving a side glance to the man next to her.

Aniya glances in the same direction. Seeing a nervous-looking guy, she asks, "And you are?"

"Nick—I'm Nick, Rachel's boyfriend."

"Well, Nick, I need to examine Rachel and take some x-rays. Would you mind waiting in the waiting room? You could go down to the cafeteria and get a cup of coffee. We are a bit busy, so this might take some time," she tells him, using her most persuasive voice, knowing he will obey her. She has always been able to do that—one of her gifts.

"Umm . . . Sure." Confusion on his face, he looks at Rachel and walks out.

Aniya waits until he is far enough away before looking at her patient. "Okay, let's take a look. Can you lift your shirt for me?" Rachel slowly and, with shaky hands, lifts her shirt; it appears she is afraid for anyone to see her.

Aniya can see why the minute her shirt comes up. Rachel's abdomen is severely bruised, as if someone punched her repeatedly. She knows exactly what happened to her and it sure as hell wasn't a fall. Aniya pulls out her stethoscope and asks Rachel, "Are you having any trouble breathing?"

"No," she tells Aniya, shaking her head.

"Take a deep breath for me?" Aniya asks, listening to her lungs and hearing the air move through them, letting her know that there are no issues with her breathing.

Continuing her examination, she presses on Rachel's stomach and asks if there is any pain. She uses her hands and focusing on her stomach and ribs, using another of her *gifts* to see inside her body, checking for any other injuries or internal damage. Aniya has been able to *look inside others* since she was a child, and her abilities have only become stronger as she has gotten older. These gifts helped her through med school and her hospital internships as well. She has never told anyone about her gifts and always makes sure she appears normal so her gifts are not exposed to the outside world. She also has the ability to see people's souls. This is a blessing and a curse because she can see the good and the bad souls of those she touches. Looking into Rachel, she can see that her soul is a pure white light, brightest around her heart. This tells her that the young woman is pure and she has a good soul. There is not a dark spot on her, making Aniya want to help her even more. Rachel is a bright light in a world where violence and darkness grow each and every day. "Okay, how about you tell me what really happened? I can't help you if you are not honest with me." Persuasion is in Aniya's voice so that Rachel will talk to her.

"He doesn't mean to hurt me—it was my fault. I made him angry. He said he was sorry." Rachel tries explaining, saying each word faster than the last so everything runs together.

Aniya looks at her and tries to calm her. "Ssshhhh, okay, okay, we don't have to talk about it right now. I don't think anything is broken, but I want x-rays to make sure."

"Oh, okay," Rachel says, taking a deep, calming breath.

Leaving the area and making sure to close the curtain, Aniya walks back to the nurses' station, where the nurse is sitting behind the desk.

"Hey, Jean, I have ordered x-rays for bed 3. Can you call the hospital therapist and send her in there? That young woman needs to talk to somebody. Her boyfriend has been beating the shit out of her for a while now."

"Absolutely, Doc—I mean, Aniya." The nurse smiles as she sees the look she was given.

Aniya walks back over to Rachel and says as she closes the curtain, "Okay, I ordered your x-rays. Now . . . next to Nick, do you have any family we can call, parents, a sister maybe?" She uses her persuasive voice again, so the information is given freely.

"Umm, yes, my parents live in the next town over. I could call them. Can you hand me my phone?"

"Sure." Smiling, Aniya reaches for the phone that is sitting on top of Rachel's purse on the chair next to the bed and hands it to her.

"Thanks, do you think they will come? I haven't spoken to them in months. We had an argument because I left to live with Nick and they don't approve of him."

Aniya replies, "Yes, I do. You are their daughter and they love you. It doesn't matter what occurred, your parents love you and will always be there for you." Having reassured Rachel, Aniya turns to leave so Rachel can make her call.

"Hey, Doc, the therapist is on her way down."

"Thanks, Jean."

"No problem, do I need to call the police?"

"Not yet. I want to get the x-rays first. I need to see if I can get an idea of how often this is happening." Aniya believes she already knows the answer but also knows it's better to have evidence, especially if the cops get involved. "But we might need to. I'll let you know, Jean."

"Dr. Filmore, you sent for me?"

"Hey, Bess, yes, bed 3 looks to have some domestic abuse going on. Would you mind? The girl's name is Rachel."

"Look, Aniya, you know as well as I do that girls in these types of situations don't always think they need help or they are too afraid to ask for help, so she might not say anything to me at all."

"I know, but I think she does want help, just doesn't know how to ask for it."

"Okay, I'll talk to her, and you know that if there is any abuse, it will have to be reported, and that is where the problems come in. She might not want to press charges."

"I know. I already have Jean on standby. I want the x-rays first, and if there is any proof, the cops will be called," Aniya reassures Bess.

"Okay, then here I go." And with that, Bess disappears behind the curtain.

A while later, the phone on Aniya's desk rings; the voice on the other end tells her that the x-ray team has headed down to pick up Rachel.

"Thanks," she answers, then hangs up the phone and turns to leave her office, but before she can reach the door, it's swung open from the other side and Bess comes through, not waiting for an invite. "That girl has definitely been beaten repeatedly for months now."

"I thought so, damn it," Aniya says, exhaling the breath she didn't realize she had been holding. "I was just on my way to see her, x-ray is on their way."

"Her parents just arrived—that's why I left. I thought maybe they might need a minute. It's time to call the police. We can't let that girl leave with him."

"I need to wait on the x-rays so I have undeniable proof, if there is any. I will make sure he goes to jail and she leaves with her parents."

"And if she doesn't press charges, or won't go with her parents?"

"She will. I have a way of convincing people to do what they need to. Rachel has a feel to her—there is something special about her. I just don't know what it is. I have to help her or at least try."

"Well, good luck with that," Bess says as she turns and walks out of the office.

Aniya knows she won't have a problem getting Rachel away from Nick. Persuasion can be a powerful thing, and she has used her gift in similar situations. She walks back to the ER, going straight to bed 3, pulling the curtain aside, but Rachel isn't there. "Jean, where is Rachel?"

"X-ray came to get her. They said they called you?"

"They did, but I thought I would arrive here before them. I didn't want to scare her."

"She seemed okay, her parents were with her and she was smiling, so I'm sure she is fine, Doc."

Aniya smiles and nods at Jean. "I'm going to go over these charts while I wait for her x-rays to come in. If anyone needs me, I'll be in my office." She grabs a pile of folders off the nurses' station and turns to walk down the hall back to her office.

About forty-five minutes later, she is reviewing the x-rays, and they confirm what she already knew; she can see that both of Rachel's arms, left wrist, and two fingers on her right hand have signs of healing fractures. Well, it's time to involve the police. She starts walking back to where Rachel is waiting, stopping by the nurses' station to tell Jean to call the police. As Aniya approaches bed 3, she can hear Nick accusing Rachel of saying something to her about what really happened. The poor girl is denying she said anything and is apologizing for having to come to the hospital, saying she just hurt really bad. Aniya doesn't give any warning; she throws the curtain aside. Nick turns around fast, looking at her, anger on his face, but hoping to mask the look, adds a smile. Too late—Aniya saw the look but pretended not to. Using persuasion, she smiles and says, "Hello, how was the coffee?" Aniya looks at Rachel so that she knows she isn't alone.

"Um . . . fine, Doc. Can we leave now?" Nick asks. "I'm sure Rachel wants to go home and rest." He is trying to sound thoughtful.

Aniya doesn't need a special gift to hear the lie in his words. Walking over to him, she puts her hand on his arm, as if to show comfort, and focuses on his soul. She waits for the picture in her head to form. As it does, she can see that his soul is as black as a starless night, with no moon for even a sliver of light to combat the dark. He is pure evil. Aniya lets go of him and looks at Rachel.

"We got your x-rays back." Looking in Nick's direction, she asks, "Would you mind going to get Rachel's parents, please?" She pushes all her persuasive energy into her words so that he has no other choice but to obey.

"Yeah, I'll go get them." Anger and confusion are in his words.

"Thank you." Aniya looks at Rachel and listens for Nick's steps to get farther away.

"I've seen your x-rays. I can see that this isn't the first time you've been to the hospital with similar injuries."

"He doesn't mean to hurt me," Rachel whispers, more to herself than to Aniya.

"He has broken both of your arms, a wrist, and at least two fingers."

"How do you know that?"

"I'm a doctor—it's my job. Now I'm going to have to report this. The police are already on the way here. I want you to tell them what really happened, and you will press charges. He will eventually kill you if you stay with him. Nothing is broken this time, but you have some deep bruising, you are going to be sore for a few weeks. Rachel, please go home with your parents. You have a bright future ahead of you, but you have got to get away from him if you wish to see it. So tell me you will follow my instructions."

"Okay, yes, Doctor, I will. I want to take back my life and be happy, but it is so scary, he . . . is so scary." Rachel tenses when she hears footsteps.

"It's okay. Don't worry—you are safe." Aniya assures Rachel by giving her hand a squeeze, when the curtain opens and her parents come through.

"Rachel, Nick said the doctor was here?"

"Yes, I'm the doctor, Mr.?"

"Walker, James Walker, call me Jim, please."

"I'm Rachel's mother, Tish Walker. Is she all right?" Worry is in her voice as she turns to Aniya. "You are the doctor? You look so young."

"I am—my name is Dr. Filmore. Rachel has some deep bruising to her abdomen and ribs. Nothing is broken—she just needs some rest and no strenuous activities for a few weeks. Rachel, are you going home with your parents?"

"Yes, I am—" Rachel is cut off by the sound of scuffling on the other side of the curtain.

"Let me go, you sons of bitches! Rachel, Rachel, tell them it wasn't me, tell them you just fell! Tell them!" Nick shouts.

"You hit me, Nick, over and over again. I'll tell them everything you've done!" Rachel yells back, followed by an "I NEVER WANT TO SEE YOU AGAIN!" that everyone in the ER could most definitely hear.

"The police are going to need your statement, and while you are doing that, I'm going to write you up a prescription for the pain and work on getting you out of here so you can go home," Aniya tells her and walks through the curtain and toward the nurses' station, just in time to see Nick being led out of the hospital in handcuffs, still swearing at the police.

"Jean, can you please get her discharge papers ready so she can go with her parents after the police are done with her? I am going home after I finish my report and give the police all the information I have."

"Will do, Aniya. Get some rest. Have a good night." Smiling, Jean waves at Aniya as she heads to her office to finish up.

"You as well," she says, waving back.

A little while later, Aniya walks out of the hospital and pulls out her cell phone to dial her dad's number. While waiting for the call to connect, she searches for her wallet and starts walking to her favorite cafe, which is right across the street from the hospital.

"Hello?" Peter Filmore answers the call on the second ring.

"Hey, Daddy."

"Sweetie, hi, how was work, are you off?"

"Yes, I'm off, and it was okay. There was a bit of a situation, but I'll tell you about it later."

"Oh, okay, are you coming by? Maybe you could stay for dinner? I'm making your favorite."

"Um, yeah, I can come by and have dinner. Better than hitting a fast food place or ordering Chinese again. Is Uncle Mike going to be there?"

"Yes, actually, he is already here, we are watching the game. See you in a few, then?"

"Sounds good."

"Oh, would you mind stopping at the bakery on your way over? I thought I had cornbread, but I'm all out."

"Sure, is there anything else you need?"

"Nope, I think that's it. See you soon. Love you."

"Love you too, Dad. Bye."

Aniya disconnects the call as she heads into the little corner cafe for her usual coffee. She isn't paying attention as she's walking, trying to put her phone back in her purse, and runs into what feels like a brick wall. Her phone falls out of her hand and onto the floor. Murmuring a quiet "damn it" to herself, she looks up to see what she hit. It wasn't a brick wall but the broad chest of a very tall man.

"Oh shoot, I'm sorry." Aniya bends to pick up her phone off the floor where it had fallen. When she rises and looks up into the deepest forest-green eyes she has ever seen, a hundred butterflies take off in her stomach and heart. He is looking at her in confusion, almost as if he doesn't understand her at all. His jet-black hair is cut short, military style maybe; he is at least a foot taller than her 5'8", making him well over six feet tall. Aniya has to tilt her head back just to look at his face. His square clean-shaven jaw looks smooth to the touch. Wanting to find out for herself, Aniya almost reaches out to touch him, his lips full and perfect for kissing. His strong nose is straight, and those eyes—the good Lord certainly blessed this man. If women had wet dreams, he would be what caused them. He is muscular but not so built that she wouldn't be able to wrap her arms around him. His shirt stretches over his wide chest and stomach, outlining the six-pack many men would spend hours in the gym to achieve. Fitted blue jeans cover his narrow waist and his legs and calves; his well-proportioned body could be the star of the next male stripping movie, and Aniya would pay just to see it. She can see that he is pale but not an unhealthy pale. Maybe he doesn't get out in the sun much, but him with a tan, Aniya doesn't even want to try and picture that; there is no time for a cold shower.

"I'm sorry, I didn't see you." But how she missed him she has no idea.

He just keeps looking at her as if puzzled. Aniya goes to step around him, and he steps in the same direction. She steps the other way at the same time he does, blocking her again but not intentionally. Finally, she holds up her hands, signaling for him to stop. She then moves around, motioning with her hand for him to go ahead and go. He hesitates for one second, looking at her again before he starts walking between tables to the front of the cafe, turning one more time to look at her before he goes through the doors. Aniya watches him leave, wishing he wouldn't before turning around and heading to the counter.

"Hiya, Hope, how are you?" Aniya greets the barista behind the register.

"Hey, Aniya, I'm good. Your usual?" Hope is one of those girls who are pretty without trying. A ponytail and sweats would look good on her. Her blond hair is usually pulled up away from her face, blue eyes sparkling every time she sees her. She is smaller than Aniya, with a nice rack and small curves in all the right places. Aniya has more of an hourglass shape to her.

"Yes, please. Thank you."

"Sure thing—that'll be $6.50, please." Aniya hands over a ten-dollar bill and tells her to keep the change, with a smile.

"Thanks," Hope tells her as she hands over the coffee.

"See you tomorrow, bright and early."

"Absolutely."

Aniya turns and leaves the cafe. Once outside, she starts walking toward the bakery, before getting to her car and driving to her father's. Pulling into the driveway of her childhood home and putting the car in park, she gathers her purse, keys, coffee, and the cornbread then proceeds toward the front door.

"Dad, Uncle Mike?" she calls out, shutting the door behind her. The house smells of the chili her father has, no doubt, spent most of the day making. She always loved the way the house smelled: her father's Old Spice cologne, cinnamon, with a hint of the forest, all mixed together.

"In the living room, honey!" Peter calls out.

"Your dad is mad that my team is winning." Humor is in Uncle Mike's voice.

"They are cheating!"

"You just don't want to pay up the twenty dollars you're going to owe me when your team loses."

"Hey, I said no more betting after the last time this happened." She scolds them both while smiling, walking over to kiss her father on the cheek and give him a hug before moving to do the same to Uncle Mike.

"We are just having a little fun, is all. Dinner is just about finished." Peter watches his daughter move to the kitchen to check on the chili and set her items and the cornbread on the counter.

"For now, until it's time to pay up. I'll set the table." Chuckling at them, she moves to get bowls from the cupboard.

"Twenty minutes till it's done," she calls out after giving the chili a stir.

"Come and sit for a minute. You've been on your feet for hours. Take a break. That hospital works you too hard for too long."

"You know I love my job. I feel fine."

"We know, but everyone needs a break. Now come sit." Uncle Mike pats the seat next to him, backing up her father.

Rolling her eyes, she moves to sit down. With the table set and the chili about done, there wasn't much to do but what they asked anyway; she knows she could sway her father or Uncle Mike separately, but not both of them together. She wouldn't even try; she was too tired to use all that energy. She tucks her feet under her as she sits; her eyes move to the television.

"You look tired—did something happen at work today that you would like to talk about?"

"Just busy, and I had to call the police about a case today."

"You know you can't keep getting involved in stuff like that."

"Dad, it's my job. I'm required by law to report all incidents involving abuse. Don't worry, everything turned out fine," Aniya assures him and proceeds to tell them about Rachel and Nick, hoping it will ease their minds a bit, knowing he is behind bars and she is home safe with her parents and has no serious injuries.

"See, no reason to worry, it all worked out. Time to eat, let's go," she tells them, hoping to change the subject. She should have known that wouldn't work; it never has before, but it wouldn't stop her from trying.

"You need to be more careful, Aniya. You put yourself in danger every time you get involved like this. One day, you might not be so lucky, and I wouldn't know what to do if something happened to you." Her father walks over to her and softly clasps her shoulders and pulls her in for a hug.

"I know, I'm just doing my job, and part of that is having to report abuse. Besides, I have you and Uncle Mike looking out for me. It's fine and I'm fine." She hugs him back.

"Your father is right, you know. You need to be careful." Uncle Mike has moved over to stand next to them.

"Always." She nods to them both before moving to the stove to retrieve the chili, making sure to grab pot holders to carry the pan to the table.

"Okay, good, now let's eat," Peter says, seating himself at the table, clasping his hands and rubbing them together.

"Thanks, Dad, this really is one of my favorites." She smiles and fills her bowl before passing the ladle to Uncle Mike.

They eat and discuss events that have happened since the last time they had dinner a week prior. Not much to discuss, considering Aniya has only been to work. Most emergency rooms, especially those in big cities, can be an exciting place on a busy day, but her hospital is in a small town in a rural area of Wyoming, so a busy day for her usually consists of a couple sprained ankles, food poisoning, and maybe an occasional car accident and that is if it's a crazy night. Her thoughts return to the man she quite literally ran into at the cafe, remembering the odd sensation of what felt like a spark igniting deep in her soul. It was not something she had ever experienced before and it had her a bit concerned, but before she could think about it much longer, her father's voice pulled her away from her thoughts.

"Aniya, are you okay? You look as if you are deep in thought."

"Yeah, I'm fine. It's just I ran into this guy at the cafe earlier, and I got this rather strange feeling in my chest and stomach. I was just trying to figure it out—that's all. Do you really want to talk with me about boys?" she tells him with a grin, rising to clean off the table and start the dishes.

"What kind of feeling? You know you can talk to me about anything. I'll always listen."

"It's nothing. I'll probably never see him again anyway." Aniya shrugs with a smile.

Mike hasn't said a word; he has been listening intently to what Aniya had been saying. It's time for him to go and visit an old friend and ask a few questions. What she is feeling could be nothing but it might also be something, and if it is what he thinks it might be, he has a lot of explaining to do. Mike is pulled from his thoughts by Peter, who is still talking to Aniya.

"Well, if you are sure. And don't worry about the dishes."

"I'm just about done. I do need to get going though, I have work tomorrow." Aniya dries her hands on a dish towel before hanging it back on the oven door.

"I have a business trip this week, so I won't be in town for a few days." Mike tells them both, deciding to use that to explain his absence over the next few days. There are probably a few things that will change for Aniya, and he is going to need all the help he can get if he wants to help get her through it.

"Just be careful while you're away." Aniya kisses his cheek and gathers her things to leave. "I'll see you soon, Daddy. Love you both." She kisses her father on the cheek on her way to the door.

"Love you too," Mike and Peter tell her in unison, watching her leave.

A few days later, Aniya is done with a particularly slow day at the ER, where she had time to finish the book she was reading. She decides to stop by the library to pick up her favorite author's new vampire romance novel. Grabbing her things, she leaves the hospital and walks the short distance to the library. Walking through the automatic doors, she smiles at the woman behind the desk before handing her the book she had just finished. Scanning the library for the new releases, she sees him. The man from the cafe is standing and looking over what appears to be a file of some sort. Her stomach explodes into butterflies once more, and the heat feels warmer at her core.

Aniya approaches the man to see if he will talk to her this time.

"Hello again, I would like to apologize to you for the other day. I was preoccupied and didn't see you." She is looking up into his handsome face, but it seems different. He looks at her with confusion once again.

"Do you not speak English? I haven't seen you around here before the other day."

"Um, nay, I'm nae from around here. We just moved here." His Scottish accent is slight, giving Aniya a clue to where he may be from.

It seems as if he has never met her and his confusion is genuine. They didn't speak the other day; he couldn't have possibly forgotten her. She literally walked right into him.

"I'm Aniya Filmore. Are you looking into the history of our little town?" She gestures toward the city files he is holding.

"Aye, actually, I was curious about this area."

"Okay, well, I just wanted to apologize for running into you the other day, so I'm sorry. Good luck with your research though. Have a good day." With that, she turns and walks away. Aniya doesn't get his name again. Why didn't she ask him? And that heat in her chest and stomach has her in a bit of panic, not understanding what is happening. She collects her book and leaves the library, when her phone begins to ring, catching her off guard. She reaches in her purse, praying it isn't the hospital calling her in, and a sigh of relief escapes from her when she sees *Uncle Mike* displayed on the screen.

"Hey, how's the business trip going?" She answers the phone.

"My business trip? Oh right, yeah, it's been fine, you know, meetings and such. Hey, ah, can you come to your dad's tomorrow night?" he asks her, sounding a bit anxious. "We have a few things we need to talk about, and I have a gift for you. I'll be flying in tomorrow morning."

"Yeah, sure. Is everything okay? You sound worried. Is Dad okay, did something happen?" Concern is in her voice.

"No, no, everything is fine, especially your father. I just need to talk to you. Don't worry. Can you come?"

"Yes, it's my day off, so it shouldn't be a problem." The concern in her voice is gone, but now she is curious.

"Okay, great. I'll see you tomorrow."

Aniya disconnects the call as she moves to put the phone away. She begins to wonder what gift he could have for her and why the urgency in his voice and what could have happened in the last few days that he would need to talk to her about. Well, she will find out tomorrow. He said it was nothing bad. One can only hope, Aniya thinks to herself while walking to her car, not realizing that her life is about to be turned upside down in more ways than one.

CHAPTER 2

Broden McKesson's heart is beating. It's been 223 years since his heart beat. Evie had said that it would never beat again because of the lack of soul mates among the Fae. It's a slow beat but there all the same. Evie had mentioned how hard it would be to find a soul mate before she had turned him and his brother in 1797. After explaining everything to him and his brother, she told them it was their choice and she would turn them into vampires only if they agreed. The Fae Council had forced Evie on this search, and she refused to force it upon them. She isn't like the vampires of the human stories they had heard as lads.

"I'll return in two days for your answers. I know this doesn't seem fair and this shouldn't fall on the shoulders of two young men. I wouldn't even ask if there was any other way. You are important, and I promise I will help you on this journey and will be there for you both," she told them both, kissing them each on their foreheads before she walked away.

Broden can hardly believe what is happening. The thought of finding his soul mate had never crossed his mind. He wasn't even looking for her, yet here she is. The woman is beautiful. A gift he never thought he would receive is standing twenty-five feet from him. Oh shite, what in the hell is he going to tell his brother? What is he supposed to do, walk up to the lass announcing who he is, throw her over his shoulder, and run out with her? That might have worked in eighteenth-century

Scotland, but in the twenty-first-century United States, it's kidnapping. She is human as well, and that is a whole different problem all in itself. Broden couldn't help but watch the bonny lass, from outside the cafe.

Brother, I need ye to meet me at the inn. I have news.

Broden sends on their mind link.

Is all weel, are ye in need of me?

All is fine, dinna worry.

Aye, be there soon.

Broden is pacing the floor in their room while waiting for his brother. How is he to explain any of this, and will Brodrick be supportive? He can't see his brother disapproving, but will he be happy for him?

Brodrick walks through their hotel room door. Approaching, he can see his brother looks a little lost but is also smiling. What the bloody hell is going on?

"Brother, are ye weel?"

"Aye, aye, I am better than. Do ye hear it?" Broden begins.

"Ye said you have news. What news? Do I hear what?" Brodrick replies, wondering if his brother has gone mad.

"I have found her."

"Ye found the mage? Where is she, then?"

"Och, nay, no' the mage—*her*, brother. I have found my soul mate. Can ye nae hear my heart?" Looking for any sign of understanding, Broden waits patiently.

Brodrick's eyes go wide and his mouth falls agape, then realization crosses his face. "Nay, her? Truly? Ye found yer mate?"

"Aye, I have." Happiness is written all over his face.

"And ye are sure that 'tis her?"

"Aye, listen." Broden stands silently still.

Brodrick listens intently and hears the *thud . . . thud . . . thud* of his brother's heart, a slow beat but there just the same. "Aye, I hear it. I am truly happy for ye." Hugging him, Brodrick gives him a solid pat on the back. "We will celebrate later tonight. I was looking into the town's history when I heard yer call. Let me finish with that and then ye can tell me all about ye and yer bonny lass, aye?" Brodrick smiles at his brother before walking over to the door.

"Aye."

Brodrick nods to a smiling Broden and leaves the room.

Broden has found his soul mate! He is happy for his brother, but what is to happen to him? Will he be able to watch Broden and his mate, knowing he might never find his own? Will the bond he and his brother have always had stay strong when his brother's heart beats and his doesn't? What of his brother's mate? How will she feel about this search they have undertaken, with all the traveling? Will she come? Brodrick cannot see his brother wanting to spend so much time away from his soul mate.

Will I have to continue the search on my own, without my brother at my side? Is that even a possibility?

A mate was never in the plans for either of them. Is there a mate out there for him as well? Now that one of them has found his soul mate, so many things will change. Brodrick's head hurts with all the questions he has and with all that has just occurred. He walks slowly back into the library, hoping to use the research as a distraction after deciding he will sort it all out later. For the next couple of days, he keeps busy with the research on the town, avoiding his brother, not that it was a hard task. Broden has spent every waking moment he could at that damned cafe, waiting for his soul mate to show herself again. How do ye meet the one meant for ye and not get her name? Brodrick thinks with a shake of his head. He has been in the library, looking at paper after paper and file after file for days now, trying to find any sign of a mage or magical being. There has to be some sort of sign, but there is nothing.

I would think there would be rumors of magic, but I cannae find a ritual site or a place of magic.

There has to be a reason why both he and his brother were drawn to this town. Broden was probably drawn here because of his soul mate, but he still feels like he has to be here as well. Not finding anything in a town where a mage or any Fae is thought to be is very unusual. Even a new mage has to practice magic; they have to learn their craft. So there should be some scorched trees or maybe even a store of witchcraft somewhere in a town this small, but there is nothing, nothing at all, no suspicious people or unexplained happenings, just nothing. Brodrick is frustrated; he's been searching for this mage who is supposed to help save the Fae, looking at newspaper articles and historical documents, book after book on the town's folklore, or fairy tales, as the Americans call it, with nothing to go on but what a seer said and a feeling. Now he doesn't even have his brother to help because Broden is more concerned with his soul mate than this search that they decided to do together and turned vampire for, all those years ago. What is the use of having a soul mate if the Fae won't be around much longer and it all vanishes?

"Hello again, I would like to apologize for the other day. I was so preoccupied I didn't see you." The most beautiful voice he has ever heard forces him out of his mental anguish.

"I haven't seen you around here before the other day. Are you from around these parts?"

Lifting his head, he sees the most perfectly blue eyes he has ever known, looking back at him. Lost in her eyes, he begins to feel the beat of his heart. Brodrick is so lost in his thoughts that he misses most of the questions she had asked before answering. "Um, nay, I'm nae from around here. We just moved here." He does not hide his Scottish brogue. His heartbeat seems to speed up.

"I'm Aniya Filmore."

Brodrick's heart beats a little faster, starting off slow but picking up the more the woman, Aniya, talks to him. She is standing in front of him, doing her best to look up into his eyes. He is looking down at her in bewilderment. Aniya's eyes are a sparkling blue like that of the Scottish sky after a storm and are almond shaped with no hint of makeup. Brodrick is not fond of those women who paint their faces so much that you cannot see the real girl underneath. Moving down her oval face, he sees she has a nose that is not too wide and perfectly straight, her lips are full and lush, damned kissable, her chin slightly pointed. Her breasts are the size of honeydew melons and would fill a man's hands, her stomach not flat but perfect for his hands to rub down; he is fine with something to hold on to. Her hips, somewhat plump, give her an hourglass figure. He has always been attracted to women with curves—nothing better than bedding a woman who has a bit extra to kiss on. Brodrick aches to pull her to him so he can see how she would feel against him, his cock nestled against her. Just the thought has him growing hard.

"Are you looking into the history of our little town?"

Her words pull him from his thoughts again. "Aye, actually, I am curious about the area."

"Well, I just wanted to apologize for running into you the other day, so I'm sorry. Good luck with your research though. Have a good day." And with that, she turns and walks away.

Brodrick didn't even give her his name, he thinks as he watches her swaying hips moving away from him. Evie had told him what to expect if he ever found his soul mate, but he had never known it would feel so strong, and this was so unexpected. What the hell is happening? His confusion knocking him senseless was not something he was accustomed to. Realization hit him with every beat of his heart. He found her, his soul mate, the one meant for him. Happiness, hope, and joy are coursing through him. He and Broden have both found their soul mates. They will not have to separate and can keep working on finding this mage together; they can save the Fae and have a chance at a life once all of this is done. Like his brother's, his soul mate is human, and with that thought, Brodrick feels the dread and fear spread through him.

Aniya leaves the library; stopping by her car, she drops the book she had just picked up in the front seat of her car, before heading to the grocery store. She enters the store and grabs a shopping basket and walks over to the produce section.

Broden finally sees her again, walking into the grocery store. Hoping to at least get her name, he jogs over to the store. Entering the front of the building he scans the surrounding area and finds her with the fresh vegetables. Grabbing a cart, he heads in her direction, not entirely sure how to approach the woman and get her talking. He is standing next to her, hoping she won't notice he's staring but praying she will see him.

"Hello again." Broden speaks a little loudly, trying to get her attention, but instead, he causes her to jump.

"Oh my gosh." The deep masculine voice makes Aniya jump, one hand going to her heart and the other to her stomach as the butterflies once again take flight and the heat in her chest goes from warm to hot in a second, causing her to sharply inhale.

"Lass, are ye all right? I did nae mean to frighten ye." Broden feels his heart speed up to a normal human pace as if her voice alone helped to regulate the beat.

"I wanted to properly introduce myself to ye. I am Broden McKesson and ye are?" he asks.

"Oh, umm, didn't I just . . . Aniya Filmore," she answers, trying and failing to calm the butterflies and cool the heat coming from her core. Something in the deepest part of her feels like it's awakening and rising up, a piece of her that has been locked away, one she didn't even know was there. What is it, and how could she not have known it existed?

"That's a bonny name, lass. May I call ye Aniya?" Broden's voice pulls her from her thoughts.

"Yes, of course, that's fine."

"Aniya." Broden likes how her name sounds rolling off his tongue.

"I am new to this area and haven't really met anyone but ye. Would ye mind showing me around a wee bit and then mayhap having dinner with me? My way of showing ye my gratitude and to say thank ye for yer time." He gives her a grin that would send any girl to her knees.

"Um, sure, sounds great," she answers, trying not to sound too eager. Who wouldn't want to spend some time with a sexy, gorgeous man who has a Scottish accent that sends shivers straight to the junction between her thighs, causing moisture to gather there every time he talks?

"Does Friday work for you?"

"Oh shoot, I'm working until five on Friday. Are you okay with a late dinner, say, seven? That is kind of late to go sightseeing though," Aniya murmurs, biting on her bottom lip.

"Friday is fine for a late sup, we can sightsee on yer next day off, if that is fine with ye. We can even do it early morn so you can still enjoy yer day off, if ye would like, Aniya?"

"That sounds great!" It feels as if he is claiming her every time he says her name, and she doesn't even care because it feels so good and so, so right.

The light inside her is so bright but also incomplete, like a piece of it is still missing. Aniya hasn't felt anything like this before. After her mom was killed, she felt the loss, but it was nothing like what she feels now: pieces being put together but parts are still missing. It is the strangest feeling. She is becoming whole, but there are parts still needing to be found and pieced together. It seems Broden McKesson is part of this puzzle, and she didn't realize there was one. And why does she feel like she is a big piece to an even bigger puzzle?

"May I have a way of contacting ye, lass, a phone number, mayhap?"

"Oh yes, I'm sorry. Here." Aniya hands him her business card with her cell phone number on the back.

"Thank ye, and I will make sure to send a message so ye will ken my number as weel," Broden says, pulling out his phone and quickly sending her a message.

"There ye are, lass. I will go so ye can finish yer shopping. I'm looking forward to seeing ye again." He turns and walks away.

"Me too." She questions why she just gave this stranger her cell number but doesn't feel as if it was the wrong thing to do. It has got to be criminal for a man to have an ass like that, she thinks as she watches him walk away. Broden is walking around the grocery store, making it look as if he is shopping, when his phone buzzes; he sees it is Aniya confirming she got his number.

Brother, come to the library.

Broden hears the message in his head.

On my way.

Broden puts the can that he was pretending to read back on the shelf and moves to the exit. He looks around the store as he walks, hoping to catch another look at the beautiful lass, and he is disappointed when he doesn't see her. He exits the store and makes his way to the library. Entering, he looks around the building and moves toward Brodrick after he spots him in the far corner of the library, looking through some old town newspapers.

"Ye have something?"

"Nay, 'tis still nothing, and I have gone back 100 years," he replies in frustration.

"Ye called me. I thought ye might have something."

"Aye, I do. I have found my soul mate, 'tis what I had to tell ye." Smiling, Brodrick thinks about Aniya and his heart rate speeds up just a bit, and it is a rather odd sensation.

"Oh, aye, truly ye have?"

"Aye, truly and she is the most beautiful lass," Brodrick says, still finding it hard to believe he and his brother have both found the other piece of themselves.

"Do ye think 'tis the reason we were drawn to this place? Maybe 'tis not the mage but our soul mates that brought us here."

"I have nae really thought about the mage recently. To be honest, I have been so focused on Aniya that I forgot about the search for a while." Frowning, Broden admits this to his brother.

"Aniya? Aniya Filmore? Why have ye been focused on her? I thought ye were trying to find yer soul mate?" Brodrick asks, wondering what Broden would want with his soul mate; she is no mage.

"Aniya is my soul mate. I only just found out the lassie's name right before ye asked me here." Broden smiles big and a bit awkwardly.

"Brother, there mayhap be just a wee problem with Aniya Filmore being yer soul mate."

"Aye, I ken it. Her being a human is a wee issue but one that can be worked through."

"Aye, that is a problem but nae the one I was referring to. Aniya Filmore is my soul mate. She cannae be yers as weel, brother."

"Nay, that cannae be, she started my heart beating. How can it be that she is yers and mine?" Broden questions as he points from himself to his brother.

"Ye must be mistaken. As happy as I am that ye have found yer soul mate, it cannae be the same woman. 'Tis not possible to share one wee lassie." The denial is clear to hear in his voice.

"Aye, brother, she started my heart as weel. Just listen, ye will hear it."

The brothers look at each other in confusion, when Brodrick starts to chuckle and then the chuckle turns into a laugh, which in turn becomes an uncontrollable roar of laughter that has heads all over the library turning in their direction.

"What in the hell is so funny about this?" Broden remarks in a hushed scornful voice.

"One wee lassie for two brawny Scotsmen, brother," Brodrick gasps out between fits of laughter.

"What are we in for that would warrant the Goddess to give us one wee lass between the two of us?"

"Think on it." Brodrick tries hard to calm the laughter.

"Och, aye, but she is a bonny thing, is she not? What are we in for with this lass?" Smiling, Broden looks at his brother.

"What indeed? I think we may need to call Mother. She may be able to help in our search for the mage, and we can ask her how 'tis possible for us to have the same lass for a soul mate."

"Aye, I believe 'tis time to call her. We have many questions that need answers, and mayhap she has news that might help us in our search for the mage as weel." Broden nods in agreement.

CHAPTER 3

Pulling into her father's driveway, Aniya can see that Uncle Mike has already arrived. She has spent the day wondering what is going on. All he had told her was they needed to talk and he had a gift for her. Well, no use in prolonging the inevitable, Aniya thinks to herself as she proceeds to walk into the house and stops at the entryway, around the corner from where her uncle and father are talking in the kitchen when she hears their hushed voices. "I think this is what she felt. Peter, it's time to tell her." Uncle Mike's voice can barely be heard.

"We need to know for sure first. We don't want to tell her about something that may or may not be happening." Peter's tone sounds concerned.

"What are you two talking about? Tell me what?" she asks them as she moves around the corner. Peter and Mike look at each other, knowing she has heard part of their conversation. Peter looks over with a flash of worry on his face before he smiles. Uncle Mike was standing with his hip resting against the kitchen cabinet and arms folded over his chest, looking anxious.

"Can I ask you something?" Peter reluctantly asks.

"Yeah, sure, Daddy. What's up?" Aniya answers, looking down as she sets her items on the breakfast bar.

"You said you met a guy the other day and you got a weird feeling. Can you describe what you felt?" Peter asks. "I know it might seem strange that I'm asking, but it's kinda important."

"It was really no big deal, it's not the first time I had an attraction to a man. And what does that have to do with what you and Uncle Mike were talking about?" She has her own concerns about Broden McKesson and how the feelings she had felt have only become stronger with every meeting since the first.

Aniya spent the remainder of last night and a better part of today trying to understand whatever this is, and she has come up with nothing except she has this very deep need to see Broden again. It is times like this she wishes she had a female family member, preferably her mother, to talk to about these things. Her dad and Uncle Mike are great; even when she was growing up, they made sure she was comfortable talking to either of them about issues like boys or any other matters that occur in a young girl's life. If either of them were uncomfortable with those talks, they never showed it. But sometimes a girl just needs another girl, and this is one of those times.

"Please, it's important. We kind of need to know," Peter says, pushing the issue a little.

"Yes, you have said that already but still have not told me why it's so important. I've had crushes before—this is no different." Aniya doesn't understand why her father is questioning her like this; he has never done so before. Why is this time, with this guy so different?

"Aniya, please just tell me. I will explain my curiosity." He is pleading with her now.

"All right, all right, I'll tell you. Well, at the cafe, I ran into Broden, causing me to drop my phone, and when I looked up at him, I felt hundreds of butterflies take off inside here." Aniya presses her hand to her heart and stomach. "And at the same time, a warmth spread through my chest. Not understanding why, I brushed it off. Then the second time—"

She was cut off by her dad. "A second time? You've seen him more than once?"

"I've seen him three times. Daddy, why is this such a big deal?" Looking at her father, she doesn't understand why he seems so upset.

"It's not, I'm sorry. Please go on," Peter replies. She can tell he is trying not to sound alarmed, but decides to continue.

"As I was saying, the second time I saw him was at the library. He looked at me like he didn't remember who I was, and the butterflies were a bit more intense and scared me some when the heat in my chest felt more like a light coming on, cool at first but warms the longer it is on. After that, I went to the grocery store, and he approached me to introduce himself. He asked me to show him around and to dinner. He is new to this area and has been trying to learn more about our town history. That time, the butterflies were so intense that it caused me to have to catch my breath and the light felt brighter and warmer in my chest. Why does any of this matter? He is just a guy, and as for what I'm feeling, as confusing as it is, it's just feelings. I'm sure Mom felt the same way toward you and you toward her. It's seriously nothing to be worried about."

"Honey, there are some things about your mother that I haven't told you. It was never a good time or place to explain where or who your mother was, and honestly, we didn't think the need to tell you would ever arise. But before we explain this, Mike has some things he needs to talk to you about." Peter nods to Mike, signaling that it is his turn.

Aniya looks between her father and uncle, wondering what in the world are they up to. "What is going on and how does Mom have anything to do with any of this? The two of you are making no sense whatsoever." She does not like the somber looks she is getting from them both. Uncle Mike walks over to the dining room table and pulls out a chair.

"Sweetie, have a seat, and I will tell you. Peter, would you mind putting on some coffee, please?"

"Sure." Peter moves to the kitchen to start the coffee before taking a seat next to Aniya.

"How about I start from the beginning? That might help you to understand all I am about to tell you. It's going to be a lot, and I will do my best to explain it all and answer any questions you might have along the way." He reaches over and grabs her hand, trying to comfort her.

"Um, okay."

"Have you ever heard of the Fae?"

"The Fae, as in fairy tales and nursery rhymes, yes, we were taught about them in elementary school. You mean like Tinkerbell or the Tooth Fairy. Those aren't real, I've known that for years," she answers him, with a shrug of her shoulders.

"Well, unlike the Tooth Fairy and Tinkerbell, the Fae are very real." Mike can't help but chuckle at the comparison. She looks at him with raised eyebrows and disbelief on her face.

"Let me explain. The Fae are magical beings made up of different species. They consist of mages, vampires, fairies, and many other creatures of folklore. Now most of the stories you have been taught are just that—stories. But in the tales, there are always some truths. Witches of the tales you know are the mages of the Fae. Their magic comes from within them, not spells or herbs like nightshade or lavender and generally used only for good. Vampires do drink blood, but they do not kill those they feed from. Shifters are not any one thing but many different species, and there are many more, from dragons to leprechauns. Some of the Fae have long disappeared, and I plan to explain that in time. However, I'm going to talk about mages for now, and the reason for this is because your mother was mage, as am I." Mike pauses to watch Aniya's face, making sure she is following him. "You see, each Mage is born with a light. This light only presents itself when they have found their soul mate. Most Fae do not have families outside of their own races. Mages can marry a human even if the one they have chosen is not their soul mate and their light is not lit. The mage blood can then be passed to any children born even if their parents are not soul mates. Now as much as your mother loved your father, he never ignited her light because she never found her soul mate, but her mage blood was passed to you when you were born."

Mike is then interrupted by Aniya. "Okay, wait a minute, you're telling me that my mother was some mythical creature of fairy tales and she married my dad, who wasn't her soul mate, so some light inside her never ignited. They had me, which passed this light on to me through this mage blood, which for some reason has come on recently? If that is the case, why did a bullet through the chest kill my mother? And don't even get me started on the fact that you are mage as well." She stands and begins walking around the dining room, running her hands over her face, trying to make sense of what she is being told.

"And what does some guy I barely know have to do with any of this?" She raises her arms and lets them drop to her sides.

"Well, actually, your mother's light was not passed on to you. You were born with your own. Please sit back down, and I will finish explaining what I can." He gives her a pointed look and gestures to her chair.

"Dad, you can't honestly believe any of this?" Aniya looks in her father's direction.

"Honey, I don't need believe it because I know it's true. I knew who your mother was, but I loved her and she loved me. Though we were not soul mates, we knew we could be happy, and you were enough of a light in her life she wasn't worried about hers, so we decided that when and if you had signs of your light coming on, we would explain it to you at that time. We never thought it would actually happen because it never did with your mother." Peter looks back at Aniya.

"I need you to understand that we were happy with each other and had a good life together even without Marriam's magic or her light!" Aniya had no doubt her parents loved each other; the looks they sent each other when they thought no one was watching and the sheer joy she remembers seeing on their faces was proof of that, but how could Aniya not know about her heritage or her mother's life? She was only eight years old when her mother was killed, but there had to be some sign of the mage. That isn't something that can be easily concealed, is it? Wiping the tears from her eyes, not realizing that at some point they had started to fall, Aniya sits back down at the dining room table, turning back to Uncle Mike. "All right, keep going."

"If you need another minute, sweetie, take it." Trying his best to offer support and comfort, he smiles at Aniya.

"What I need is to understand what the hell you are talking about, and that's only going to happen if you keep going." Aniya doesn't care that she is using her persuasion to get him to continue. That breaks one of her personal rules, to never use her gifts on her family. However, she is starting to lose some of her patience.

Uncle Mike visibly tenses as he feels a slight push to obey Aniya, proof of her mage blood, but does she know what she has just done?

"I'll go get the coffee." Peter stands and steps away from the table, feeling a sense of uncertainty for his daughter and needing a minute to collect himself.

"All mages are born with abilities, mostly small things like the ability to move objects, start a small flame, or even the ability to persuade others. They are given their full abilities once they have bonded to their soul mates." Mike watches Aniya for any reaction that she knows what she has just done. Peter has returned with the coffee and hands them each a cup and rubs Aniya's back after she takes her mug and nods in thanks to her father. He gives her a small smile. They then both turn their heads back to Mike as he continues with the story.

"Your mother's light was never on, so she could be killed with a bullet. Even without their light, mages have a long lifespan, which is then extended once they are bonded to their soul mates, but until then, they can be killed the same way humans can be. The reason you haven't been told about us is because it has proven difficult for us to find soul mates, and we honestly didn't think it was even a possibility because the Fae races are on the verge of extinction. We didn't want you to worry, and if your light never came on, you would live a normal but somewhat prolonged existence." Uncle Mike pauses to take a sip of his coffee before proceeding.

"But if the Fae have prolonged lives, how are they almost extinct? Wouldn't they just continue living and having children in hopes that soul mates might come along?" Aniya asks out of curiosity.

"Not all Fae races can have children like mages, and even our children are rare in situations like your mom and dad's. You were eight, with no siblings when your mother died and the first child born to a mage in over 100 years that we are aware of. Children, now more than ever, are a precious thing among the Fae." Uncle Mike gets a sad and distant look in his eyes.

"Now the Fae are choosing death over life with no hope. So with no children being born because soul mates are needed for most races to produce and the few races that can have children without a soul mate are few and far between, the Fae have become fewer and fewer over the last few hundred years." Aniya nods, letting him know she understands and he can continue.

"The reason we needed to know what you felt when you met this Broden is because it seems as though your light has come on, and that means you have found your soul mate. Aniya, this makes you so important to the Fae and your heritage. It's a good thing. You are the first mage to ignite your light since your grandparents, which was many, many years ago." Uncle Mike looks at Aniya, whose eyebrows are raised.

"Wait, my grandparents? Are they alive, where are they, and how come I have never met them?" Surprise is in her voice.

"You were just a baby and they knew I wasn't your mother's soul mate but we were happy, and they could see that. Your grandparents knew the possibility of you ever finding your soul mate was so small we decided that it was best to raise you here in the human realm. You never had anything to do with the Fae world because the chances of you ever fully coming into your mage blood just weren't there. We kept your grandparents up to date with everything from your first words to graduating college and becoming a doctor. They sent you gifts and loved you from a distance, even after your mom's death. It has been extremely hard on them because you are their only grandchild and link to their daughter, but we knew it was best for you to live a normal life than in the Fae realm, where you, being the only child in the Fae realm, might have become an outcast. So to answer your questions, yes, they are alive. Yes, you have met them, and they live in the Fae realm," Peter explains, answering Aniya's questions.

"And on that note, in hopes of lightening the mood a little, I told you I had a gift for you. Your grandmother sent something for you. She chose it because it will not only guide you but also be a protector and companion. I will go and get it, be right back." Uncle Mike stands up from the table and jogs to the garage door that is right off the living room.

"Dad, a gift from a grandmother I didn't know I had, who apparently has watched over me my entire life? This is just too much to take in, so much to sort through and process." Aniya is looking for something familiar in a very unfamiliar situation.

"Honey, I know this is a lot of information, and you are going to need time to sort it all out. Your uncle, myself, and now even your grandparents will help you as much as possible. You are being introduced to a world you didn't even know existed up until today. You are going to have questions, and the four of us are going to answer those the best we can. I promise you," Peter states, trying to show his support.

"I get what you are saying, but why wait to tell me all this? If you had said something before, I might have been a little more prepared, but instead I feel like my entire life has all been a lie. Did you and Uncle Mike or even Mom, for that matter, think I might have the right to know, and after Mom died, did either of you ever think that having my grandparents around might have been a comfort?" Aniya never thought that those closest to her would ever make her feel as though her feelings didn't matter. "Did either of you think that I might have needed my grandparents or that they may have needed me after losing their daughter? The whole mage thing aside, Dad, I'm your daughter. You are supposed to love me, yet all I feel right at this minute is betrayed," she tells him honestly. How else could she possibly feel at this point?

"I can see how you would feel that we lied to you, and yes, you might even feel hurt and betrayed, but we felt we were making the right decision for you."

"Why couldn't you tell me as I got older instead of waiting until there wasn't a choice? Wouldn't that have been easier than springing all this on me at once?"

"Aniya, as parents, we have to make decisions that are in the best interest of our children. This was one of those times. We knew it was a good possibility that you wouldn't get your light. We didn't want you to miss out on something that might never happen, so we chose not to tell you. One day when you have children, you will understand." Peter hopes the explanation helps to cool Aniya's temper.

At that moment, Mike steps back into the house from the garage, halting any further argument from Aniya. He is holding a box of some sort with the most beautiful blanket draped over the top. It looks to be homemade; it has bright vibrant red, blue, and purple colors throughout, each color blending into the next more perfectly than a rainbow. Mike carefully sets the box on the table in front of her. She jumps when the box unexpectedly moves just a little.

"This is something that every mage receives once their light ignites, usually given by a family elder. It's called a familiar, and it will stay with you for the rest of your life." Uncle Mike moves to stand behind her chair as she slowly starts to raise the blanket off the box, which turns out to be actually a crate with a metal door.

Looking inside, she can see the light from the dining room reflect off the eyes of whatever creature inhabits the crate. Carefully, she removes the rest of the blanket, not wanting to damage it any; it is far too beautiful not to keep. Peering into the front of the crate again, she is surprised to see a baby tiger, and not just any tiger but a white tiger with eyes the color of sapphires and the black and white stripes running down its tiny body. This baby is only the size of a house cat at the moment. "Uncle Mike? This is a tiger!" Aniya blurts out, not sure if that is what it's meant to be.

"Yes, it is. Beautiful, isn't she?" he replies with a huge grin.

"She? It's a girl?" Aniya can hardly believe what she is seeing.

"Yes, a familiar is a mage's companion. She will protect you, and you can pull energy from her if it is ever needed," Uncle Mike informs her.

Aniya can't help but want to stroke the animal's fur and slowly goes to open the crate. She reaches her hand toward the tiger, watching for any signs the animal is frightened. The cub stretches her neck toward Aniya, sniffing her hand. Being very careful with the baby tiger, she gently scratches her behind the ear, causing her to start purring, the sound coming from deep within the cub's throat. Aniya's hands reach for the cub to take her out of the crate, bringing her to her chest to nuzzle the top of her head. Lifting her a bit more for a better position, she uses her shoulder to support the tiger, its paws resting there. Cuddling her close, she runs her hands down its back, causing the cat to purr again, louder this time as she starts kneading Aniya's shoulder as if seeking comfort. Aniya can feel the cub's kneading and carefully goes to pull the tiger away before her claws can accidentally nick the soft flesh along her shoulder; however, she is a second too late, and the cat's claws dig into her shoulder, causing her to jerk with the slight pain. The cub, feeling Aniya tense, whines as if to apologize and stretches her head toward the shoulder where a small amount of blood has soaked through her shirt. Nudging the shirt aside, the cub licks at the tiny wound. Immediately, she feels the cub's rough tongue licking at the small wound. With every lap of the cat's tongue, the stinging disappears and the punctures she had caused close up.

"And just like that, the bond is made," Uncle Mike says, watching his niece and her familiar.

"Bond? What bond?" She is not sure what he meant by that, but in complete awe over what she is seeing.

"What's going on? What are the two of you seeing? I don't see anything." Peter is looking utterly confused and at a loss as to what they are talking about.

"Sorry, I forgot you can't see familiars," Mike says, with a flick of his wrist.

Peter's eyes widen. "A tiger, they gave her a tiger. What in the hell are they thinking?"

Mike laughs a little at Peter's response before turning his attention back to Aniya and the tiger. "To answer your question, a bond between a mage and their familiar is formed by blood. If the familiar accepts the mage, then it will take a small amount of blood to seal the bond. Your familiar not only accepted you but also healed the wound she created."

"So she meant to claw me?" Uncertainty and a small amount of apprehension are in her voice.

"No, a familiar will never hurt its mage on purpose, but she recognized what she did, so she healed the wound. She also took your blood and sealed the bond, kind of claiming you as hers. It's a very strong connection between you and her," he tells her before asking, "So what's her name? We can't keep calling her cub or familiar."

"The first thing I noticed about her was her beautiful blue eyes." She lifts the cub to eye level to get a better look. "They are the color of sapphires, so I think that should be her name—Sapphire," Aniya proclaims.

"It's a good name," he tells Aniya, reaching over her shoulder to pet Sapphire behind the ear, and he kisses Aniya on the top of the head. "You can communicate with her, you know."

"How can I communicate with her? She's a tiger. I don't know about other mages, but I do not have the ability to speak to or understand animals, Uncle Mike."

"All mages I have met, which is only a few, have never had the ability to speak to animals, but they can communicate with their familiars through their minds. From what I'm told, the ability comes from the bond created when the familiar accepts the blood from the one they have chosen. Give it a try."

"Um, okay." Aniya looks at Sapphire, not knowing exactly what she is supposed to do. She decides to try a simple *hello.*

Hi. Aniya hears a childlike voice echo in her mind.

Sapphire?

Oh, is that the name you chose for me?

Aniya looks from Sapphire to Uncle Mike and back.

Yes, is it okay? Do you like it? I chose it because the blue of your eyes reminded me of sapphires.

Yes, I like it, sounds pretty. I'm cold. Can you hold me against you again? I like to hear your heartbeat, please? Sapphire sends, showing how young she really is.

Oh, I'm sorry, yes, of course.

When Aniya brings Sapphire back against her chest, she snuggles in close, laying her head right over Aniya's heart. Aniya holds her close and pets the sweet cub.

"So did you talk to her?" both men ask in unison.

"She asked me to hold her against me because she was cold and likes to hear my heartbeat." Aniya is in disbelief. She had just had a full-blown conversation with a tiger cub. Could this day get any weirder? she thinks as she continues to pet the cub.

Not weird, interesting maybe, Aniya hears Sapphire say in her head, sounding sleepy. Looking down, she sees the cub falling asleep.

Sleep, beautiful girl, we both have had a crazy day. I've got you.

Sapphire snuggles in close and nods just enough that Aniya knows Sapphire agrees.

"That's a good girl." Uncle Mike gives Sapphire a gentle pet from her head to tail. Her purring is almost completely quieted as the cub drifts off to sleep in Aniya's arms.

"Do not even think that this conversation is over." Aniya gives a pointed look at her dad and uncle. "I have so many more questions, and giving me a gift isn't getting you out of explaining yourselves, even if I absolutely love her."

"We know you will have more to say, honey, but don't get too agitated. Sapphire will feel what you feel, and both of you need time to adjust to this," Mike tells her, gesturing to the sleeping Sapphire still in Aniya's arms.

"We will have plenty of time to talk through everything. For now, take some time to digest and sort through everything you have been told and get to know Sapphire. We can finish this conversation later." Peter reaches over and gives Aniya's hand a squeeze. Standing up from the table, with Sapphire in her arms, she moves to the couch in the living room to lie down. Curling up on her side, Aniya repositions Sapphire so she is tucked in against Aniya's stomach and chest, for a more comfortable position to sleep in, but keeping the cub close to her heart as she had asked.

Meanwhile, Broden and Brodrick are waiting in their hotel room for their mother to arrive. Broden is sitting in an oversized chair, watching his brother pace the room in amusement. They have contacted her through their mind link, telling her they need to talk and have some questions. She replied almost immediately, letting them know she will be there soon. A knock at the door stops Brodrick's pacing, and he looks up.

"Enter," both twins say in unison.

The door opens, and Evie glides into the room with a naturally sensual sway. Before she can even greet and hug her boys, they both start talking at once.

"What are we going to do? One of her, two of us." Brodrick is in a panic.

"She is beautiful! She has this long hair and blue eyes," Broden remarks while staring off into the distance. Caught off guard by both of them, she raises her hands to hold them up, trying to silence them.

"Boys, boys, what are you talking about? I can't understand you when you're both talking at the same time." She interrupts their chaotic ramblings. Both of them quiet immediately and take deep breaths. Walking toward them, she stops in her tracks as she hears the thumping of not one but two heartbeats. She runs to take them in her arms and hug them. Seeing her cry, the boys accept the hug and look at her.

"What's wrong?" Brodrick asks.

"Why are ye crying, is all weel?" Broden follows up.

"Happy tears," she assures them, wiping at her eyes. "My sons have found their soul mates." Excitement and relief sound in her voice.

"Soul mate," they reply in unison.

"Wait? Soul mate? What do you mean?"

"One woman, Mother," Brodrick says, holding up one finger to emphasize his words.

"I'm not understanding what you are talking about." Evie looks at them in confusion.

"Mother, that's why we called ye. Our soul mate is the same woman," Broden states.

"*And* she is human," Brodrick adds.

"Oh dear," Evie says in a sigh.

CHAPTER 4

The room falls silent at this revelation. The boys watch their mother as she starts pacing, taking a few steps then looking up at the boys, taking a few more, and looking up at them again. She finally stops in front of both twins, looking very anxious.

"One girl is soul mate to both of you, and you are absolutely sure it's the same woman?"

"Aye Mother, very sure," Broden answers.

"Absolutely, without a doubt the same girl," Brodrick confirms.

"I don't understand how this has happened. I've never heard of such a thing." Evie thinks out loud to herself.

"And how does she feel about this?" Evie looks from one of her sons to the other.

"Weel, we have nae told her yet. We only just discovered this a day ago and contacted ye right away. She does nae even ken we are twins," Brodrick explains.

"And when do you intend on telling her?"

"Weel, Mother, 'tis one reason why we called ye. We ken not how to tell her." Broden looks at his brother for backup.

With a stern tone, she tells the boys, "She is going to find out soon enough. You may be identical twins, but your personalities are as different as night and day, completely opposite of each other. You must come out and tell her everything, from you being twins to soul mates and who you are as well. It wouldn't be right to continue hiding it."

"We are nae trying to hide it from her, Mother," Brodrick tells her before the boys go on to explain how they came to meet Aniya and all that has transpired since.

"Here is what I want you to do. First tell her you are twins, then you need to explain soul mates to her. When are you to see her again?"

"Broden has a date with the lass on Friday."

"That's a couple days away, enough time to bring this to the council and hope they know what is going on."

"Aye, Mother."

"Oh, my boys, we will figure this out." Evie holds out her arms and hugs them. "I can't wait to meet the woman who has started my son's hearts beating again. She must be special."

Over the next couple of days, Aniya continues her daily routine without too many changes, other than Sapphire going everywhere with her. At first, she wasn't sure what to do about the cub, but Uncle Mike has assured her that only those with magic can see her, so Sapphire just follows her around, making sure to stay close but never in the way. It's now Friday night, and she has her date with Broden. She had almost canceled because of all that has transpired in the last few days but decided that was pointless. They are soul mates, and even though she doesn't quite understand everything that entails, apparently it's fate, and who is she to question fate? Besides, she really wants to see him again and spend time getting to know him. Getting home to get ready, without a clue as to what to wear, she settles on jeans and a sweater, perfect for a late winter outing! She feeds Sapphire a raw steak, silently thanking her uncle for teaching her about Sapphire's eating habits. She stops at the closet to get her coat before leaving the house and locking the door.

Come on, Sapphire, stay close.

Oh, time to ride! Sapphire pounces around in excitement.

Aniya giggles at her and strokes the cat as they leave the house. Sapphire has grown some in the last couple days. She is now the size of a medium dog. Uncle Mike said that familiars grow faster to mature quicker so they can better protect their mages. Opening the car door, she waits for Sapphire to jump in before getting behind the wheel and pulling out of the driveway toward the direction of the mom-and-pop restaurant where she and Broden have agreed to meet.

Aniya parks her car across the street from the restaurant and gets out, waiting for Sapphire to follow. Next thing she knows, the tiger is running into the street.

Sapphire, STOP!

Aniya runs to follow the cat, not paying any attention to what's going on around her. Headlights flash, and Aniya stops in the middle of the street as she sees the car coming straight for her at a high speed. Broden is watching his soul mate as she gets out of the car; he then sees a white tiger come out from behind her and bolt onto the road. He watches as Aniya begins chasing the tiger, only stopping when she sees a car is headed right for her. He jumps from the table and, a second later, is grabbing her around the waist to take her back to the sidewalk, out of the speeding car's path. The driver slams on the brakes, which then halt the wheels with a screech. Jumping out of the car, he runs over to them.

"I'm so sorry, the car wouldn't stop. Is she okay?" The driver is panicked and slightly out of breath.

"Weel, mayhap had ye hit the brake and nae the gas, ye would have stopped." Broden clenches his teeth and sneers at the driver.

"I did, but the car just kept going. No matter how hard I stomped on the brakes, it just kept going, it wouldn't stop." The driver tries explaining.

"Are ye all right, love?" Broden concentrates on Aniya, ignoring the daft driver. "And why were ye chasing a tiger?"

"A tiger? You were chasing a tiger, where?" The driver's gaze searches for any sign of the animal.

"How can ye miss a bloody tiger?" Broden snaps as he escorts a frightened Aniya back across the street to the diner.

As they approach the door to the diner, Sapphire comes running back to them from behind the building. She then nudges Aniya's hand when she approaches.

Why did you run, Sapphire? You've never run away from me before.

I smelled evil, Iya, so I follow to check.

A warning next time would be good, okay?

It my job to protect, and I fail. Sapphire drops her head just a bit.

You were trying to protect me, but even you can't be in two places at once, beautiful girl.

I felt your fear, so I come back right away.

I know, but next time, tell me what is happening. Promise me?

Promise. Sapphire nudges at Aniya's hand again.

Brodrick runs over to his brother and Aniya.

"I saw what happened. Are ye both all right?"

Aniya is a little confused because now she is seeing double. "Did I hit my head? Because I am seeing two of you, Broden."

"Och, nay, lass. We have something to tell ye, but let's go in and sit ye down first. Aye, lass?" They walk her into the restaurant and ask for a table for three.

The restaurant is small, with tables throughout, spaced far enough apart that it won't look or feel crowded when it's at full capacity; low lights give the place a calming feel. The walls are carved to make it look like the inside of a log cabin complete with a wood-burning fireplace. Pictures hang all around, showing scenes of decades past, when the restaurant first opened, to the most current years. White tablecloths are spread over each table. The hostess walks over and escorts them toward a circular table in the back of the restaurant. The twins seat Aniya before they seat themselves across the table from her, their backs to the wall. Sapphire sits down on the floor between her and Brodrick. "Okay, so care to tell me what's going on?" She looks at both of them, slightly disoriented from the recent event. Reaching down, she strokes Sapphire, searching for some comfort.

I here always.

"And how is it that you can see Sapphire?"

"Weel, before we get into that, lass, are ye mage?" Broden takes a long look at her.

"I guess, but I only just found out about that since you apparently lit my mage light." Her light is shining so bright Aniya wonders how she isn't glowing, and the butterflies have extended their flight to her whole body—flutters from head to toe.

Their waitress, a young girl with red curly hair pulled back in a half ponytail and hazel eyes highlighted with painted-on eyeliner, glued-on lashes, and a face so full of makeup you can't see even a hint of her natural look, approaches the table. She is wearing short cutoff shorts and a low-cut tank top barely covering her breasts that have started to push out the top of her tank. The joys of a good push-up bra! Before looking both the boys up and down with a seductive smile, she quickly glances at Aniya, then looks back at the men.

"I will be happy to get either of you absolutely anything you want." She flirtatiously winks at them and completely ignores that Aniya is even there.

Sapphire lets out a slow growl directed at the girl.

"Please do your job or leave us alone." Aniya's look of disgust at the waitress has the guys smirking.

The woman's motivation is clear with her next words.

"But there are two of them. You couldn't possibly handle both. Well, then again, maybe you can, they are a scrumptious dessert." The waitress looks at the guys with lust in her eyes.

Aniya, having had enough of this woman, stands up from the table, looks the girl squarely in the face, and using the strongest persuasive voice she tells her, "GO AWAY."

And she watches in complete satisfaction as the waitress practically runs away from the table. Broden and Brodrick are looking at one another and grinning.

This wee lass is already very possessive, brother.

Aye, she is.

"What are the two of you grinning at?" Aniya interrupts their mental conversation.

"Nae a thing." Broden's grin never leaves his face.

"Nay, not a thing, but ye just sent our waitress running." Brodrick laughs just a bit.

Rolling her eyes, Aniya flags over a waiter and asks if he will please take over their table. After he agrees, they place their orders. Aniya orders a burger and fries, and both twins get steak and a baked potato with everything and a very rare steak for Sapphire.

"She should have kept her mouth shut and just done her job," Aniya murmurs after the waiter leaves the table.

I go bite her. Me not like her, Iya.

Sapphire's comment causes Aniya to laugh.

No, beautiful girl, leave her be. She is gone.

Aniya scratches her behind the ear, which starts Sapphire purring.

But good girl.

This brings them back to the situation at hand.

"I now know you are twins." Lifting her eyes to theirs, she cocks an eyebrow. "One of you is Broden, and the other?" She is looking at the one whose name she doesn't know.

"Brodrick McKesson." Raising his hand to signal she was correct in the assumption that he wasn't Broden.

"Well, that does explain why you didn't remember me when I saw you in the library." Her eyes are on Brodrick.

"And why you didn't remember I had given you my name already, at the grocery store." She turns to Broden.

"Aye, lass, I did nae ken you had met Brodrick, nor that ye are his soul mate as weel as mine. But ye failed to mention to us ye are mage," he says in a questioning tone.

"We thought we were drawn here because of what we seek, and instead we found ye and we did nae sense that ye are magic when we first met."

"What do you mean I'm his soul mate and yours? How is that possible? And I didn't know I was mage when I met you," Aniya informs them.

"Aye, lass, ye are my soul mate as weel. Did ye not feel anything when we met in the library?"

"Yes, I did, my light seemed to grow brighter. I thought that was Broden but it was you, which might explain why I could feel my light get brighter but not complete, like it was still in pieces." All of this is making much more sense to Aniya.

"Aye, that could be it, lass." Both men are in agreement with her.

"How does your light feel now?" The question comes from Broden.

"It feels the brightest it has ever felt but still incomplete, not tied together yet," she answers after taking a minute to focus inward and think about how to phrase what she is feeling. "How can I be soul mate to both of you? How would that work?"

"Lass, 'tis something we have asked as weel. We have never heard of this happening, and we are as confused as ye are about that. We have someone helping us to figure it all out." Brodrick looks up as the waiter comes to drop off the food and refill their drinks, causing them to halt the conversation for the moment. Passing their orders to each of them, the waiter asks if they need anything else before he leaves them to their food.

"How is it that you can see Sapphire? Are you both mage as well?" she asks them before anyone can take a bite of food, excited that she might have someone to explain more of this to her.

"Nay, loving, we are nae mage but we do have magic, and that is how we can see yer tiger." Broden hands Sapphire a piece of steak he has cut off for her.

I like them, Iya—they feed me steak.

Hey, I feed you steak too.

I like them, I love you. Sapphire rubs her head against Aniya's leg.

I love you too, beautiful girl. Aniya grins down at her.

Cutting into his steak, Broden pauses, looks up at the beautiful woman, and asks, "Are ye going to let us in on what she is saying?"

"Dinna ye know we cannae hear her?" the other twin pipes up.

Aniya smirks before biting into her burger. "She was just saying how she likes the two of you but loves me," she gets out, between bites of her food.

"I dinna understand what is so funny." Broden takes a bite of his steak and realizes for the first time in over 200 years, he can actually taste the meat. It isn't bland or plain-tasting. He can taste the seasoning used to flavor the meat, the melted butter to help tenderize. The texture is wonderful. He can even taste the slightly gamey flavor coming out in every bite.

Brother, eat the meat. Can ye taste it?

Ye ken we cannae taste human food.

Taste it!

His brother's insistence has Brodrick giving him a questioning look before he takes a bite of the steak, immediately realizing why Broden had pushed him to eat the normally flavorless food. Sitting back in his chair, closing his eyes, he just revels in the flavor that is exploding in his mouth. Next, he tries the baked potato, deciphering each flavor—salt, pepper, sour cream, chives, melted butter, and starch. Brodrick turns to his brother to see him doing the same, with a look of pleasure identical to his own, like every taste bud has awakened with the beat of their hearts.

We can taste food again!

Aye, brother, more proof of who she is to us.

With a joyful, happy laugh, Broden catches Aniya watching them. "You two look as if you have never tasted steak and potatoes before."

"Aye, sweetling, 'tis been a while since we have had a good steak." Brodrick takes a few more moments to savor the food they can now taste.

"How is it possible that ye did nae ken ye were mage? Ye said ye only found out just two days ago." Brings them all back to the original discussion.

"From what I was told, my mage blood comes from my mother, who was killed when I was eight. Before that, they thought it best not to say anything. My parents were not soul mates, and after Mom died, my dad and uncle thought it better to continue keeping everything a secret. I guess it's been hard for the Fae to find soul mates, so they figured I'd be better off not knowing. That is, until you two came along. I didn't even know the Fae existed," she informs them.

"Och, lass, to lose someone so important at such a young age. A mother is the hardest. Ye said she was killed. Might I ask what happened?" Wiping his mouth with his napkin and pushing his plate away, Broden gives her a sympathetic look.

"Thank you, there are times I wish she was here. It would have helped with all of this. She was shot during an attempted mugging after we left a restaurant we had eaten dinner at that night. It was the night we also met Uncle Mike. He came to try and help us." Sapphire, feeling Aniya's sadness, nudges her hand, sending comfort.

Do not worry. It was a long time ago.

I here, Iya.

"I know." Lost in her memories of the past, she speaks out loud.

"And ye were almost run down by a car tonight," Brodrick remarks while deep in thought.

"Yes, well, I'm quite accident prone. It isn't the first time something like that has happened." She comes back to herself and answers him.

"What do ye mean *nae the first time*? Have ye had many accidents, then?" Broden asks her, concerned that something nefarious may be going on.

"The mugging was the start of a lot of bad luck. Just after Mom died, I fell off some playground equipment and broke my leg. At one point, I got really sick and was in the hospital. The doctors thought for sure I wouldn't live, but I got better. And then once I was in college, I was in a car accident. That's what I can remember off the top of my head. I seemed to heal quickly, so I didn't have to stay in the hospital long, and my dad and Uncle Mike were always there for me, so I was never alone." Aniya shrugs her shoulders nonchalantly about everything.

"Ye said that ye healed quickly and yer dad and uncle stayed with ye, they were also the ones who told ye about being Mage. By chance, are either of them Fae?" Broden asks her, just a bit curious about all these "accidents" she mentioned.

"Oh yes, my uncle is mage. He is also the one who figured out my light had come on and brought Sapphire to me." She looks down at her cub, smiling.

"And he was there the night yer mother was killed too, but could nae save her?" Brodrick seems to be putting some puzzle together in his head but isn't ready to voice his opinion yet.

"If you are thinking Uncle Mike had something to do with my mom's death and my accidents, you are wrong. Mom was shot in the heart, there was nothing anyone could do and my *accidents* are just that—accidents. I'm just extremely accident prone." Feeling the need to defend her uncle, she says that a little too loudly. Looking around, she is confident no one overheard her or is staring.

"Nay, lass, we are nae thinking that at all. It seems though ye may have been unlucky with accidents and very lucky to have him there to heal ye. Something is amiss though, ye are young and it appears strange for someone to have had so much happen to them. It just makes one wonder, 'tis all," Broden informs her, matching his brother's thoughts.

"What do you mean?"

"Dinna fash yerself, sweetling. We will see what else we can find out before we make any assumptions." Brodrick assures her, but he is looking at his brother, telling him this would be taken seriously and they would get to the bottom all of all her "accidents."

"Okay, then, but I'm telling you, I'm just clumsy. Now do I get to hear more about the two of you, or are we going to sit here all night only talking about me?"

"Weel, what would ye like to ken, lass?"

"How old are you? I can hear your accent, so I know you are not from the United States. Any brothers or sisters?" Aniya asks them, wanting to learn as much as she can about her soul mates.

"Nay, no other siblings and I am older than him." Broden nods at his brother, teasing him with a smack to his back and a roguish grin on his face.

"Only by a couple of minutes, ye arse. We are from Scotland and a wee bit older than ye! Our brogue, or accent, as ye put it, isn't as strong as it used to be, either."

Seeing how close the two of them are, she is a bit envious. Aniya can't help but wish she had someone growing up, to share memories and time with.

"Aye, Brodrick was a surprise as weel. Our birth mother was nae expecting two bairns, but I'm glad to have him."

"Weel, I have saved yer arse a time or two, brother."

"Aye, 'tis true, and I have ye as weel. What are brothers for?"

"Your birth mother? What do you mean?"

"Och, lass, a tale for another time. 'Tis time to go." Brodrick gives Sapphire a pat before reaching for Aniya's hand. Flagging the waiter over and getting the check, Broden and Aniya both go to grab the ticket.

"Nay, loving, I invited ye, I will pay."

"That's okay, I don't mind." She reaches for the check again, and Broden pulls it out of her grasp.

"But we do." He rises from the chair and waits for her to do the same.

"Well then, I thank you both!" They make their way to pay the bill, through the restaurant, toward the register, where Aniya sees the waitress from earlier standing behind it and watching them approach. She sends Aniya a look of hatred before putting on the same seductive flirty smile she wore earlier.

"Ugghhh, you can't be serious. This girl is ridiculous!" she murmurs to herself.

I can still bite her.

No, Sapphire, no biting.

"And how was everything? Are you sure there is nothing I can do for the two of you?" The waitress takes the money she is given and cashes them out.

She writes something on the receipt before handing it over to Brodrick, ignoring Aniya once again.

Before she can say anything, Aniya hears Brodrick say something that takes her by complete surprise. "Listen here, wench, we showed no interest in ye when ye sought out our attentions before, but the fact that ye blatantly sought us out in front of Aniya again makes us even less interested in ye now. That alone shows us what type of woman ye are and more, proves we want naught to do with ye at all. Lucky it was she who said something to ye earlier and nae me. Keep this to yerself. We have no need for it. Come, sweetling." Brodrick tosses the receipt back to the waitress, and both men make a point of putting their arms around Aniya as they walk toward the restaurant doors. Sapphire in tow looks back at the waitress and growls. Not being able to help herself, Aniya looks over her shoulder to sneer at the woman, putting one arm around each of the twins as they leave.

We need to take her to Mother. I think there is more to this than Aniya being clumsy. I feel she is in danger.

Aye, I feel the same as ye. We can also find out what other accidents this wee lassie has been in.

And, mayhap, if someone is trying to kill her.

Aye, we agree, time to introduce her to Mother. With the mental agreement made, they turn to her. "We would like to take ye to meet someone. Do ye think ye would mind?" Broden asks her while opening her car door, preparing to leave the restaurant.

"Aye, they are very important to us, and we would like to introduce them to ye."

"We are supposed to go sightseeing tomorrow, but it's still early, and if it is important to you, then yes, I would like to meet them." Aniya isn't really ready to be away from either of them just yet. This soul mate business is no joke. She can't love them yet, can she? What in the hell is she thinking? There is no way that could be possible.

"Weel then, let us go, if ye are sure." Brodrick's words pull her out of her head.

"Yes, I'm sure, let's go." Smiling, she nods at them in agreement.

Mother, can ye meet us in our room? We have our soul mate with us and would like to ken what the council has told ye.

I get to meet my new daughter tonight? Yes, I will meet you in your room.

Evie is bubbling in excitement, and both men can feel her loving energy.

CHAPTER 5

Evie arrives at the hotel room first. She sits to wait for her sons and to welcome her new daughter. Her excitement is almost overwhelming! Looking around the room, she realizes that her sons have not cleaned in a long while. She doesn't want her new daughter to see the room with dirty clothes and unmade beds. Setting the spiced wine she has brought with her for Aniya on the table, she starts zipping around the room to tidy it up, reminding herself to get after her boys for this mess when the hotel room door opens.

Never in her life has Aniya ever gone to a hotel room with a guy after only one date, but here she is, walking hand in hand with not just one but two of the most gorgeous men she has ever seen, doing just that, and surprisingly, she feels no shame in it either. They are soul mates, after all, and she can't help but want to be close to both of the men. The guys are in front of her as they approach what she can only guess is the door to their room. She is feeling a bit nervous about meeting whoever this person is, but they seem to be important to her guys, which makes them important to her as well.

"Weel, here we are, lass." Brodrick enters the room, followed by Broden.

"Oh, she is here already!" Both the guys are gone from her, hugging some woman and kissing her on the cheeks.

"SHE?" Aniya is surprised at the scorn in her voice, looking at the most beautiful woman she has ever seen holding on to her soul mates.

The woman has a small figure and gorgeous, flawless pale skin, long wavy hair down her back, and she is wearing the most beautiful long blue gown that Aniya has ever seen; it hugs her perfectly shaped curves. Everything about this woman shouts sensual. All of a sudden, she is very aware of her shorter, more rounded figure with wide hips and her brunette hair not nearly as beautiful as this woman's mahogany tresses that sparkle even in the low light of the hotel room. Who is his woman, and why the hell is she holding on to Aniya's soul mates like they are her lifeline?

You can bite this one, Sapphire, if she doesn't let go of our men.

Jealousy spreads through her like a wildfire in a California desert.

I give her a chance first, we not know who she is. Sapphire is watching the scene as intently as Aniya. *I not smell evil, only good.*

What about the girl at the restaurant? You were willing to bite her— was she evil?

She smell dirty, not evil, and I not know about this lady. She smell pretty, Iya.

Aniya slowly backs out of the room. There is no way that she can be the soul mate to both Broden and Brodrick; she is no competition to this woman. Fate is wrong. Aniya's only thought now is to get out of there, but fate has other things in mind.

"Lass, where are ye going?"

"There has obviously been some mistake. You two have your hands full, so I'll be leaving now." She tries and fails to hide the hurt in her voice.

"Sweetheart, where are you going? I've been looking forward to meeting you. Please come back in?" The woman's voice sounds just as beautiful as she looks.

"No." Looking at both of the guys, she says, "Thank you for dinner and have a good life." The jealousy comes out before Aniya can stop it.

"Did the two of you not tell her who she was coming to meet? Please tell me you did not bring her here without explaining who I am?" Exasperation is clear in Evie's voice as she addresses her sons.

"We told her ye are important and wanted her to meet ye." Watching their mother cross the room to Aniya, they do not understand what the problem is. Why would the lass get so angry? What have they done now?

"No wonder the poor dear looks like she's running away." Carefully approaching Aniya, Evie stands in front of her, when Broden begins to understand.

"Lass, ye misunderstand. Let us introduce ye to our mother, Evilyn." He smirks at how jealous their soul mate has become in mere hours!

"Your mother? She's your mother? How can she be your mother? She looks my age." Shock has replaced the jealousy that radiated through her.

"Yes, you can call me Evie if you like." Smiling and with an exasperated shake of her head, Evie continues, "Please let me apologize for my sons' lack of manners and explanation." She glances at the twins while informing them with a *we will discuss this later* look.

Evie envelops Aniya in a hug, which she awkwardly returns, not really knowing how to react.

See . . . I tell you she not evil. Glad I no bite her.

"And who is this beauty here?" Evie bends to Sapphire, giving her a rub behind her ears.

Then a realization hits Evie—her daughter is a mage, and this is Aniya's familiar. Evie's family just got a bit bigger and she couldn't be happier, but a mage and vampire? This just got more complicated as well. A problem for another time—right now, Evie just wants to get to know her daughter, and they can figure out the rest later.

"This is Sapphire," Aniya answers Evie, forgetting for a second that they all can see her. Evie stands and wraps her arm around Aniya's shoulders and guides her back into the room to the oversized chair that Broden likes to sit in.

"How about some wine? I brought it as a welcome gift for you, Aniya. It's one of the best Fae wines I could find." Evie walks to the sink against the far-left wall to pick up a few of the hotel's plastic glasses off the counter. Pouring four glasses, she hands one to each twin and Aniya, taking the last for herself even though she can't taste it. Evie sips the wine and looks at Aniya. The girl is beautiful. Her eyes move to her sons, who are watching Aniya like she is their everything. Evie can't help but smile; she can see how much they already feel for Aniya, and joy fills her unbeating heart. If her boys can find their soul mate, then that gives her hope for herself and the Fae.

"Mother, any news from the council?" Broden pulls Evie from her thoughts.

"Yes, my dear, I have some, but being your soul mate is mage, that does require another visit home and to the council. You told me Aniya was human, not mage, and this is something that has never occurred before. We will go to the council together with Aniya and discuss it with them," Evie tells them all. "We are a family, and though I only just met you, Aniya, I already love you. Thank you for bringing us so much happiness and hope. You are my daughter, soul mate to my sons, and I vow to protect you and Sapphire always." Evie makes the statement as though she has known Aniya all her life.

"You don't even know me. Why would you protect someone you don't know, and what are you protecting me from?" Aniya asks.

"We don't know what could happen. Each species keeps to their kind. A mage and vampire have never been soul mates before and—" Evie gets cut off.

"Vampire? Who's a vampire? I'm a mage, not a vampire!" Aniya exclaimed.

"They didn't mention they are vampires?"

"They're vampires! No, that was never brought up." Aniya sends the guys a sideways glance.

"Broden and Brodrick McKesson, I remember telling you both that you needed to tell Aniya everything. Would you care to explain why she seems surprised to know you're vampires?" Evie scolds the two. Aniya looks from Evie to the twins, who are looking disheveled under their mother's scolding and look of disapproval.

Yep, she is definitely their mother.

Aniya stifles a giggle.

I not want to be them right now, me not want to upset her . . . ever! Sapphire sends a mental picture of her shaking her head.

Me neither.

"Weel, Mother, it just had nae come up yet." Brodrick raises a hand to the back of his neck to rub away the tension.

"We had nae really had a chance, after the car almost hit her then learning she is mage and her mother's death then there was the fact that she has had a few accidents while growing up and we called ye because we wanted ye to meet her, and weel, here we are." Broden hopes to maybe ease his mother's anger a bit.

"There is still no excuse, and what do you mean by accidents?" Evie sets down her wine and walks over to Aniya, placing a protective arm around her shoulders again, then calls Sapphire over for added security.

"Really, they are just accidents. I am a clumsy person, always have been." Aniya looks up at Evie but doesn't move away from her embrace. Strangely, she finds it comforting.

Mother, we will explain more of our worries once we take Aniya home. For now, get to know her—she is so special. Brodrick doesn't say anything out loud, knowing Aniya will argue against it.

"Well, we can talk about that another time. Right now, I want to spend some time with my beautiful daughter." Evie sends a radiant smile to the three of them. Aniya is really coming to like the woman. She handles Brodrick and Broden well, and Aniya can see how much Evie loves them and isn't afraid of putting them in their place.

I like her already.

Aniya smiles at Sapphire's comment.

"Aniya, tell me about you. I want to know everything." Evie sits on the arm of the overstuffed chair. Aniya takes her first sip of the wine and is amazed at the flavors. It's berries for sure but also something else she has never tasted.

"Wow, this tastes amazing." She lifts her glass and looks at the red liquid.

"Do you like it? It's one of the oldest wines from the Fae realm, berries with a touch of magic," Evie explains.

"I love it." Aniya takes another sip before continuing. "Well, I'm twenty-five. I have my father Peter and my Uncle Mike. They raised me after my mom died. I work at the hospital, my mother being the reason

I wanted to be a doctor. I like to save lives and help people." Aniya tells them all about her life.

"Oh, so you are in school, then?" Evie asks.

"No, I'm a doctor. I graduated high school and went to college then med school," Aniya states matter-of-factly.

"And so young, quite an accomplishment, my dear," Evie says proudly.

"I've always been able to see people, on the inside."

"See people? You mean inside of someone, injuries?" Evie's curiosity is genuine.

"Well, yes, but also see the souls of people. The good and the bad but I have to be touching them and then focus inward. I can also persuade people." Aniya has never told anyone about her gifts, and it feels so good to talk to someone about this.

"Oh my, that must be difficult. If you can see their souls, I can imagine being a doctor can be a burden," Evie says, seeing how hard that could be on someone.

"It isn't. I love what I do, and yes, I do use my gifts but I don't always look inside someone. I think that's just my way of keeping their privacy. I'm a doctor first, and it's my job to heal and help those who need it, good or bad. When I do use my gifts, I always back it with my skills, and if I feel the need to, I will look at the person's soul." Aniya goes on to explain Rachel and Nick as an example.

"You see, yes, I used my gift to get Nick away from Rachel, followed the law, and Rachel is home safe with her parents. That young girl is so special, but I still haven't figured out why," Aniya finishes.

"My sons are lucky to have a soul mate who is so good and kind. To do a job like yours, and even faced with evil, you were able to save a young girl and bring her justice as well. Please always be careful—you could get hurt."

Aniya smiles at Evie's words. "My dad and Uncle Mike tell me the same thing. May I ask a few questions?" Aniya directs the question to Evie.

"Of course, my dear."

"I only just learned of all this, and Uncle Mike explained the mages' light and said each species has their own way of knowing when they have found their soul mates. How did Broden and Brodrick know I was theirs?"

"Well, with vampires, there are several things that happen. Our hearts start to beat, and that is usually the first thing that occurs. Our sense of taste comes back, meaning we can now taste food and drink, but to keep our strength, we still have to feed. Also, all emotions are enhanced a hundredfold, and we can withstand the sun. We can always handle some sunlight, but usually only dawn and dusk. After we find soul mates, we can actually walk in the sun with no adverse effects," Evie explains.

"You haven't found your soul mate? You seem to love them so much, and the way you welcomed me, I would have never thought you can't feel." Disbelief is in Aniya's tone.

"I can feel but not the same as my boys do now that their hearts beat. Broden and Brodrick have been the one thing that has kept me alive all these years." Evie sends the twins a loving look. "I may not have birthed them but they are my sons, and them finding you has given me hope that I will still find my soul mate," Evie tells Aniya.

"You didn't give birth to them, but you call them your sons? So how did they become vampires?" Aniya is a little confused about this.

"Until a vampire has found their soul mate, we cannot have children. Our hearts don't beat, which means the only thing that keeps us here is hope and the love of and for our families. Because vampires can only have children after our hearts beat, the love between the soul-mated couple brings the children up with love and kindness which does help after we are raised and searching for our own soul mate. My parents are the last mated vampire couple, and when they had me, they raised me with love. So I do know how to love, and that helps me get through every day without my soul mate. And on the rare occasion that I feel like giving up, I remember my parents' love and the love I have for Broden and Brodrick. Because I'm the last blood-born, meaning child born from a mated couple, I was called on by the Fae Council to help them by finding the Finder, who is supposed to find the mage who is to bring soul mates back to us all. That's why I turned Broden and Brodrick, even though it goes against everything I was taught. You see, it is against our laws to turn humans unless they are soul mates, but because of being the only blood-born and capable of being able to turn a human, I was forced to search out the Finder, and I believe they are the Finder. A seer said that only the Finder could find this mage and save the Fae from extinction." Evie pauses to look at her, hoping she doesn't seem resentful of her for doing what had to be done. All she can tell is Aniya is listening intently, so she continues.

"I wasn't sure if they were who I had been searching for, but their pure hearts and kind nature as well as their ability to find anything made me believe they were who I had been seeking. Vampires have to not only prove they are soul mates to a human but also have permission from the council and the one who is to be turned. They may have forced me on this journey, but they were not going to force me to turn a human who refused to be turned. So I explained to the boys who and what I am as well as told them who I thought they were. I asked if they would allow me to turn them into vampires so they could help save the Fae. I gave them two days to decide and promised Brodrick and Broden I'd always be there for them as a mother, knowing I could never replace their birth mother. I accepted them as my sons, and together, we are still searching for the mage meant to save us all. This is so much to put on one person, mage, vampire, or human, but as I did with my boys and you, I will offer my love and protection to this mage as well, when we find them," Evie tells them all before adding, "As for soul mates, I knew my boys had found you when I heard their heart beats, and it was the most beautiful sound to me. I have you to thank for that, my darling. You will never know what that means to me and what all of you have given me. Now have you two regained your tastes yet?" Evie asks, looking from Aniya to Brodrick and Broden.

"Aye, Mother, we have. The wine is very good." Broden takes another sip from his cup.

"What happens if someone is turned and not a soul mate?" Aniya asks Evie.

"That has happened, and sadly, the human, if they are not a true soul mate, tends to go crazy, bloodlust happens, and our hunters are sent to dispose of the rogues." Sadness is in Evie's voice.

"Bloodlust?" Aniya looks at the twins.

"Yes, that means the newly turned vampire becomes crazed and kills humans, vampires, or anything they can find. That is where your stories of vampires come from. This has been happening a lot in more recent years because soul mates are so few, vampires are losing hope and, in turn, just choose a human whom they have some type of liking for, and hope that the small bond created is enough when sadly, it never is." Evie looks at Aniya and sighs.

"But this didn't happen to Broden and Brodrick? What about the bond they have with you? If I'm their soul mate and that's our bond, what is your bond with them?" Aniya asks.

"Yes, you are their soul mate, make no mistake about that, daughter. The bond I have with them is that of a mother to her children. I watched them as they turned, being reborn with my blood in their veins, and that might sound morbid to some but I promise you it's not. I had hoped that their pure hearts would keep them safe, and my love and pure blood helped with the transformation." Evie hopes that the description doesn't scare Aniya off, but she knows that right now, they need all truths out in the open.

"Now my sons have a beautiful soul mate who has given them back the sun, their tastes, and a chance at a life I thought they might never have. I get a daughter and hope for the Fae as well. You have brought us so much to look forward to. I do and will treasure you for that alone." Evie pulls Aniya close for a hug as tears of happiness fall. Aniya hugs her back, taking in everything she has just learned.

"Sweetling, we have questions, would ye mind?" Brodrick approaches the two most important women in his life, and his heart fills to almost bursting, seeing Aniya and Evie together, knowing both have accepted each other.

Brother, this sight alone has made all of this worth it.

Aye, brother, truly a beautiful sight.

"Of course, Brodrick, I'll answer the best I can," Aniya replies.

"Have ye noticed any changes in yerself since finding us?"

"I didn't even know of the Fae or any of this until recently. I can say from the first time I met Broden and you, my light is only getting brighter and stronger. All I can tell you is what I have learned. Sapphire is important to me. I can hear her and talk to her in my mind, and she sends energy to me as well as comfort. She stole my heart the minute I met her." Aniya lays her hands on Sapphire, who stands and purrs to Aniya.

Beautiful girl.

I know.

"How can ye tell us apart, lass?" It's Broden's turn to interrupt the mind conversation she was having with Sapphire.

"I'm not sure. I just seem to just know. It's a feeling—maybe it has to do with you both being my soul mates," Aniya tells them while still petting Sapphire.

"How do mages secure the bond to their mates?" Broden can't help but wonder.

"I'm not sure about that either. I know a blood bond was needed for Sapphire, but a mage's bond? I will have to ask Uncle Mike." Aniya hadn't thought to ask him about that yet; it was the last thing on her mind when she was learning about all of this.

"How do vampires complete the bond?" Aniya asks. Broden and Brodrick look to Evie for help to answer that question.

"Well, dear, it is actually a blood exchange." Evie notes Aniya's worry.

"They have to bite me?"

"Yes, and you them as well. It does not hurt, from what I'm told, and not much blood is needed. Don't worry, love. The boys will know what to do, and if you truly are their soul mate, which I know you are, you will know what to do as well," Evie explains while trying to reassure and comfort Aniya.

"The best I can say is we can go talk with Uncle Mike. He would know more about mages than I, and we can get the answers together." Aniya's words are for all of them.

"Aye, lass, 'tis a good plan," Broden tells her.

"'Tis time we take ye home, lass." Brodrick walks over to Aniya and holds his hand out to help her rise from the chair.

"Yes, it is late, but I can drive myself. No need for all of you to go. Visit with your mom." Aniya tries to convince them.

"Och, lass, what sort of Scots would we be if we did nae escort ye home?" Brodrick smiles at her.

"They do have manners, daughter. I will be fine," Evie assures her.

"Aye, and we would like some time to prepare ourselves for her wrath, seeing as we both ken it is coming because we did nae tell ye everything as she had told us to," Broden says jokingly, kissing his mother on her cheek.

"You two will answer for that." Evie pulls Aniya to her for a hug, and bending to Sapphire, she hugs the cat. "Watch over her, beautiful girl."

Iya, she call me beautiful girl like you.

I heard.

"What did she say, dear?" Evie asks and looks up at Aniya.

"You could tell she spoke to me?" Aniya is a bit surprised.

"Yes, I felt it. I will explain next time we meet," Evie replies.

"She said you called her beautiful girl—it's what I have called Sapphire since she was given to me." Aniya pets Sapphire as she answers.

"I'm sorry. I wasn't aware, I don't have to. Do you mind?" Evie hopes she hasn't upset Aniya or Sapphire.

"No, no, not at all. It's an endearment and also very true," Aniya tells Evie honestly.

I not mind either.

I didn't think you would.

"Well, off you go. I can't wait for our next visit and look forward to meeting Peter and your uncle." Evie hugs Aniya one last time and kisses her on the cheek.

You both protect her and make sure she gets home safe. Evie sends the mental message to both Broden and Brodrick as she watches them leave the hotel.

The three walk out to Aniya's car. As she moves to get behind the wheel, Broden moves in front of her.

"I'll drive, lass."

"But you don't know where I live," Aniya protests.

"True—ye can tell me though."

"Yes, I can, but it would be better if I drive and the two of you don't have to come." Aniya tries one more time to convince Broden and Brodrick that she can get home on her own.

"Is there a reason ye dinna want us to escort ye, lass?" Brodrick asks.

"Well, no, but—"

Aniya is cut off by Broden. "Then get yer beautiful arse in the passenger seat, loving. I'm driving." Broden's boyish grin has her knees going weak.

"Ugh, fine." Aniya is not at all happy but then her heart skips a beat and she realizes she has lost this little fight.

"In with ye, then, beastie." Brodrick smiles as well, opening the back door for Sapphire.

I not a beast.

I don't think he meant it in a bad way, sweet girl. Aniya reaches into the back seat to comfort Sapphire and sees Brodrick climbing in next to her.

"I'm going to need a bigger car." She watches as the big Scots do their best to get comfortable in her four-door sedan.

"Och, love, I do believe so." Broden has put the driver seat all the way back, and he is still hunched over quite a bit. Aniya laughs at this ridiculous sight as he pulls the car onto the road, and she directs him to her home.

"How will the two of you get back to the hotel?" she asks as they pull into her driveway.

"Did ye already forget we are vampires, sweetling? We have speed on our side, so 'tis only a few minutes' run for us," Brodrick answers with one of those breathtaking side smiles.

"Oh, right. Well, thank you for dinner and a great night. I loved meeting your mother. She has a good soul." Aniya accepts her keys from Broden and walks toward her front door, and she realizes Broden and Brodrick are walking on either side of her. "What are the two of you doing now?"

"I thought that was obvious," Broden replies.

"Really, there is no need for that."

"Mayhap not, but we would nae risk angering Mother any more tonight. She will ask us if we made sure ye got inside before we left. We dinna want to lie." Brodrick gives Aniya a pleading look.

"Indulge us, will ye, for our safety?" Broden smiles.

"Okay." Aniya approaches the door, but before she can insert the key, she is turned around and in Broden's arms.

"I bid ye good night, loving."

Broden bends his head, and Aniya's heart skips a beat as his lips come down on hers. Broden watches Aniya as he moves toward her lips, seeing only surprise, he continues his descent. His lips touch hers, soft, supple, and tasting of the wine she drank. Aniya gasps as Broden's lips touch hers. Strong, firm and when her lips part, he takes the invitation and deepens the kiss; his tongue is hot as he invades her mouth. Aniya can't help herself at the sweet invasion, and her response is automatic as her tongue dances with his softly, but before she can do anything more, Broden pulls away and simply says, "Good night."

Before she can recover from Broden's kiss, she is whirled around, and Brodrick is crushing his lips to hers. Caught off guard, she takes a second to respond to him, with his much fiercer kissing. She is soon matching his tongue with hers, thrust for thrust. Where Broden is soft and gentle, Brodrick is hard and demanding. Aniya pushes herself against Brodrick as he is crushing her to him. She can't get close enough to him and wraps her arms around his neck, trying to close the smallest gap between them, not that there is one. Abruptly, he backs away from her, and the crisp winter air rushes between them, cooling the overly heated flesh of Aniya's face.

"Och, sweetling, I had to pull away, or I would nae be leaving ye this night. Sweet dreams to ye," Brodrick says. Aniya felt the same but did not say it as Broden and Brodrick took turns to drop one more kiss on her lips.

"Go in, loving, and lock the door behind ye." She turns and unlocks the door to enter. She turns back to tell them goodbye, but they are both gone. For a second, she believes all that just happened was a dream, but her swollen lips are proof that it wasn't.

Come on, beautiful girl. She moves aside to let Sapphire in, closes the door, and locks it as Broden had told her to do.

Broden and Brodrick glamour themselves so Aniya can't see them as the two decide who will stay with her and keep watch and who will face the wrath of their mother.

Ye stay the night and watch her. I do feel something is amiss, and we will take turns keeping watch over the lass, Broden reluctantly tells Brodrick.

Aye, brother, ye are better at calming our mother than I am. I do tend to say things I dinna mean when Mother is angered. In a glance, Brodrick enters the house before she closes the door and locks it.

Ye did nae fight me on that even a wee bit, brother. Ye stay the gentleman we claimed we are tonight, Broden warns him.

Och, brother, she is no wench I'd spy on, she is our soul mate. She is to be respected. I vow it.

Good sleep, brother.

Ye as weel and good luck with Mother, ye are going to need it.

CHAPTER 6

Aniya awakens the next morning and her eyes move directly to the chair she keeps in her bedroom. She can feel eyes on her, but looking around, she sees only Sapphire, who is still sleeping at the foot of her bed. Pulling the covers off and throwing her legs off the side of the bed, she stands to walk toward the bathroom, again feeling eyes on her as she moves. Who is here? Could it be Broden or Brodrick, and how can she not see them if they are?

"Broden, Brodrick?" Aniya asks, feeling crazy as it appears to be a quiet and empty room.

She must be going crazy. Walking into the bathroom, she closes the door, which is not something she would normally do. Sapphire usually waits right inside the bathroom while Aniya takes care of her morning needs, but she decided to close the door in hopes of shutting out her feelings of being watched.

Brodrick is surprised when Aniya wakes and her eyes move straight to where he is sitting. He watches her as she moves to the bathroom. He stills as she calls out to him and Broden. *She cannae see me*, he thinks to himself and almost answers her, sensing she is unsure of herself. He begins to feel a little guilty. She closes the bathroom door, and Sapphire, hearing the click, wakes, scanning the room and stopping when she sees Brodrick. He notices her. Knowing Sapphire's connection to Aniya, he approaches the cat, who has to have grown at least a few inches during the night, because she is noticeably bigger this morn.

"Dinna alert her to my presence, wee beastie. We want to protect her, for we feel our Aniya is in a wee bit of trouble. Can ye keep this between us?" Brodrick watches as Sapphire drops her head as if to acknowledge him and agree.

"'Tis a good girl ye are." Brodrick gives her a pet from her head all the way down to her tail. Sapphire purrs and nods off to sleep again.

Aniya reaches for the towel hanging on the wall and steps out of the bathtub, drying her hair and wrapping the towel around her as she leaves the bathroom. Opening the door, she looks at Sapphire, who must have heard her getting out of the shower.

"Good morning, beautiful girl," Aniya says, talking aloud to her as she walks over to the bed and sits down, reaching for Sapphire, to hug her before getting dressed. "How about I let you out and you can try hunting your breakfast?"

Easier if you just give me steak.

"Yes, maybe it is, but you need to learn to hunt."

Okay, fine.

Aniya watches as Sapphire jumps off the bed and stretches, with a yawn.

But I not happy about it.

Sapphire walks by Aniya and rubs herself against her legs, showing her she isn't really all that upset. "Come on," Aniya tells her, smiling as she starts walking over to the French doors in her room that lead outside and into the forest behind her home. Sapphire walks out the doors and then jogs off and into the woods, disappearing into them as she stands there watching. *Be careful.*

I will.

Aniya turns away and moves toward the closet to choose what to wear. She unwraps the towel and throws it to the bed.

Upon seeing what his soul mate is doing, Brodrick turns around to give Aniya some privacy. Damn, a mirror—and her bare body is reflected in it. Brodrick can't help but stare at the beautiful woman. Watching as she runs her hands through her wet hair, Brodrick's eyes travel downward. Aniya's breasts could fill a man's hands to bursting, her nipples the color of a soft pink rose and hardened by the cooler air in the room. She has left the doors open to the outside, and he would be damned if any other man who isn't her soul mate should see her like this.

Brodrick is slamming the doors before he can stop himself.

Startled at the sound of the French doors slamming, Aniya jumps.

"Who's there?" she yells as she begins looking around the empty room. How and why did the doors slam shut? Aniya hurries to put on a pair of black silk panties with a black lacy bra, grabbing a set of pink scrubs and throwing them on. Running to the doors, she throws them open and looks around.

Sapphire!

Aniya grabs her cell phone and dials Broden. She waits for the ring and for him to pick up.

"Broden, I think someone is in my house. Is Brodrick there with you?"

"Nay, lass, he is on his way to ye. What happened?" He listens as Aniya quickly explains.

"Okay, loving, let me call Brodrick and see how close he is to ye. Where is Sapphire?"

"I called for her. She is hunting."

"Okay, stay calm."

Brother, are ye with her?

Aye, brother, 'tis me who slammed the doors. She was dressing and had left them open. The thought of another man seeing her was too much. I overreacted.

Move to the front door and ring the bell like ye have just arrived. Can ye do that?

Aye, I can.

Brodrick moves quickly to do just that.

"Loving, Brodrick should be there any second." Just as he tells her, the doorbell chimes.

"I think that might be him. How did you call him if you were on the phone with me?" Aniya asks the question as she moves through the house to the front door.

"I will explain later. Is it him?"

"Yes, it is. Thank you," Aniya says while looking through the peephole.

"'Tis fine. We are here if ever ye have need of us," Broden says before he disconnects the phone. Aniya hangs up the phone, unlocks the door, and runs into Brodrick's arms before he can say anything.

"Hush now, sweetling, ye are fine." Feeling quite a bit guilty that he is the one who frightened her, he wraps his arms around her and gives her a slight squeeze.

"Can you check the house? I felt like I was being watched and then the doors . . ." Aniya trails off, trying to slow the adrenaline rushing through her.

"Of course, lass." He begins to walk the house, knowing he won't find anything.

Sapphire chooses that moment to come running through the front door.

You closed the doors. I couldn't get in through the back.

I didn't but someone did.

What you mean? Sapphire's eyes are on Brodrick as he walks back to the front of the house.

"Nothing and nobody is here, sweetling." Brodrick's eyes are on Sapphire. "No worries, beastie, yer mistress is safe."

"Okay, well, if you are sure there is no one here, I need to finish getting ready for work." Aniya looks over for confirmation.

"'Tis fine, sweetling, I promise ye," he says as he bends to kiss Aniya's forehead. "I will even wait and go with ye to the hospital if it pleases ye," Brodrick assures her.

"Thank you." Aniya moves to her bedroom to finish getting ready for work.

"Thank ye, Sapphire, for not giving me away this morn. It was I who frightened her and closed the back doors on ye. She was dressing, I feared someone would see her. I do apologize, beastie." Brodrick bent to whisper so only Sapphire would hear. He gives her a pet before standing to wait for Aniya.

"I'm ready. We are going to stop by the cafe first for coffee, if you don't mind. I haven't had a chance to make any, with all that happened this morning," Aniya says as she walks toward Brodrick and Sapphire.

"Aye, 'tis fine, lass," Brodrick tells her as she smiles at him and rises up on her tiptoes to gently kiss his lips before continuing to the front door. "Come on, beautiful girl."

We go to work now?

"Yes, we go to work," Aniya answers aloud with a smile.

Aniya parks outside the cafe and moves to get out of the car. Brodrick is already there, offering his hand to help her out of the driver's seat.

"Dr. Filmore!" Aniya hears and turns to see Rachel coming out of the cafe doors.

"Rachel! Hi, how are you doing?" The young woman is in Aniya's arms, hugging her before she knew it was coming.

"I'm great. Things are going so well for me now, and it's all thanks to you." Rachel is all smiles and pure joy.

"No, you made the choice, not me, but I'm still so happy to see you," Aniya remarks

The two start talking, not really paying attention when a loud *pop* sounds in the distance. The girls are pushed out of the way but not before Aniya feels a searing pain run through her left upper arm. Brodrick heard the unmistakable sound of a gunshot, and he immediately pushes the girls out of the way but hears Aniya's inhalation, and then the smell of blood and gunpowder permeates the air.

"Dr. Filmore!" Rachel screams.

Sapphire takes off in the direction of the noise.

I smell evil, Iya!

Sapphire, wait! Aniya's mental plea is a second too late as Sapphire runs toward the danger.

"Sweetling, are ye all right?" Brodrick's worry is apparent in his voice.

"I was shot, I think." Aniya is holding her upper arm and pulls her hand away to look as the blood flows from a little hole. She replaces her hand to cover the wound and then applies pressure. "Rachel, go across to the hospital, tell them Aniya's been shot." Brodrick looks away from Aniya to give Rachel his instructions.

"Okay! Hang on, Doc," Rachel tells Aniya before taking off at an unnaturally fast speed.

Brodrick only spends a second taking note of how very fast Rachel moves.

"Sweeting, I need to communicate with Sapphire. Can ye relay my words to her?"

"Yes," Aniya answers through clenched teeth. He can also see she is unfocused and in a lot of pain.

Mother, Broden! Aniya's been shot.

Brodrick can hear the panic and fear for Aniya in his own voice as he tells them what has happened.

Mother, I need to communicate with Sapphire. How does the connection work?

I'm not sure you can. This is a mage trait brought on by a blood bond to their familiar.

So if I take Aniya's blood, will I be able to talk to Sapphire?

I don't know, son, but try. If nothing else, you will have some type of bond to Aniya.

Brodrick can feel how worried his mother is.

"Sweetling, I'm going to take a bit of yer blood. This isn't a full exchange, but I'm hoping it will open a link to Sapphire." Brodrick is holding Aniya as she nods her head in agreement.

Brodrick dips his head to the open wound on her arm, taking only a small amount of the blood that is trickling out from between her fingers. She tastes of the sweetest wine. Her blood is intoxicating, but he only takes enough to hopefully open the mind link.

"I'm taking ye to the hospital now." Brodrick lifts Aniya into his arms and is across the street in the next second. Sapphire comes running back and falls in next to Brodrick as he enters the emergency room doors.

Sapphire, can ye hear me?

Brodrick prays she can, but when he gets no response from Sapphire, he knows it didn't work. "Damn it!" he murmurs, and he feels Aniya shift in his arms.

"What's wrong?" Aniya's voice is quiet.

"Nothing for ye to be concerned about right now," he tells her.

Evie and Broden arrive a second later and glamour themselves as they enter the hospital and follow Brodrick.

"Rachel," Brodrick calls out to her as he approaches where she is standing, which is next to the nurses' station.

"They are bringing a gurney for her now." Rachel answers the unspoken question.

"Thank ye, lass." Brodrick tells her as the nurse behind the desk sees them.

"Aniya?"

It's at that second the ER erupts into chaos as everyone works to help one of their own.

"You call the police. You and you come with me, and someone get Peter on the phone now!"

Jean starts giving orders to those closest to them; no one asks questions or argues, and no one tries to stop her.

It's a while later when Aniya is in bed and resting, when she learns that they had to surgically remove the bullet. Peter had arrived shortly after they had taken Aniya into the operating room, and he has been trying to get Aniya's uncle on the phone, with no luck.

"I'm going to step out and try to call Mike again," Peter informs Brodrick and Rachel as he rises from the chair next to Aniya's bed and walks out of the hospital room.

"Rachel, can ye go and get us some coffee, please?" Brodrick asks her.

"Sure, I could use some as well," she answers him, and she leaves the room.

Brodrick watches as his mother and Broden come into view, dropping their glamour.

Evie moves over to the now-sleeping Aniya and reaches for her hand, looking her over closely now that she can see for herself that Aniya is safe. The boys watch their mother with their soul mate, when they realize that there is a fourth heartbeat in the room. Looking around the room and then at Evie, they are shocked to realize she is the fourth heartbeat.

"Mother, yer heart!" Broden says in complete shock.

"Aye, it beats," Brodrick confirms with the same look of shock and awe on his face as well.

"Yes, it does," Evie tells them, her eyes still on Aniya.

"But who, how?" Broden stumbles over the words.

"Peter. But we can deal with that later. Right now, Aniya is our first concern. She needs our attention at this moment." Evie is ignoring the looks from her boys and keeps her full attention on Aniya.

"But ye found yer soul mate, Mother," Brodrick tells her.

"I am well aware of that, my son, and he will still be my soul mate once his daughter is home and recovering. Leave it for now, boys." Evie makes this stern statement hoping to put an end to the conversation.

"Now that we have that out of the way, Brodrick, did you take Aniya's blood? Are you able to talk to Sapphire?"

"I did take a wee bit of her blood, but nay, it did nae work," Brodrick answered. Then he has an idea and bends down to Sapphire.

"Beastie, I need yer help. I need to talk to ye and ye be able to talk to me. Can ye trust me and take a wee bit of my blood to see if it opens our minds to one another?" he asks.

Sapphire only takes a second before she nods. Brodrick then bites his wrist and offers it to Sapphire. She licks at the puncture marks and then closes the wound even though it would have healed on its own. Sapphire doing so means she accepts Brodrick. She then walks over to Broden as if waiting for him to offer his wrist as well. Understanding Sapphire, Broden bites his wrist and offers it to her. She again licks the marks and closes the wound. "Now what?" Brodrick asks, knowing this is completely new to them all.

Did it work?

Sapphire makes sure to send her question to both Broden and Brodrick.

Aye, beastie, I can hear ye. Smiling, Brodrick answers Sapphire and gives her a pat on the head.

"She spoke?" Broden asks. "I did nae hear anything."

"The only difference is I took a bit of Aniya's blood," Brodrick informs them.

"Then maybe Broden needs to do that as well," Evie offers.

"That might be it, brother.' Brodrick suggests.

"But I cannae ask her, she is unconscious." Broden looks at the sleeping Aniya.

Evie steps toward Broden.

"She gave Brodrick permission. I'm sure, under the circumstances, she would you as well. Only take a small amount though, son." Evie steps to the side so Broden can approach the bed.

"Do ye think 'tis okay to do so?" Broden is a little worried about Aniya's reaction when she wakes up and finds out.

"I'm sure it is." Evie is confident.

Broden steps over to the bed and bends to take Aniya's wrist, and with the slightest nip of his teeth, he can taste her. She tastes of honeyed wine, strong, sweet, and warm. He lifts his head and watches as the wound closes, leaving no sign of the small marks he had just given her.

Can you hear me now? Sapphire sends the message and waits.

Aye, I can. Ye have a beautiful voice, Sapphire, Broden sends back.

At least you not call me beastie like him. Sapphire tilts her head toward Brodrick.

'Tis an endearment, I'm sure, lovely.

I like your enderment better.

Hearing Sapphire try to pronounce *endearment* causes a small laugh to escape Broden.

"So can you both hear her, then?" Evie asks.

"Aye, Mother, we can," Broden answers. His eyes move over to Sapphire again.

Sapphire, do ye sense anything? Can ye tell us what happened?

Broden makes sure to include his brother in this mental conversation.

Now I only smell Iya, and medicine, Evie too. But I smelled evil when the loud sound came. I followed the trail, but it just disappeared. No other trace. Just gone. How can that be?

Brodrick and Broden can hear the confusion in Sapphire's voice.

Sapphire moves over to Evie, resting her huge head on Evie's lap and looks at Aniya asleep on the bed.

"She will be fine. She has magic and her light is bright—that will all work together to heal her, beautiful girl. No need to worry so." Evie tells her with comfort in her voice, knowing that is what Sapphire needs right at this moment. Evie runs her hands down Sapphire's back, the soft fur sliding between her fingers.

"I hope she comes to trust us like she does ye, Mother." Brodrick watches her and Sapphire.

"She already does. Otherwise, she wouldn't have taken your blood."

"But she doesn't seek comfort from us like she does ye," Broden tells Evie.

I'm right here!

Sapphire's sarcasm is clear to hear in both Broden's and Brodrick's mind.

"She sees me like a mother, I think, but I am not sure," Evie explains.

So many new aspects to try and work through.

At that moment, Rachel reenters the room, followed by Peter, whose eyes are on his phone. "I've finally gotten ahold of Mike. He is going to meet us at my house." Peter lifts his head and realizes the room is a lot fuller than it was when he left.

"Who are all of you?" he asks, his eyes falling on Evie as she looks back at him.

She is the most beautiful woman he has ever seen. Wait . . . What is he thinking? She is Aniya's age; he can't see her that way, plus he should be focused on Aniya right now anyway. His eyes move toward Brodrick and Broden next. Twins? What the hell is going on?

"Brodrick?" Peter guesses, making it obvious that he cannot tell them apart.

"Nay, I am Broden McKesson. Ye must be Peter, Aniya's father?" Broden walks over to Peter and reaches to shake the man's hand. Slowly and a little confused, Peter grasps Broden's hand, not paying much attention to it.

"This is our mother Evilyn, Evie if ye prefer." Broden introduces Evie, who is approaching slowly, her heartbeat getting a little quicker.

"Hello, nice to meet one of the men responsible for raising a wonderful and remarkable young woman." Evie's singsong voice penetrates Peter's mind.

"Hi, um, hello." Peter seems to shake out of his trance, recognizing Broden's name and realizing that he is Aniya's soul mate.

"You're the one responsible for lighting my daughter's mage light." Peter doesn't try to hide the accusation or his anger.

"Aye, I am, 'tis a truly wondrous thing." Broden smiles and looks at Aniya.

"Wondrous? Her life has been turned upside down!" Peter raises his voice a bit.

"Peter, calm down. There is much to discuss." Evie tries to defuse the situation before it escalates.

"And how are you their mother? You are no older than Aniya." Peter lowers his voice; he doesn't want to frighten Evie or wake Aniya, but he is trying to figure out what is really going on, why all of a sudden he feels something toward this woman. His daughter is lying in a hospital bed with a gunshot wound in her arm, for god's sakes.

"Dad, is that you?" Aniya's sleepy voice has everyone turning to her and forgetting the conversation for a moment.

"Hey, sweetie, how are you feeling?" Peter asks, bending to kiss her forehead.

"Like I've been shot. Sapphire?" Aniya calls out, and Sapphire is there, jumping carefully onto the bed so she doesn't jostle Aniya.

I am here, Iya.

"Dr. Filmore." Rachel walks to the bed.

"Rachel, please call me Aniya," she tells her.

"Aniya, are you okay? I'm so sorry. I hope you can forgive me." Rachel lowers her head, feeling some guilt.

"Why are you sorry, Rachel? You didn't shoot me."

"Well, no, but had I not stopped you . . ." Rachel trails off.

"Do not be sorry, Rachel. This was not your fault," Aniya says firmly.

"Okay, but what are they talking about? What light?" Rachel asks, remembering what she heard Peter and Broden discussing.

"I'll explain that later. Right now, I want out of this hospital." Aniya tries raising herself to move out of the bed.

"NO!"

Aniya stops and looks at everyone, realizing they all spoke at the same time.

"Evie, Broden, Brodrick, what are all of you doing here?" Aniya asks, but before anyone can answer, the door swings open. Dr. Craine, another ER doctor comes in, looking around the room almost bursting with bodies before his eyes land on Aniya.

"Hi, Aniya, I see you have guests. I can come back," he tells her.

"No, it's okay, Gary. Come in."

"If you're sure." Dr. Craine enters the room and closes the door before he continues talking.

"We removed the bullet and sewed you up. There shouldn't be any permanent damage—it was lodged in your flesh, so it didn't tear any muscles but you are going to need to rest. You are to take a few weeks off, with pay, of course, and you are not to overdo it," he tells her.

"But, Gary—" Aniya is cut off by the doctor.

"No buts, Aniya. I know you don't like being the patient, but in this, you will listen and follow my orders. Peter?" Dr. Craine looks for him in the crowded room.

"Yeah, Gary." Peter moves between Broden and Evie to the bed.

"These are her prescriptions: something for the pain, antibiotics, and one to help her sleep." He shows the paper to Peter then looks back at Aniya.

"The stitches can come out in two weeks. You will probably remove them yourself, but I'd rather you come in so I can do it and check the wound."

"Fine. Can I go home tonight? I don't want to stay in the hospital." Aniya uses what little bit of energy she has to put as much persuasion in her voice as possible when she asks the question.

"I'd rather you stay, but I'll agree if you go to your dad's," Dr. Craine tells her.

"Okay, as long as I can leave tonight." Everyone can see that Aniya isn't at all happy, but they know that if she can leave the hospital tonight, she will deal with it.

"I'll go write up your discharge papers. Peter, make sure to get those meds today," Dr. Craine says as he turns to hand the script to her dad.

"I will, Gary," Peter assures the doctor, taking the small piece of paper and putting it in his pocket.

"All right, Aniya, I want to see you back here in a couple of weeks, and if you need anything between now and then, let me know. Get some rest," Dr. Craine says as he leaves the room.

Aniya looks around the room at everyone before she says anything. "Should we continue our talk now or wait until I'm discharged?"

"Aye, loving, we will continue our talk at yer da's," Broden answers.

"Then can all of you guys leave the room so I can get dressed?" Aniya looks at all three of the men in the room.

"Daughter, do you need help?" Evie asks. "Rachel and I will be more than happy to assist you."

"Yes, please, if it's no trouble," Aniya agrees, realizing she is still a bit weak.

"Daughter? What do you mean?" Peter starts asking as the men are being backed out of the room so Evie can gently shut the door, bringing an end to all his questions.

"Now let's get you dressed, my dear," Evie walks to the bed and begins to dress Aniya with Rachel's assistance.

Everyone arrives at Peter's house within moments of one another. Evie and Brodrick drove Aniya's car, with Sapphire. Aniya rode with her father and Broden, Rachel followed in her own car, and Mike was already there.

"Broden, I can walk. I was shot in the arm, my legs are just fine," Aniya protests as Broden sweeps her up and starts walking to the front door with her in his arms.

"I'm weel aware, loving, but why would I pass up the opportunity to hold ye in me arms?" Broden bends his head to whisper in her ear.

"You are shameless," Aniya whispers back with a smile.

Peter walks ahead to open the door for Broden and stands aside to let them pass.

"Can you put me down now? Evie and Rachel can help me to my room."

"Aye, lass, but take it slow." Broden sets her on her feet and dips to press a kiss to her lips before anyone notices. Brodrick then does the same as he passes her, both catching Aniya off guard. It was so quick she doubted anyone saw it even if they had been watching.

"Careful, sweetling," Brodrick quietly tells her upon entering the house.

"All right, daughter, show us to your room so we can get you resting," Evie says, standing next to Aniya.

Relay what you know and tell Peter everything. Evie sends the message to Broden and Brodrick on their shared mind link.

Aye, Mother.

Everything.

We will tell him everything, they assure her.

CHAPTER 7

Peter watches the women as they make their way up the stairs to Aniya's old bedroom, Sapphire following close behind them. Looking at Broden and Brodrick, he listens for the *click* of the bedroom door.

"What in high hell is going on? You show up and turn on my daughter's mage light, this woman who looks no older than Aniya says she is your mother and calls Aniya daughter, and then to top it off, Aniya gets shot? Care to enlighten me because honestly I'm not impressed with any of this, and it all started when she met you," Peter starts demanding once the door is closed.

"Wait a minute—ye are thinking this is our doing? Ye cannae be serious, ye really think all her accidents are nae a coincidence? Ye would have us believe ye ken nothing? The car accident in high school, falling off playground equipment, she got deathly ill, the car that almost hit her the other night, and Aniya getting shot is nae at all related and ye ken nothing? Her mother's death was also a freak accident? Ye would have us believe ye never thought for a second something else might be happening? Ye cannae be serious, Peter," Broden shoots back at Peter angrily.

"Wait, what do you mean Aniya was almost hit by a car? When?" Peter is surprised Aniya didn't say anything to him.

"Aye, Peter, the other night before our dinner date," Brodrick confirms.

"Hold on, you both are dating her?" Peter thinks he might need to have a talk with his daughter.

"Peter, let us sit and talk. We will figure this out, but fighting will nae solve anything," Broden tells him, moving in the direction of what appears to be the living room

"Peter, I put coffee on and took the liberty of ordering pizza for dinner, thought we might have guests." Mike walks toward them. "And I can hear I was right if your raised voices was any clue," he adds.

"Ye must be Uncle Mike. Are ye thinking the same as Peter, clueless to the fact that Aniya may be in danger?" Brodrick wastes no time with introductions.

"We will discuss this once everyone is seated with coffee." Mike turns back to the kitchen.

"I think I need something stronger than coffee," Peter murmurs under his breath, moving into the living room.

The men have all sat down. Broden and Brodrick are next to one another. Peter and Mike sit across from them on the much smaller loveseat.

"Now can you tell me about this car that almost hit my daughter?" Peter sits with coffee in hand. Broden relays all that had happened before dinner. Brodrick tells his side and what he saw from his angle.

"And you think it was intentional? This short, bald older man aimed for Aniya?" Peter asks.

"He said the car would nae brake," Broden says.

"Now you tell me about the gunshot." Peter thinks he is talking to Brodrick but can't be sure.

"I will tell ye what I told the police. It all happened too fast. Rachel greeted Aniya. They were talking to each other when a shot rang out. I tried to push them both out of the way but was nae fast enough. I told the police everything I could tell them." Peter sympathizes when he hears the hurt in Brodrick's voice.

"Now I can tell ye Sapphire said she smelled evil, but the trail just disappeared, vanished," Brodrick adds.

"You can see and hear Sapphire—how is that possible?" Peter asks.

"Peter, those with magic can see Sapphire, but I'm a little curious about hearing her myself." Mike looks at the twins.

"Weel, the obvious answer is we are magic so we can see her. As far as hearing her, 'tis a bit more difficult," Broden tells them.

"Okay, this is my daughter we are talking about, so maybe you boys can start explaining everything." Peter feels like they are reluctant to explain it all but isn't sure. So he waits patiently for one of them to continue with all the information he knows he doesn't have.

"Weel, Aniya is soul mate to both of us. We are vampires, as is Evie—" Brodrick starts but is interrupted.

"Soul mate to both of you, vampires. Mike, what in the hell is going on?" Peter asks the only person other than Aniya that he trusts.

"Peter, I have never heard of this happening. I know I have been away from the Fae realm for a long while, but I can't imagine that it has changed that much. Aniya's grandparents didn't mention anything when I went to them about her mage light." Mike does not understand this himself.

"This never happened before us. Mother wants to ask the council, but before she had a chance, Aniya was shot," Broden tells them.

"If ye like, I will proceed, 'tis more." Brodrick looks at Peter.

"More? There's more?" Peter takes a drink of his coffee, unsure if he is going to be able to handle much more.

"Aye, Peter, we will tell ye all we ken. Mayhap together we can figure all this out." Broden looks at Brodrick. "Brother, continue."

Brodrick tells Peter and Mike how they met Aniya and about the mage they are seeking and that that is what they thought brought them here. He goes on to explain why they were turned and how Evie considers them her sons and Aniya her daughter. Broden throws in a few other details.

"'Tis the truth and the whole of the story up to this point," Broden finishes.

"So you think something or someone is trying to kill Aniya, but why? She is mage, but she had no idea about you or the Fae. We never thought her light would come on." Peter anxiously tries to take everything in. He now knows how his daughter felt when they told her she was a mage.

"Aye, Peter, 'tis the only thing that makes sense, but as to the why of it . . ." Broden shrugs.

"We have nae figured that out. If she is the mage we were searching for . . ." Broden trails off.

"Nay, brother, ye cannae think . . ." Brodrick picks up on his brother's thoughts.

"Aye, brother, why else? Two attempts in a matter of days. Think on it." Broden watches Brodrick.

"Think on what?" Mike isn't sure he wants to know but asks anyway.

"Boys, fill us in, please." Peter waits.

"If Aniya is the mage we are seeking, then all this makes her even more important, not just to us but the entire Fae. But then why try and kill her if she is meant to save us?" Brodrick asks them all.

"What makes you think the person doing this is Fae?" Mike asks.

"Aye, 'tis true whoever it is has made us think 'tis a human. They used a car and a gun, nae magic, but Sapphire said she smelled evil and then the trail vanished," Broden explains. "Humans cannae vanish into thin air without leaving a trail, but Fae can," he continues.

"How would they know she is the mage? Nobody does—that is why you were created, isn't it? To find the mage? And if your suspicions are correct, why kill Marriam? Aniya was already born. Wouldn't they have tried to kill Aniya?" Peter is trying to put everything together and make some sense of all this new information.

"Mike, ye were there, do ye think the bullet was meant for Aniya's mother or her?" Brodrick looks at him.

"It happened so quickly. Aniya was next to Marriam, but she pushed Aniya behind her when Peter started to grab for the gun. It's possible the shooter was aiming for her and Marriam got in the way. The police arrived before he could get off another shot," Mike tells them.

"Do ye ken what happened to the killer?" Broden asks.

"He was tried for murder and convicted, still in prison to this day," Peter answers.

"The police said it was just a robbery gone bad," Mike says.

"The police didn't say whether it was his intention to kill either of them, but I never really asked." Peter finishes.

Evie and Rachel help Aniya upstairs and into some pajamas, settling her into bed Evie pats the end of the mattress.

"Up, girl," Evie tells Sapphire, which she carefully does as she lies with her head next to Aniya's waist, near her hand.

"Good job, beautiful girl." Evie reaches to give Sapphire a rub down her back.

"Who are you talking to?" Rachel asks, looking around but not seeing anything.

"Can she not?" Evie looks at Aniya.

"No, she can't see her," Aniya's reply is slightly groggy since she had taken her meds before leaving the hospital.

"Oh dear, Rachel, why don't you have a seat?" Evie tells her.

"I'm not going to like this, am I?" Rachel's confusion is plain to see.

"It's not bad, it's quite extraordinary actually." Aniya starts giggling.

"The pain meds," both Evie and Rachel say together, joining in on the giggles.

After a moment, the girls settle in.

"You asked what light had been lit. Are you sure you want to know? This will drag you into a different world, one of fairy tales," Aniya asks Rachel, giving her the option to back out if she wants to.

"If it helps me to understand what happened today, then yes. Are you sure you want to talk about it?" Rachel asks her in return.

"Honestly, it would be nice to be able to share it with someone outside my ever-growing family, which reminds me. Evilyn, this is Rachel. Rachel, Evilyn, Evie for short. She is kind of my mother-in-law." Aniya introduces the two because she can't remember if that had already been done.

"When did you get married, or were you married when we met?" Rachel asks.

"I'm not married."

"Aniya, you aren't making any sense."

"Daughter, if you would allow me, I will explain it to Rachel." Evie realizes the pain medication is having quite an impact on Aniya's thought process.

Evie gets Rachel to sit down next to Aniya on the bed, making sure Sapphire is out of the way, and she begins to explain everything. Once she is finished, Evie looks at Aniya, who seems a bit more aware now.

"Did all that make sense, Rachel?" Aniya looks at her.

"Yeah, if we were in a TV show, maybe. As a reality show, you'd flop big time. Seriously, a tiger that can only be seen by those with magic? A witch and vampire twins who are soul mates? A different realm where fairies live, and can you imagine baby vamps with witch powers?" Rachel points out. Aniya realizes nobody thought about the children she, Broden, and Brodrick might have. Not the time for that right now, she tells herself.

"Rachel, it's all true—except for the baby thing, which nobody is thinking about right now," Aniya tells her.

"Aniya, come on. The joke is over." Rachel laughs it off.

"You want proof?" Aniya challenges.

"Sure, say a spell, or better yet, can you conjure up Mr. Right for me? That would be awesome!" Rachel starts laughing.

"Fine, watch." Aniya waves her hand. "There, that's Sapphire," she tells Rachel.

"Aniya, there is no tiger lying next to you. Stop."

Sapphire raises her head at the comment. *I right here.*

"I know, beautiful girl. Hang on, let me go get Uncle Mike." When Aniya goes to stand, Evie pushes her back down.

"No, you don't. I will go get him."

"Evie, I'm okay just going to walk down the stairs and get him. I was shot in the arm, my legs are fine." Aniya, getting tired of how overprotective everyone is, echoes the same argument she gave Broden.

"Fine, just take it slow. The meds could still be affecting you," Evie warns while she helps Aniya stand up.

"Thank you." Walking slowly, she makes her way to the bedroom door, and when she opens it, she can hear the murmurings from the men talking.

Making her way to the stairs, she carefully starts the descent to the bottom floor.

"Hey, Uncle Mike, I need your help . . ." Aniya trails off as the view to the living room comes into her line of vision.

Uncle Mike looks about twenty years younger; his auburn hair that only a week ago was streaked with gray is now healthy, with no gray whatsoever. The laugh lines and wrinkles that were starting to show around his mouth and blue eyes have all but disappeared, leaving smooth perfect skin on his oval face. His frame seems slightly slimmer but healthy, and he looks a bit taller even though he is sitting.

"UNCLE MIKE! Nope, nope, no, uh-uh, I'm seeing things. These meds are messing with every one of my senses. I'm so not doing this, I'm done and going back to bed now. This is just too much." Aniya turns and starts walking back up the stairs.

"Uncle Mike looks more like he's thirty. He is Dad's age. I am so not taking those meds again," Aniya murmurs to herself.

"Aniya, wait, you're fine. I just dropped my glamour is all. Please come back!" She can hear Uncle Mike call after her.

"This is so not happening. I need to wake the hell up," she whispers to herself. Hearing several footsteps following her up the stairs, she makes her way toward her bedroom.

"I'm good, I just need Uncle Mike to show me how to reveal Sapphire to Rachel." She turns her head and calls down over her shoulder to the four men chasing her.

All four men follow Aniya, one after the other, up the stairs.

"Sweetling, wait."

"Loving, stop."

"Sweetie, Uncle Mike . . ." Peter raises his voice over the others.

"Honey, it's still me. I just dropped my aging glamour."

Aniya turns when she gets to the top of the stairs, to look at them all.

"I just need Uncle Mike. No, I can't call you that anymore. You look too young to be my uncle now. Mike, I just need Mike to show me how to make it so Rachel can see Sapphire, that's all. We can talk about this" Aniya holds her hands out as if to circle Mike, "later. I can only deal with one life-changing event at a time." She turns and walks back to her room.

I really need to lie back down, she thinks to herself, entering her room. Aniya goes back to her bed and waits for all the men to come in. As they enter, Mike makes his way to the head of the bed and looks at Sapphire where she lies.

"You can still call me Uncle Mike."

"One life-changing event at a time. I'm sorry, but that will be discussed later. Now please just do the hand-waving thing so Rachel can see Sapphire and stops thinking I'm crazy, but I'm beginning to wonder about that one myself." Aniya talks to Mike but doesn't look at him.

"I will show you, but I'm not going to do it for you. You need to learn your magic."

"Now I want you to close your eyes and focus inward, look for your light. That's it." Mike watches Aniya as she appears to do as he requests.

"How will I know where to look? I've never done this before."

"You'll know. It's going to feel warm and be very bright."

"I think I see it. It's beautiful. How is that inside me?"

"It's part of you, just like your heart or any other organ. It's your magic, your source, always there. Now you need to pull it forward, but just a little, we don't know how powerful you are yet. Gently focus on the magic and mentally picture what you want it to do," Mike instructs Aniya.

"Is it working?"

"Mentally see it and wave your hand, letting the magic flow through your arm down to your fingertips with a small wave."

Everyone is watching her intently. Aniya's eyes are closed. She can see the picture of Rachel looking at Sapphire and seeing her. She focuses on her light, watching as it rises up from her chest, and on bringing it to the surface; it takes some energy to push her magic in the direction she needs it to go, remembering to not push all her magic out of her, just a little, enough for Rachel to see Sapphire. She pushes her magic through her arm, to her hand, and out of her fingers. Aniya must have done it correctly because then she hears Rachel's next words.

"What the hell!" Rachel's surprise is clear to hear; she jumps off the bed as the white tiger comes into view.

"You weren't joking, you're serious! That's a tiger!" Rachel's hand is over her heart as if that will help slow the pace of its pounding.

You told her I was here. Why is Achel scared, Iya?

Aniya opens her eyes and looks at Rachel. "Rachel, this is Sapphire. She doesn't bite."

"I think she is just surprised, beautiful girl." Aniya answers Sapphire's question out loud.

Sapphire watches as Rachel slowly sits back on the bed only a few feet away from her. She starts to belly crawl toward Rachel, asking for a pet, but Rachel moves away and Sapphire can't help but open and close her mouth in a biting motion to see Rachel's expression, then looks toward Aniya as if laughing a bit.

"Sapphire, stop that. You'll scare her more." A small laugh escapes Aniya, knowing Sapphire would never bite her friend.

Sorry, Iya, couldn't help it.

"I thought you said she doesn't bite?"

"Rachel, she doesn't. Sapphire was messing with you. No more jokes, Sapphire." Aniya hugs the cat and pats the empty spot on the bed next to her, urging Rachel to sit.

Let her pet you so she won't be scared anymore.

Of course, I would never bite Achel. She smell like the forest. I like her smell.

Like the forest, are you sure? I can't smell the forest on her.

My nose more sensitive. Achel smells like the forest, Iya.

Rachel's hand reaches out, and Sapphire pushes her head against Rachel's palm. "Oh my gosh, I'm petting a tiger! She is so soft." Rachel bends down and rubs both her hands and head into Sapphire's fur.

"How is that reality show looking now, Rachel?" Aniya cocks her eyebrow at her and laughs.

"I'm so sorry I didn't believe you, Aniya. Sapphire is beautiful." Rachel is still petting the cat while in complete shock. She isn't sure if it's more shock at seeing the tiger or shock that all of what Evie and Aniya have told her is true.

"Rachel, you don't need to be sorry. Welcome to my life. Every day is a new adventure. If you're willing to walk through this with me, then I'd be glad to have you!"

"I'll be here whenever you need me, Aniya, thank you for telling me." Rachel's sincerity is genuine, and Aniya is happy to have her as a friend.

"There you go. Now the more you practice using your magic, the more it will become second nature to you. You also won't have to pull it out. It will just come to you naturally," Mike tells her.

"Sweetling, is yer arm bothering you?" Broden asks when he notices her scratching at it.

"No, just itches some. I think I need to check the wound and change the bandages." Aniya hadn't noticed she'd been scratching, but now that the itching has gotten pretty bad, she can't seem to stop.

"Weel, we can help ye heal it. Just a bit of our blood and it will be a scar," Brodrick adds, a little irritated with himself for not thinking of it sooner.

"Let's get it unwrapped and have a look." Evie approaches the bed and slowly starts to unwrap Aniya's bandaging.

Aniya watches as the bandages slowly come off, and when her arm is bare of the wrapping, everyone in the room is gasping. The wound is almost completely healed, and the only reason it isn't is because the damn stitches have irritated the healed skin, causing it to pull.

"How does a less-than-day-old gunshot wound close so fast?" Rachel asks the one question everyone else is wondering.

"Dad, can you go get the suture scissors out of the first aid kit in the bathroom, please?"

"I have always been a fast healer, Rachel, but this is faster than it's ever been," Aniya answers as she is turning her arm in many different directions to try to get a better look at the injury.

"Mayhap it has something to do with yer light. Mike, do ye ken?" Broden asks.

"My light has never been on. We are mage, so we do heal faster than humans even without our mage light. It would make sense that our magic would help with healing once our light is lit," Mike answers Broden, but it is the only thing that would make sense.

"Something to ask your grandparents, honey." He offers the suggestion.

"I think we need to go to the Fae realm as soon as possible, daughter. We need to speak to the council and the seer, so we will stop in to see your grandparents as well," Evie says.

Peter is back with the scissors, and he hands them to Aniya.

"Here you go, sweetheart, be careful." Peter moves to stand next to Evie without thinking about it.

"Daddy, I am a doctor."

Before she can start to cut the stitches, Broden steps forward. "Let me. It might be a little difficult because of where your injury is," he tells her as he goes to grab the scissors from Aniya.

Once Broden has finished cutting out the stitches, five in total, Aniya cleans the area—no blood and the wound is completely sealed now. She raises her head and looks at everyone in the room. "I can go home now. The wound is healed, and if we are going to the Fae realm, I need to take care of a few things and get ready."

"Maybe it would be best for you to just stay here tonight. I'd feel better if you didn't stay by yourself," her father tells her.

"I'll be fine. Sapphire will be with me, so I won't be by myself."

"Peter, one of us will stay with her if ye like. We had already planned to have one of us with her at all times, even if she stayed here," Brodrick interjects.

"Yeah, Dad, Brodrick or Broden can stay with me. It'll be fine." Aniya rises from the bed and moves to get her stuff.

"If you're determined to go, I would feel better knowing that one or both of them as well as Sapphire will be with you. Before you leave, at least have some of the pizza Mike ordered—it should be here any minute." As if on cue, the doorbell rings.

"I'll get it." Mike goes to leave the room.

"Thanks, Mike, next time, dinner is on me," Peter says.

Everyone moves downstairs just as Mike closes the door, walking into the dining room to set the pizzas on the table.

"Come and get it." Mike grabs some plates to set out.

They all eat, talking about nothing in particular, just getting to know one another. Once all are finished and have visited a little while, Rachel is the first to leave.

"I'm gonna head out. Aniya, I'd really like to come with you to the Fae realm. Would that be okay?" she asks.

"I'd like that. It will be my first time as well—is it okay to bring her?" Aniya looks to Mike, Evie, Broden, and Brodrick for an answer.

"I can't see a problem with it." Mike shrugs.

"It might be good to have her there," Evie agrees.

"We've only been a few times, but it should be fine." Brodrick looks at Broden, who confirms by a nod of his head.

"Great! I can't wait," Rachel says, with a smile.

"Meet us at my house tomorrow morning. You can park your car there," Aniya tells her.

"I'm coming too." Peter makes the statement as if they all would tell him no.

"I'll be going as well."

"Okay then, this is going to be interesting," Aniya says.

"See you all tomorrow, then." Rachel hugs Aniya and Evie and says her goodbyes before leaving.

"I'm ready to go too," Aniya announces.

Me too.

Aniya looks down at Sapphire as the cat yawns and stretches.

"All right, beautiful girl, let's go. Dad, Mike, see you tomorrow." Aniya hugs them both. "Be safe."

"Love you, sweetie."

"Love you both," Aniya tells them both.

"Mike, Peter, thank ye and we can talk more tomorrow." Brodrick shakes hands with the men.

"Peter, we have some things to discuss as well. Thank you for everything." Evie kisses his cheek, which sends a jolt of electricity through them both.

"Mike, lovely to meet you too." Evie nods her head to him.

Aniya, Brodrick, and Broden along with Evie all leave together, heading to Aniya's house. When they arrive and get inside, Sapphire heads straight to the bedroom and is on the bed, curled up and fast asleep.

"Well, that didn't take long." Aniya laughs at Sapphire.

"She's had a busy day." Evie smiles at the sleeping cat.

Should we both stay with her or just one?

Brother, I'd like to stay with her tonight. She was hurt while I was right there. The guilt has eaten at me since. Can ye understand and give me this?

'Tis not yer fault, but I can understand. Besides, we will need to check out of the hotel tomorrow. I will give you this night, brother. In return, I want just one night as weel and then neither of us will leave her. We both will stay by her side from then on.

Aye, I'll agree to that. Thank ye.

"Aniya, I will be staying with ye tonight. Broden and Mother will meet us here in the morning, and we all will go to the Fae realm together," Brodrick tells her.

"Okay, but you're on the couch," she says.

Broden walks over and kisses Aniya. The gentle touch of his lips on hers starts her heart fluttering and she opens to him, meeting his tongue. He pulls away before he loses his control and decides he wants to stay instead.

"Good night, loving," he tells Aniya, dropping one more kiss on her lips before turning to the door.

"Sleep well, daughter." Evie kisses Aniya on the cheek and hugs her before turning to Brodrick to say good night.

"Good night, Mother, we will see ye both in the morning."

"I'll have breakfast on the table," Aniya promises.

Brodrick follows them to the door, closing it after showing Evie and Broden out, making sure to lock the door before turning to Aniya.

"If ye think for one second I am sleeping on the couch, Aniya, ye be wrong. I will be holding ye while we sleep," he tells her with a wicked smile.

CHAPTER 8

"Any other time I'd argue that, but right now, all I want is a shower and clothes that do not have blood on them. So you can have a seat or make coffee, but I'm getting under some hot water." With that, she walks to her bedroom, leaving Brodrick to entertain himself.

Brodrick watches her as she walks from her bedroom to the bathroom. He hears the shower turn on and can tell the moment she steps under the spray. Brodrick decides he could use a shower himself.

Without a second thought, he walks to the bathroom, removing his clothing as he goes.

Aniya steps into the spray of the steaming water, feeling it run down her head and body. She tilts her head back, letting the water run over her face, her hands in her wet hair as the water rinses away the smell of the hospital and the dried blood from her wound. It takes her a moment to realize she is no longer alone. When another pair of hands is in her hair, she jumps slightly. Turning, she sees a very wet and naked Brodrick.

"Brodrick! Wha— wha— what are you doing?" she demands while trying to cover herself.

"I only wished to help ye bathe. Yer arm may be healed, but I thought mayhap ye might be sore. No need to cover yerself, it will make it a bit difficult to bathe ye with yer arms in the way."

"I am capable of bathing myself!"

"I ken ye are." He slowly turns her around so her back is to him. "But I would nae want ye to cause more pain to yer arm when I can help." Brodrick reaches around Aniya for the shampoo and puts a small amount into his palm before rubbing his hands together and massaging the shampoo into her hair, and soon enough, the smell of roses fill the air.

"Really, I'm fine." Aniya's protest dies as Brodrick starts working the shampoo through her hair and massaging her scalp. Closing her eyes, she tilts her head back, giving him better access.

"That's it, sweetling. Relax, enjoy, and let me take care of ye." He begins rinsing the shampoo and moves to get the conditioner. After he has rinsed her hair again, making sure everything has come out, he grabs her body wash.

"Here, I can do that." She reaches for the bottle, but Brodrick is much faster.

"Nay, lass, let me." He opens the bottle and squeezes a good amount onto his hand before replacing the body wash.

"I have this," Aniya says, raising a loofah.

"I'll be using my hands. Turn around."

She slowly faces him, her awkwardness showing.

"Beautiful, absolutely perfect." Brodrick's eyes move over her breasts, nipples taut from the shower spray, curved hips, and the patch of brunette curls at the junction of her legs dripping with water. He works a lather up in his hands and starts washing Aniya. His hands on her shoulders move down each of her arms, up her rib cage, over her full beautiful breasts, paying extra attention to the soft pink nipples that only harden more at his touch. Kneeling down, he moves down her stomach, making sure every inch of her legs and calves are covered with the lather. Aniya inhales as his hand moves up between her legs to her thighs, but it isn't his hand she feels touching her most intimate place. He catches the small stream of water falling from her curls with his tongue before kissing her most sensitive spot.

"Brodrick!" she moans.

"Aye?" He rises, making sure to run his thumb over her bud of nerves between the pink lips of her mound. The soap is gone from Aniya's skin, only to be replaced with trails of fire where he touched her.

"It's your turn," she tells him.

"For what?" Brodrick looks at her with desire burning in his eyes.

"For me to wash you." A seductive smile is on her lips.

"If ye insist, but be careful. Ye had better be prepared to put out the fire yer going to start, sweetling."

Aniya grins and reaches for the soap. "Don't worry. I would never leave a fire to burn out." She lathers her hands with the body wash. She moves her hands to his chest, rubbing in slow circles, reaching her arms around him to get to his back, causing her breast to rub against his stomach, hardening her nipples again. She moves her hands lower over Brodrick's butt before moving to his front again. Her body sliding down his, she is soon face to face with his cock, already hardened as she looks at him. She isn't even a little frightened by his size, though he is quite a bit larger than the men she has been with in the past. His girth alone has to be two to three inches, and near nine inches in length from tip to base. She wonders what he might taste like, and before she thinks about it too much, her tongue is licking him from balls to tip. Brodrick inhales and lifts Aniya to her feet.

"Keep that up, sweetling, I'll spill my seed before we make it out of the shower." Then he bends to capture her lips in a hard and demanding kiss. Rising on her tiptoes to meet his kiss, she presses her wet body to his, feeling his erection against her stomach. She pushes herself hard against him, needing to feel his touch almost as much as she needs air to breathe.

"We might want to get out of the shower. I could nae bear it if ye fell," Brodrick says as he feathers kisses down her jaw to her neck. He then reaches around Aniya to shut off the water.

"Oh, right." His words, as soft as they were, are enough to bring her out of the haze of desire. The water is off and the shower curtain is opened, causing cool air to hit her heated skin.

Brodrick reaches for the towel hanging on the wall and steps out of the tub. He turns and helps her out before wrapping her in the towel.

"Thank you." She dries off before handing the towel to him and walking naked out of the bathroom to her dresser.

"Nay, I like seeing ye this way." Brodrick's husky voice is in her ear.

As if sensing it is time to leave, Sapphire jumps off the bed and heads out of the room.

I go sleep on couch for now.

Brodrick chuckles and Aniya smiles as they watch Sapphire leave.

Looking at him, she notes the towel she had given him was knotted around his narrow waist and water spots still drip from his chest, catching the light as they slide down, before the towel absorbs the droplets. This man is a Greek god.

"Brodrick."

"Aye, come to me."

She begins walking toward him and he meets her halfway. He drops his head to kiss her. His tongue dances with hers, deepening the kiss. He lifts his head and turns Aniya in his arms so her back is against his chest. He bends to kiss the curve of her neck.

"If this is nae what ye want, all ye need to do is tell me to stop and I will. However, I have hope ye dinna," he whispers in her ear, sending shivers of desire through her. Every nerve in her body comes alive with each kiss.

Aniya leans her head to the side, giving Brodrick better access to the sensitive spot at the base of her neck.

"Don't stop." Her voice comes out in a sexy whisper.

Brodrick's hands cup her breasts, his thumbs rubbing over her nipples, sending shocks right to her clit, which has her wet and dripping down her thighs. He takes her nipples between his thumb and forefinger, pinching and releasing them, leaving her panting and softly moaning in desire. He moves his left hand down her stomach before going lower still to cup her before sliding a finger between her wet slit to caress the bundle of nerves. He circles her clit with his thumb, moving his finger to her opening and slowly slides his finger then another into her. Once his fingers are as deep inside her as he can get, he withdraws and pushes in again, his thumb lightly circling her clit. Scorching heat rises in her with every thrust of his fingers and every circle of his thumb. She can feel the pleasure as she climbs, reaching higher and higher as her hips meet the thrust of his fingers deep inside her. Her body craves the release she feels building inside her. Brodrick kisses her neck, moving from one side to the other, his hand rubbing and slightly pinching one of her nipples while his other hand works to push her over the edge. His teeth softly scraping her neck, he can feel her heart beating frantically, and before he can stop himself, his teeth sink deep into her tender flesh. He drinks her in while his fingers keep thrusting, his thumb working at her clit. He feels her muscles clench at his fingers, followed by her scream of ecstasy. Aniya feels the pleasure building. Her eyes close, head rolling back and forth as he uses his hands and mouth to keep her climbing even higher toward her peak. She feels a small sting where her shoulder meets her neck which sends shocks of bliss through her. The orgasm sets off an explosion of wave after wave of pleasure as she reaches the top of the cliff and falls.

"Brodrick!" Her moan comes out more as a scream.

"That's it, come for me, lass." Brodrick licks her neck and watches as the marks he created heal before taking her in his arms and carrying her to the bed, where he lays her down and lets the towel fall, dropping to the floor. Aniya's eyes run up and down his body as he climbs onto the bed. She reaches for him, pulling his head down to hers. Their tongues dance as Brodrick moves between her legs. He raises his head and looks at her.

"Sweetling, I am going to bond with ye now. I dinna think I will be able to stop myself. I will take yer blood and give ye mine. This will seal us together for all eternity in the way of vampires." His voice is husky with his desire for her and a look filled with an emotion she has never seen on him before—tenderness, maybe even the spark of love?

"You already took my blood. Could I not just take yours?"

"We have to do this while our bodies are joined."

"Ummm, in case you haven't noticed, I don't have fangs."

"'Tis why I will make a cut for ye to drink from. Dinna worry—it won't hurt." Then he bends his head and begins kissing her. Aniya is still on fire for him, her desire not yet sated. She returns his kiss. The fire in her rages on with every kiss and caress he gives her as he moves down her jaw to her neck before moving to the valley between her breasts and settling on her right nipple, causing a low moan to escape. Brodrick sucks on the nipple, running his teeth and tongue back and forth over the tip then moves to repeat the action on her other one, both now hard from his attentions. He nips at her slightly, the sting sending more electricity through her again. She arches her back, pushing her breast into his mouth asking. No, begging for more. Slowly moving lower over her stomach, nipping and kissing every spot he stops at before he opens her legs and moves his head between her thighs to taste her. When her hands find his hair, he increases his flicks and nibbles. She can hardly control her muscles as they jerk with every lap of his tongue.

"Ohh!" Aniya moans.

Brodrick is over her in the next second, and with one thrust, his cock is buried balls deep inside of her. "Uhh!" She cries out.

"I did nae hurt ye, did I?"

"Ohh no, not at all. Don't stop." She tells him, moving her hips, encouraging him.

"Impatient, are nae ye?" Grinning, Brodrick begins thrusting.

"You feel so good," she whimpers

"Aye, so do ye." He pulls out almost all the way before thrusting in again, and pleasure rocks his body. Never has it felt so good to be buried so deep in a woman. He rises up on his hands so he can look down at his soul mate as he continues to thrust in and out of her wet, hot, and tight pussy. Her little moans of delight added to his heavy breathing ignite the fire in his belly that burns. Lifting his hand to the spot just above his collarbone, he cuts himself, feeling the blood start to flow.

"Sweeting, drink from me, help to seal our bond," he whispers as he lifts her head while still thrusting into her body, moving faster and faster. Bending to her shoulder, he sinks his teeth into her, drinking deep, enough for a full exchange this time. It seems so bright Brodrick closes his eyes but doesn't stop his hips as he moves in and out of Aniya and they drink from each other. Aniya is the first to pull away, her eyes searching out his. Brodrick lifts his head and goes to close the small puncture marks on her neck but watches and sees that they are healing on their own. He is soon distracted as Aniya lifts her hips to meet his next thrust, feeling her body is ablaze but not painful. Her light is so bright it seems to be projecting out of her and hovering above them. She watches the beautiful light as it splits into three different pieces.

Brodrick keeps thrusting into her as the three lights surround them, hurting his eyes slightly. His hips move faster and faster as Aniya's vaginal walls contract around his cock; still he keeps thrusting, knowing her climax is close.

"Oh my god!" Aniya shouts as her orgasm rocks her and the waves of pleasure spread through her body. Brodrick pushes into her before pulling out and pushing in again and again. Another release causes what look like stars to form all around Aniya. He feels her second climax hit her, squeezing his shaft tighter and tighter. Unable to hold himself back anymore, his body seeking its own release, he thrusts one, two, three more times before his seed fills Aniya's womb. Brodrick's moans match hers as they scream out each other's names while they both ride the wave of their shared release together.

Brodrick sits up and goes to move off Aniya, but before he can one of the three lights shoots toward him, hitting him in the chest over his heart, throwing him off Aniya until he hits the wall on the opposite side of the bedroom.

"Brodrick! Are you all right?" Aniya sits up on the bed and looks for him.

One of the two remaining lights looks to be searching for something and when it seems to not find it, shoots back into Aniya along with the other one that is floating with it, causing her to be slammed into the bed on her back.

"What in the bloody hell was that?" Brodrick asks.

"I think that was my light!" Aniya replies with a slightly pained voice full of confusion.

"Why the bloody hell did it throw me across the room?" he asks while trying to stand. Aniya jumps off the bed to help him rise.

Brodrick, you broke the wall!

Sapphire sends to them both after hearing the loud crash and running into the room.

"Weel, beastie, the wall broke my arse, so we're even."

What's arse? Sapphire tilts her head to one side.

"Nothing, beautiful girl, sorry if we scared you." Aniya helps Brodrick dust wall plaster off himself.

"Well, that was unexpected, lass. Do ye ken if that is supposed to happen?"

"Why yes! It's happened every time I've had sex. A light comes out of me, turns into various shapes, and shoots into every man I've been with." Her sarcasm is apparent, but he doesn't think her being with any men other than him and his brother is funny in the least and shoots her a look telling her so.

No other man will touch ye unless it's my brother.

"What are you talking about? I was being sarcastic, Brodrick. I don't want any other men if they aren't you or Broden. Why would you even say that?" Aniya looks at him, folding her arms over her bare breasts.

"Aniya, I didn't say that."

"Yes, you did, just now. I heard you."

"Nay, I did nae."

"Yes, you—"

Brodrick cuts Aniya off. "Nay, lass, I did nae say it, I thought it," he explains.

"You thought it . . . But how? I heard your thoughts? What the hell is happening now?"

"Weel, we are now bonded in the way of vampires and I'm assuming the mage way as weel, but damn, that hurt!" Brodrick rubs his chest where the light entered him.

Well, if that doesn't ruin a beautiful moment.

Brodrick puts his finger under her chin, raising her head so she can look him in the eyes.

"It did nae ruin it, lass. I enjoyed it very much." Bending, he drops a gentle kiss on her lips.

"Okay, this is unreal. I think we should just go to bed. We have to be up early anyway. I would love a repeat, but after finding out my light can throw you across the room," *I hope that doesn't happen every time.*

"Aye, I too hope it doesn't happen every time but I'd like to find out." Brodrick flashes her a grin and walks to the bed to remake it before they lie down.

"You being in my head is going to take some getting used to," Aniya says she walks over to help straighten out the bedding.

"Ye have Sapphire in yer head, is nae that the same?"

"No, Sapphire can only talk to me in my mind, so it's different."

As if hearing her name, Sapphire is standing at the foot of the bed, with her head resting on top, looking up at them.

Come up, beastie.

They both watch as Sapphire jumps on the bed, taking her claimed spot at the foot. Aniya bends to pet and hug her before climbing under her comforter.

Good night, beautiful girl.

Night.

Brodrick scratches her behind the ear before climbing in next to Aniya.

Aniya waits for him to lie down before moving her head to lie on his chest and feels his arm come around her.

"Will this ever be normal?" Aniya's voice is getting slightly heavy with sleep.

"It will become our normal, sweetling. And we will figure it out, dinna ye worry." Brodrick kisses the top of her head.

"It just seems like so much and it's all at once."

"Aye, but we are soul mates and that means we are meant to be. 'Tis not something we can change, nae that I would want to. Sleep now, tomorrow is going to be another big day for ye." Brodrick runs soothing hands over her back.

"More to deal with." Her voice is low.

"Aye, we will deal with it together, ye are nae alone anymore." Brodrick can hear her breathing relax and become deeper.

"Together," she whispers as sleep takes her.

Brodrick just holds her for a while, listening to her even breathing and thinks over everything that has been happening and pulls her closer before sleep claims him as well.

Aniya wakes the next morning to banging on her front door.

"What the . . . Oh shit, Dad?" She looks around the room and sees a naked Brodrick next to her. Remembering what happened the night before, she jumps out of bed, looking at the hole in the wall and the mess all around it. How on earth is she going to explain all of this?

"Please work, please work," Aniya whispers as she focuses inward, ignoring her father's pounding. She pictures the wall, whole with no damage, and the mess is all gone. Everything is back to where it needs to be. Waving her hand after directing her magic through her, slowly she opens one eye and then the other, praying that everything is fixed. With a relieved sigh, she looks at the wall, and the hole is gone and everything is fixed.

"Nice job, lass," Brodrick says, laughing a bit at Aniya's frantic behavior. "Ye are a quick learner," he says, trying to keep his laughter from showing.

"You aren't going to be laughing when he remembers he has a key and can open the door and bust in here. Like he really needs to see you naked," she tells him, watching him rest his back against the headboard of the bed and put his hands behind his head.

"I am nae ashamed. Let him see," Brodrick says, with a grin. Looking him over, she can't help but want to climb back on top of him for a repeat of the previous night. The blankets have pooled around his waist on the bed, and his bare chest is just begging for her kisses.

"Aniya Elizabeth Filmore, you have three minutes, or I'm using my key," her father yells through the front door. That shocks Aniya out of her thoughts.

"Come on, get up—he isn't joking!" Aniya is throwing on some jeans and the nearest shirt she can find.

"Ye really think he will come in?"

"Yes, please get dressed. Coming, Dad!" Aniya yells in the door's direction, hoping to buy a minute or two to collect herself before facing her father. She walks to the French doors to let Sapphire out. "Sapphire, time to go out, get some breakfast."

Iya, I still sleepy.

"I'm sorry, but we have to get going soon and I know you are going to want to eat." Aniya watches as Sapphire jumps off the bed and stretches. "Good girl." Then Sapphire heads out the doors. Aniya looks around the room to make sure everything is looking as it should, before leaving the bedroom and walking to the front door, taking a deep breath before turning the lock and opening the door, with a smile.

"Hi, Dad—" she starts to say, but her father is rushing through the door and he takes her in his arms for a hug.

"You scared me. What took so long for you to answer the door?"

"Sorry, we overslept. I am fine though."

"I can see that, but I was so worried when you didn't answer."

"We are both fine. He's in the bathroom. Sapphire is hunting. Come in and help me start coffee and breakfast—everyone will be here soon." Aniya moves to the side so her father can pass.

"What are you wearing?" Peter asks.

"Huh." Aniya looks down and realizes that in her hurry to get dressed, she had put on Brodrick's shirt. Damn it, how embarrassing, Aniya thinks to herself.

Why? I think ye look sexy in it.

She can hear Brodrick's voice in her head.

You knew and didn't tell me.

Aye, I kenned it, but I like you in my shirt.

Oh you!

"Honey, are you all right?"

"Yes, I'm fine, just a bit embarrassed."

"No reason to be, it's just a shirt."

Ye can wear my shirts anytime with naught underneath. Brodrick sends a mental picture of her and him. She is sitting in his lap, straddling him, and his hands are all over her body with nothing but his shirt on. Aniya's cheeks heat with a blush.

"Aniya, are you feeling okay? You look flushed. Are you sure the stitches were ready to come out?" Peter asks, and a roar of laughter comes from the direction of the bathroom.

"What's he laughing at?"

"Nothing, I'm fine. Let's go to the kitchen." *Will you stop? My dad is here.*

All the more reason to tease you. Wish I could have seen yer blush.

I didn't blush. Aniya sends him the denial, and laughter can be heard once again.

Sure ye did nae.

"Hey, Dad, can you make the coffee and I'll start the bacon? Everyone is going to be showing up soon, and I would like to have something ready when they get here," Aniya asks Peter, purposely ignoring Brodrick's comment.

Aniya and Peter are in the kitchen together, talking and cooking when Brodrick comes out of the bedroom. He is freshly showered, with a dark burgundy shirt and jeans that hug his butt and waist, along with a pair of black boots. Aniya looks up as he enters the kitchen and smiles at him. He walks right over to her and drops a kiss on her lips, which she returns.

"Good morn, Peter." Brodrick greets him as if this is an everyday occurrence.

"Morning—oh, how'd you sleep?" Peter looks at him with a raised eyebrow. Brodrick can now see where Aniya got the "look" from.

"Great, Aniya made sure I had all I needed." he says, with a wink to Aniya.

"That's good." Peter looks between the two of them. Something is different about them, but before he can question them, the doorbell rings.

"I'll get it." Wiping her hands on a kitchen towel, Aniya walks to answer the door.

"Hey, Rachel, come in. Coffee is in the kitchen, and the food is almost done," Aniya says after she opens the door.

"Good morning. Great, I was so excited I didn't get any this morning. Smells good, bacon and egg?" Rachel guesses as she enters the house

"Yep. Dad and Brodrick are in there as well."

"You look like you had a pleasant evening," Rachel says in a giggly hushed voice.

"Is it that obvious?" Another blush rises to her cheeks.

"I want all the details, and yes, it's *that* obvious. A shower might help. Is this Brodrick's shirt?"

"Yes, I was in a hurry to get dressed and grabbed it by mistake."

"Go get showered and dressed, on your own . . . unless you want everyone to know you got some last night."

"No! But breakfast—"

"I'll take over. Go get showered."

"Thanks." Aniya smiles and sighs, walking back toward the kitchen.

"I'm going to go take a quick shower. Rachel will finish breakfast," Aniya tells everyone.

Need any help, lass? I quite enjoyed last night's shower and would love to wash ye again.

I think a cold shower is what you need.

With ye, it would nae be a cold shower.

"Oh good lord," Aniya mumbles under her breath, with a roll of her eyes as she walks to her room.

Sapphire had come back at some point and was fast asleep again.

"Sapphire, time to wake up, I'll give you some bacon."

I don't want to get up.

"Okay, you can sleep until I'm out of the shower, then no more excuses, okay?"

Thanks, Iya.

By the time Aniya is out of the shower and dressed, she can hear that Evie, Broden, and Mike have arrived and Sapphire is finally up as well. She throws her wet hair into a ponytail and puts on some comfortable walking shoes. Today they will be going to the Fae realm. A lot has happened, and she has a feeling more is to come, leaving her room and walking back to greet them all.

"Good morning, everyone. Did you all eat?"

"Aye, we did and even made ye a plate as well." Broden walks over to her with the plate and kisses her before handing it over.

"I'm never going to get used to this," Peter says.

"You will—it may just take some time, Peter. I was shocked as well when the boys told me they had the same soul mate," Evie says, giving Aniya a hug and handing her a cup of coffee. "Hurry and eat, we need to get going." Mike kisses her cheek.

Looking up at him, Aniya asks, "How long are we going to be gone? I still have to pack."

"I took the liberty of packing for you. I hope you don't mind. While you were in the shower, I threw some clothes in a bag for you," Evie says.

"Thank you, Evie, I didn't even hear you."

"Perks of being a vampire, which, if I'm correct, you will learn soon enough," Evie says.

"What do you mean by that?" Aniya looks at Brodrick.

"We will talk about it later."

I did nae say anything, sweetling. Brodrick sends to her, catching some of her thoughts.

"Eat, lass, so that we may go." Broden offers her his seat.

Nodding in thanks, she sits to eat.

After Aniya has finished, she moves to start cleaning up, and everyone moves at once. Evie, Broden, and Brodrick zip around the house. Rachel and Aniya work on the kitchen, while Peter puts dishes away and Mike moves around, checking windows and locking doors, making sure everything is secure. After everything is finished, they all meet back in the kitchen.

"Everyone ready?" Mike asks. "We will need to walk a bit." Peter grabs bottles of water and starts passing them around. Everyone moves to the front door.

"Let's go," Evie says.

We are going on the trip?

"Yes, beautiful girl," Aniya answers out loud.

"She's excited." Rachel laughs at Sapphire.

Achel is right. I'm very excited.

Sapphire starts excitedly jumping around everyone.

Waiting for everyone to leave the house before following them, Aniya turns and locks the front door, not sure how long it will be before she returns.

"All right, ready?"

Six yeses can be heard from everyone. Evie and Mike take the lead, followed by Broden and Brodrick then Aniya, and last are Rachel and Peter. Sapphire is everywhere as they start walking into the forest behind her house.

CHAPTER 9

Aniya is walking through the woods, with everyone around her. She keeps thinking of what could happen once they get to the Fae realm, when Evie slows from walking next to Peter to walk with Aniya.

"I know you probably have a few questions. I can sense a change in you."

"Is it really so obvious? Do I have a mark or something?"

Laughing, Evie replies, "No, but I am a vampire, so my senses are sharper."

"So what happens now?"

"While your mage abilities will probably take a while to develop, you may also develop some vampire abilities, but with the mix of both mage and vampire, none of us really know what will happen."

"Is that a bad thing?"

"Well, I can't say whether it's good or bad, because this has never happened. Each species usually keeps to their own kind, but I am happy you have become part of our family. I don't want you to worry, Aniya. We will protect you." Evie wraps her arm around Aniya's waist and hugs her as they walk.

"Evie?" Aniya isn't quite sure how to ask the next question but gives it a try anyway.

"Yes."

"Last night, when Brodrick and I were . . ."

"Together?" Evie offers.

"Yes, together, my light came out of me and shot into him, throwing him across the room. Is that normal?"

"Well, I'm not sure what happens when mages bond. Maybe you could ask Mike?" Evie suggests.

"I thought maybe I should."

"He might be able to give you some answers. Are you comfortable with talking to him about . . . that?"

"I've always been able to talk with both Dad and Mike, and he is the only other mage I know. I wish my mom was here." Aniya lowers her head to hide the grief and longing that have begun to fill her.

"I'm sorry I couldn't be more helpful with all of this, but I'll always be here for you," Evie assures her, with another hug.

"Thanks." Aniya, saddened at the loss of her mother, is happy and grateful that she at least has Evie here to help when she can and to talk to when she needs a friend.

"Okay, this should be far enough into the woods to call the portal," Mike calls out to everyone.

"Mike, I can call it if you would like," Evie offers.

"Sure, Evie, that would be fine," Mike says, walking over to her and Aniya.

Pulling out a small dagger, Evie makes a cut on her palm then wipes her hand across what looks to be an invisible wall but is just air surrounded by woods, murmuring. Aniya can't hear what she is saying but it looks like a spell.

"I thought we didn't use spells."

"It's not a spell, Aniya. She is calling the portal."

Aniya watches as the forest in front of them shimmers and a different view opens in front of them. Through the opening, Aniya can see snow and what appear to be flowers. Blues and purples shine through, with green popping up here and there as if spring is on the way.

"That's so awesome!" Rachel says, approaching the portal, circling it until she walks back around to the opening. "Wow, it's like a mirror, but the reflection is different," she says, circling the portal a second time.

"Come on, everyone, let's go. Peter and Rachel, you might feel some resistance when you enter the portal, but you will get through," Evie warns them.

Aniya, Brodrick, and Broden go through first. Aniya feels as if she is being welcomed, with the feel of coming home. The second her feet touch the ground in the Fae realm, she feels a surge of power, like she is being recharged.

"Wow, that's different. Sapphire, come on." Aniya watches as she goes through the portal and prances around the three of them.

"Happy to be back, beautiful girl?" Aniya laughs while watching her antics.

I'm home and you are here too! It feels so good.

"I'm glad you're happy."

I'm happy wherever you are. Sapphire runs to Aniya and nudges at her legs.

"Beastie, careful, you'll knock us all over." Brodrick smiles at her.

I will knock you over, Brodrick.

As if to make her point, Sapphire runs a few feet away, stops and turns toward him, drops to the ground, and takes off toward Brodrick.

"Sapphire, don't you—ugh!" Brodrick lands with his back on the ground and Sapphire's paws on his chest.

Told you! She jumps off him, and he tackles her to the snowy ground.

"Oh, ye want to play?" The two of them start wrestling in the snow. Brodrick pins Sapphire; she turns and pins him.

"Brother, I believe ye've met yer match." Broden is laughing along with everyone else as they all watch the wrestling match for a few minutes.

"Aye, that was a bit of fun." Brodrick is sitting in the snow after getting up from Sapphire's last pin. "Come on, beastie, everyone is waiting," he says, laughing and giving Sapphire's head a rub.

"Dad, are you okay?" Aniya asks when she sees Peter looking a bit exhausted.

"Yeah, just a bit difficult getting through the portal. I had forgotten the amount of strength it takes, and I'm not as young as I was when I last went through."

"We can rest for a minute. Rachel, are you okay?" Aniya looks at her friend, who doesn't seem affected the same way her father is.

"Yeah, I felt a bit of resistance, but next to that, I didn't have a problem."

"Hmm, okay," Mike says but doesn't elaborate.

Aniya looks around the area that now surrounds them. The scenery is beautiful; even with all the snow, there are flowers all around. The trees are tall, and some have icicles hanging from them. The flowers stretch over the ground. Dark reds and dark purples, different shades of blue, and deep-green leaves can be seen in every direction. Broden and Brodrick are on both sides of her, watching her face. She starts walking toward one of the bushes of flowers to get a better look, and it seems the flowers turn toward them as they walk; it appears they're watching, and as they pass, the flowers seem to bow.

"Why do the flowers look as if they are bowing slightly as we walk by?" she asks Broden and Brodrick.

"I dinna ken, loving. I have nae seen them do this before." Broden is a little puzzled himself.

"Nor have I." Brodrick seems just as curious as he starts looking over the flowers Aniya is admiring. Aniya bends down as she approaches some of the blue flowers. They start to shake a little and seem to look right at her. She lifts a hand to touch the flowers, and they stretch out as if they want to take her hand. Once her hand is close enough, the flowers stretch out their stems and wrap them around Aniya's wrist as if to hug her before they lie and rest in her palm.

"Are the flowers trying to nuzzle me?" Aniya wonders aloud, as she has never seen or experienced anything like this before.

"Aye, it does look that way." Brodrick squats down to get a closer look, and the flowers turn toward him with a bow as well.

"'Tis different, 'tis like they are accepting you and bowing down to you." Broden, doing the same as his brother, squats down as well and watches the flowers as they do the same with him.

"Well, they are absolutely beautiful," Aniya says and just watches them for a minute. When she stands, the flowers lift and watch her move away.

"Your grandparents have a home about a day's walk from here. If we get moving, we could be there before night falls," Mike tells Aniya. "We can stay the night there and take the portal in the morning," he informs them all.

"Okay. Have you ever seen anything like what just happened, Mike?" Aniya asks as they start walking again.

"No, I haven't. That was a new one to me." Mike had watched, with awe, the plants and trees. They gravitated toward Aniya and her soul mates—that is something he probably should try to figure out when he has a moment to do so.

"Let's keep moving, the winter season is beautiful but can also be dangerous."

"Winter season?" Aniya asks.

"Yes, the Fae realm has four parts to it: winter, summer, spring, and autumn, each with its own area in the realm. The center of the Fae realm is where each area meets, and that's where the council is located," Mike explains.

Aniya starts following Mike as he walks the path. She can't help but admire the beauty of this area. She can see lights that seem to be floating in midair.

"Evie, is it normal to see lights that seem to float?"

"Those are fairies, Aniya. They help keep each part of the realm balanced. It's been a difficult job for them the last few hundred years because they are having a hard time finding soul mates as well. That's why my boys have been trying so hard to find the mage. All Fae help by doing their part to keep the balance, but there are so few of us left we all have to work harder." Aniya can hear the sadness in Evie's voice.

"Well, once we get the soul mate business taken care of, I will help with the search. This place is so beautiful I want to save it," Aniya says, while mentally making this a promise, not just to herself but to all of the Fae.

"I knew you would feel that way, and we will be happy to have the help. Who knows, maybe you are the missing piece we need to help save our world," Evie says, smiling down at Aniya.

They have been walking for a while when Mike stops in a small clearing.

"We can stop here for something to eat and a small break. There is a stream just through the line of trees there." He points to his left.

"Sapphire, go hunt and get some food for yourself, but don't wander too far," Aniya tells her.

Okay, Iya.

Sapphire takes off into the nearby woods.

Aniya looks to the right of where she is standing, and in the distance, she can see green-covered mountains. Broden looks in the same direction she is and spots the spring-season part of the realm. "Ye can see the spring season. It is farther than it looks, lass."

"Spring." Aniya looks in the opposite direction. "So does that mean autumn is that way?"

"Aye, it is."

"It's quite different here."

"Dinna worry, we will explore all four parts of the realm once we have figured everything out. Brodrick and I would be happy to show ye the little we have seen." Broden stands behind her and wraps his arms around her waist and just holds her as they both look around the area. Sapphire comes trotting out of the nearby woods, holding something in her mouth.

Sapphire, what is that?

She proudly continues walking to Aniya and then drops a rabbit at her feet.

I went hunting for everyone, Iya. I'm not the only one who needs to eat.

"Oh, Sapphire, you are so sweet." Aniya looks the rabbit over.

"This is huge and will feed everyone," Aniya says, bending to kiss Sapphire on her white-and-black striped head.

"Well done, beastie, I will get it ready to roast." Brodrick picks up the rabbit and looks for some place he can skin and clean it. Just a few yards away is a rock that would be perfect for the job, but Brodrick doesn't recall it being there a minute ago.

"I think I have some matches in my hiking bag, so I will get a fire going." Aniya walks off to collect some dried wood. This could prove to be difficult with all this snow on the ground. Strangely though, it isn't; she comes back with arms full of sticks, all dry and one or two decent-sized logs to use once she gets the fire going. Aniya builds a small pit, but in no time she is working to build the fire. When she has a good small fire going, she adds one of the bigger logs and watches as the flames lick at the bark. Aniya stands and stretches, her back aching just a bit from being hunched over for so long, wishing she had a place to sit. To her surprise, before she thinks any more of it, a rock rises up from the ground, pushing through the snow, and then stops at a perfect height to make a decent seat. "What in the world? Did anyone else see that?" Aniya's surprise catches everyone's attention.

"Honey, how did you do that?"

"That was amazing!" Rachel bursts out.

"I didn't do it. My back was hurting when I stood up from building the fire and I thought how nice it would be to have a place to sit, and the next thing I know, that rock just came up and out of the ground."

"You didn't use your magic?" Mike asks.

"I don't think so. I only *thought* about having a place to sit, that's all," Aniya answers.

Brodrick has come back with a fully skinned and ready-to-cook rabbit on a spit, and he jabs the stick into the ground over the fire.

"Nice job with the fire, sweetling. Our rabbit should be ready in a short while." Brodrick looks around and sees all the surprised expressions.

"Ye all are looking a bit astonished. I ken how to get a rabbit ready to cook. Broden and I did it a lot when we were wee lads."

"No, it wasn't that. Let me try something."

Aniya thinks how great it would be for everyone to have a place to sit and rest around the fire. All their eyes grow big when six more rocks push up and out of the snow. The snow completely melts in an area next to Aniya as grass grows and forms a lush green patch for Sapphire, who wastes no time in claiming the spot.

"What was that, lass? Did you do that?" Brodrick exclaims.

"I don't know. Oh, that's what we were all talking about right before you came back with the rabbit."

"Well, that is something new," Evie says, sitting on one of the rocks and holding her hands up to warm them with the heat of the fire. "But it does feel nice to rest my feet a bit, so thank you," she finishes on a sigh.

"Well, let's all sit and warm up while the rabbit cooks. We will all need to get up and be on our way soon enough." Everyone agrees with Evie and starts to take their seats. Broden and Brodrick are on either side of Aniya, and Sapphire lies slightly in front of her on the ground.

Once they have all had their fill of the food and they each take a few minutes to attend to their personal needs, they are ready to continue on. Aniya doesn't know why or to whom, but she feels the need to say thanks. As they all start walking out of the clearing, she turns to where they were all sitting, and the clearing looks the same as it was when they arrived: snow-covered with no sign of rocks anywhere.

"Thank you," she whispers, with a slight bow of her head.

"What was that, daughter?"

"Oh, nothing," she answers with a smile and follows the others.

Everyone is walking and talking among themselves. Peter and Mike are chatting about the terrain and trees. Aniya is talking to Evie and Rachel; Broden and Brodrick are in a deep conversation, but they keep a close watch on her. Evie has asked a question that Aniya misses because she was trying to hear her soul mates.

"Hello, Fae realm to Aniya, are you listening?" Rachel starts waving her hands in front of Aniya's face, trying to get her attention.

"Oh, sorry. What was that?" Aniya looks back toward Rachel and Evie.

"I hope one day I find someone that can knock me senseless in the middle of a conversation like that."

"I'm sorry. I was trying to hear what they were saying."

"Eavesdropping now too?"

"No! I just wanted to know if Brodrick was telling Broden anything about last night." Aniya blushes slightly with the thought.

"Don't worry. I can hear them, and they are not talking about that. It sounds like they are making some plans." Evie waves off the conversation the boys were having.

"Well, I wouldn't mind the details."

"Rachel! My dad and Mike are right there!" Aniya is pointing at the two men and shaking her head.

"Ugh! Fine, but as soon as we girls can get away, you better spill." Rachel turns and starts looking over all the trees and notices something in the distance.

"What is that?"

"What is what, Rachel?" Aniya follows Rachel's line of vision, when she feels it. Someone is watching them. Concentrating to see if she can tap into her magic to help her figure out what it is, she feels something but it isn't directed at her, but at Rachel.

Sapphire, do you smell danger?

Sapphire inhales deeply. *Iya, it's a wolf, but I don't smell a threat. He seems to just be watching Achel.*

"It's a wolf!" From where she is, Rachel can now see the creature. The wolf seems to be watching her. She can see that he is big. His face is black outlined in gray, and it's those colors that flow along its body. He is the most beautiful wolf she has ever laid eyes on, but the way he is following her with his eyes makes her feel very uneasy.

"Why is that wolf looking at me like I'm his next meal?" Rachel asks Evie and Aniya.

"Sapphire says she doesn't sense any threat—that it's only watching you."

"He." Rachel corrects Aniya.

"He?"

"Yes, the wolf, it's a he."

"And how do you know that, Rachel?"

"I'm not sure, I just know."

Iya, he won't hurt Achel.

How do you know that, beautiful girl?

Because he smells of the forest too.

What do you mean?

Him and Achel have the same smell. Achel isn't bad, he isn't, either.

"Well, let's just keep walking," Aniya tells them all.

"Yeah, that wolf is making me nervous, the way he keeps watching me. Let's just go." Rachel is walking a little faster as if trying to get away from the wolf.

I have a feeling the wolf will keep following Achel.

Well, let's not tell her—she's worried enough. Just keep your guard up and warn me if you sense a change, okay?

"So how much longer, Mike, are we close yet?" Aniya asks, trying to distract Rachel.

"Still a ways. We can take a small break if you would like, but only a few minutes if we want to have beds to sleep in tonight and not the forest floor."

Aniya takes a moment to look at the group. "Dad, Evie, Rachel, are you guys okay to keep going or want to take a couple minutes?"

"No, honey, I'm good to keep moving."

"Yeah, me too, my pocket warmers are cooling, so I'd like to be indoors soon."

"Okay then, we keep moving," Aniya announces.

"I can carry ye if ye would like?" Brodrick asks.

"I actually feel fine." Aniya gives him a sly seductive smile.

Lass, if ye keep looking at me like that, I'll carry ye off into the woods.

Don't you dare, I will shoot you with my light again.

Brother, we need to talk. Broden interrupts the mental flirtation.

Aye, I ken it.

"I sense a change in ye. Did the two of ye bond last eve?"

"Aye, we did, but I need to warn ye."

"I thought as much. I'm happy for ye, brother."

"Thank ye, yer in for a surprise though."

"What do you mean?"

Feeling Broden's confusion, Brodrick replies, "Just be prepared for when the mage light enters ye. It's powerful and stings a bit." As if remembering the feeling, Brodrick's hand rubs his chest where the light entered him.

"Are ye okay?"

"Och, aye, 'tis nae painful now."

"Painful?"

"My arse was more sore than my chest where the light entered."

"Why would yer arse be sore from a bonding?"

"I cannae give it all away. Ye will soon see, brother."

Brodrick chuckles a little before walking ahead a bit to be next to Aniya. Broden moves up to her other side. Aniya looks at them both. Brodrick looks pleased with himself, and Broden looks bewildered and deep in thought.

"What did you tell him to make him look so lost?"

"I only tried to warn him about yer light."

"Brodrick, you told him?" she asks him, embarrassed.

"Nay, he guessed. I merely gave him something to be aware of, 'tis all."

"Broden? What did he tell you?"

"No details, lass, I promise ye. He just did nae explain his meaning of what he did tell me."

"We can talk about this later, when your mother and my father along with everyone else aren't within earshot of the conversation."

"Only about a mile to go. We are almost there." Mike interrupts them.

"How long till it's dark?" Rachel asks.

"A couple hours, we will make it before then." Mike looks up at the sky to guesstimate what time it is.

"Great! I could use a hot cup of coffee," Peter says.

"Now that's something we all could agree on." Aniya lets out a sigh of longing.

It's been about an hour when Aniya looks up from talking with her dad and sees a house in the distance. It looks like a cottage; it's made of wood logs with huge windows on either side of the door that leads inside.

"Mike, is that the house?"

s, don't let the outside fool you. It's quite cozy on the inside."

s they move toward the cottage, Aniya gets a much better look. re are no lights on, so the windows are dark. There is a porch that s chairs and tables set up close to a fire pit; flowers in oddly shaped pots are placed in various places on the porch.

"Do we need a key?" Peter asks.

"Peter, we are in the Fae realm, locks aren't necessary."

"So anyone could just walk in?"

"Well, no, a family member or close friend of those who have lived here has to be given permission and they must enter first. Aniya's grandparents granted her entrance long ago. They had hoped she would one day find her way to them. When or if she did, they made sure she would be able to enter any and all of their homes. Aniya, let's give it a try. I have been granted permission to enter, but I'd like you to try first."

Aniya walks up to the door and slowly reaches for the doorknob. "What if it doesn't work?" she stops and asks.

"There is only one way to find out," Mike tells her.

She reaches for the doorknob again. This time when her fingers wrap around it, it turns with a click, opening up and causing her to release the breath she had been holding. Pushing the door open, she steps inside and jumps a bit when lights come on. To the left of her in a sitting room is a large fireplace that ignites a moment after she enters.

"How did that happen?"

"The house recognizes you. It's your magic, Aniya. The Fae realm works differently. Here, your blood, magic, and family ties make things work."

"So now what?"

"Invite them in."

"Ummm, okay, please come in." One by one, they all step into the house.

"Hopefully this will all make sense one day."

"It will," is all he says.

"So, coffee first then we figure out something to eat." Peter walks around, looking in each room.

"First we need to find the kitchen."

"Let me show everyone around the house," Mike says, looking them over.

"How do you know where everything is?" Aniya asks.

"I've been here a time or two. The times I came back from the human realm, I stayed here or whichever house your grandparents were at. So they created portals going from one of their homes to the other."

"This is all just too confusing to think about right now."

"I know you're tired, so let me give you the tour of the house so we can eat and get to bed." He shows them around, pointing out all the bedrooms, bathrooms, and eventually the kitchen, which surprisingly has a fridge full of food and all modern appliances from a dishwasher to stoves. Rachel, upon seeing a coffee pot, seizes the moment and starts searching through cabinets for the coffee and mugs, while Peter starts to prepare the coffeemaker for the first pot to be brewed. Rachel and Aniya look for something to cook for everyone and settle on something simple, chicken and mashed potatoes. While Evie watches the girls prepare the meal, she realizes she has never learned to cook and now that she has a soul mate, she is going to need to eat as well. She will still need blood but not as often; she is going to need to take some cooking lessons.

Once dinner is ready, they all sit around the dining room table to eat and discuss the day's journey and all that happened. The conversation then turns to sleeping arrangements. Aniya assumed she would sleep in a room with Rachel and maybe even Evie. However, Broden and Brodrick had other ideas. So in the end and without much of a fight, she and the guys would sleep with Sapphire in the master bedroom, and everyone else would take the other rooms.

"The two of you had better not think of trying anything though. I'm too tired and need to sleep," she tells them.

"Sweetling, I dinna have it in me, as much as I'd like to."

"Aye, loving, ye need nae worry. We ken ye be tired and we are as weel."

If she wasn't so tired, the reassurance in their tones might have been a disappointment.

"Rachel, would you mind helping me clean up? The quicker we get done, the quicker I can crawl into a bed," Aniya says while stifling a yawn.

"Sure, I am exhausted and wouldn't mind crashing either." Rachel stands and stretches.

"I'll help too. Many hands make light work. Come on, my dearest, let's get the dishes done." Evie stands and starts cleaning off the table. Aniya and Rachel head into the kitchen, loading the dishwasher and washing the pots and pans, putting each dish back where they had found it. Before they knew it, everything was done.

"That didn't take long. Evie, do you have any of that wine left from the other night? I wouldn't mind a glass."

"No, but we could ask Mike if this house has a wine cellar, if you don't think they would mind that we open a bottle."

"Mike, do my grandparents have any wine?"

"Look in the cupboard above the microwave. I think there might be a bottle or two."

Aniya moves to look, and sure enough, there it is. She looks at the label, but she has never heard of that brand.

"It smells amazing." Rachel says after she opens the bottle. "Evie, would you like some?"

"Oh yes, absolutely!" Aniya pours a glass for each of them.

"This is really good." Aniya groans after taking a sip.

"I like it too," Rachel agrees.

"It is delicious, isn't it?" Evie asks.

"You can taste the wine, Evie?" Aniya knows what that means for a vampire.

"You know what, don't tell me. I'm too tired and have hit information overload. But after some sleep and everything else, I want to know who. I'm so happy for you." Aniya walks over and hugs Evie.

"Thank you and you will know soon enough, I promise."

"Cheers, to soul mates, family, and great friends." Aniya lifts her glass of the amber-red liquid.

"Cheers."

"Cheers."

"Well, I'm ready for bed, I think," Rachel tells them after she finishes her wine.

"Yeah, so am I." Aniya walks to the sink and rinses her glass.

"I agree," Evie says.

"Aye, we are as weel, good sleep all," Brodrick says.

"Good sleep." Broden reaches for Aniya.

"Good night, Daddy and Mike." She gives them all a hug and follows Brodrick to their room, with Broden walking behind her.

"I think we are all headed in that direction. Good night, everyone," Mike says.

"Sapphire, come on," Aniya calls from the bedroom and closes the door once the cat is inside.

Iya, I'm so sleepy.

I know, jump up and let's get some sleep, beautiful girl.

Sapphire climbs onto the bed, curling up, and is soon fast asleep.

"Into bed with ye as weel," Broden tells Aniya.

"Let me get changed." Aniya grabs her bag that was set in the room sometime while she had been cooking and goes into the bathroom. Once she is out, Aniya moves to the center of the bed and gets under the blankets, lying on her stomach. Broden and Brodrick watch as their exhausted soul mate falls asleep immediately.

"She was tired," Brodrick says, grinning at the sleeping Aniya.

"Aye, she was and so am I. Good sleep, brother." Broden strips his clothes off, sleeping only in his boxers, and climbs into the bed on the right side of Aniya, kisses her on the shoulder before putting his arm around her.

"Good sleep." Brodrick strips off his clothes as well and climbs into the bed on the other side, kisses her exposed cheek, before getting under the blankets. It takes no time for them all to fall fast asleep.

CHAPTER 10

Aniya wakes the next morning with Broden and Brodrick on either side of her, each with an arm around her. With a little smile, she gently moves their arms from around her chest and waist so as not to wake them, then begins to climb over Broden in order to get off the bed. Very carefully, she gets one leg over his waist, when he begins to stir. While waiting for him to settle once more, she realizes the position she is in and prays to whatever gods, goddesses, or any other beings that they believe in, that Broden doesn't wake up and catch her like this. Finally after what feels like hours, she is able to move her other leg over Broden so she can stand up.

"Sapphire, time to get up," Aniya whispers gently.

Iya, time to go?

Not yet, beautiful girl, but you need to eat.

You mean I have to go hunt.

Yes, you're a tiger. That's what you do.

But I also have to protect you.

Right now between them (Aniya points to the still-sleeping men) *and Dad, Mike and Evie, I think I have more protection than I need. Go hunt.*

Okay.

Aniya lets Sapphire out of the room, then moves to the front of the house to open the door for her. *Be safe.*

I will.

Aniya watches as Sapphire takes off in a run.

Aniya goes to the kitchen and sees everyone is awake except for Broden and Brodrick.

"Good morning. At least you are wearing your own shirt this time." Rachel laughs. "Coffee is ready and we were going to start breakfast but we were waiting for the three of you."

Good-mornings come from around the room.

"Morning," Aniya answers, moving to the coffee pot.

"So what are we making for breakfast?"

"French toast, and I think there might be some sausage too," Rachel answers.

"That sounds great! I'll help."

"I do not have any idea of how to cook, but I'll do my best to help," Evie offers.

"No problem, Evie, we can give you a lesson this morning," Rachel suggests.

"That would be wonderful."

The girls pull out all the ingredients for breakfast and start preparing the food. While they are cooking, Broden and Brodrick wake and join everyone.

"Good morn," they say as they walk to Aniya, who tilts her head from side to side to receive each of their kisses.

"What are ye doing?" Broden asks, looking at the mess the women have created.

"Teaching your mother to make French toast."

"Mother, ye want to learn to cook, we could have taught ye our way." Brodrick smiles.

"Oh, son, what can you cook, next to a rabbit over an open fire on a spit? Which I'm sure you've guessed at that," Evie says jokingly.

"That rabbit was quite good!" He defends his skills.

"Go sit and have a cup of coffee. Broden, can you see if Sapphire is back yet? Maybe she brought Brodrick something else to 'cook.'" The girls all laugh.

"Wenches," a smiling Brodrick murmurs.

"What was that?" Evie turns and says, giving him her mom look and tone.

"Nothing at all." Brodrick smiles.

"Aye, Mother." Broden moves to check on Sapphire, and she runs into the house when he opens the door.

Good hunt, lovely?

Yes, I am so full. It's so pretty here.

Ye are right, it is. Did ye see the wolf from yesterday while ye were out?

Yes, but still no danger. He just seems to be watching. Should we tell her? Iya says no because it could scare her.

I think Aniya is right. We don't want to scare Rachel.

Okay.

Everyone is in the kitchen.

They are all seated, eating breakfast and discussing today's plans.

"So first the council then my grandparents and last the seer, if we can find her. That's a full day," Aniya comments.

"Aye, but a lot of questions may finally be answered, and once 'tis all done, we can start our lives together."

"That will be so nice," Evie comments while looking at Peter.

"So once everyone is ready, we can take the portal to the center city and go to the council room from there," Mike says between bites of food.

Aniya finishes eating and moves to stand when she feels a tug from deep inside her. What is that? She thinks to herself. She tries to ignore it and moves to take her dishes to the sink when another tug comes. Not sure what it is, she decides to ignore it again.

"The guys have the dishes this time," she says, once everyone is done eating.

While the men work in the kitchen, the women get showered and dressed. Once the guys are done, they get cleaned up and prepare to leave as well.

"Ready, Sapphire?"

Yep, yep.

"I'll call the portal if everyone is set." Mike looks around and yeses come from everyone.

"Okay." He calls his magic forth and waves his hands in a weird pattern when the portal opens in front of him he moves to the side to let everyone walk through.

"Still so awesome," Rachel says as she steps through.

One at a time, everyone enters the portal, and it closes when Mike, being last, is through.

The tug Aniya felt while in the winter cottage has become a strong pull. However, they have a destination that they need to get to, so she ignores it again, which is getting much harder to do. Along with the pull, Aniya now feels a deep sadness deep in her heart. Well, that is just one more thing to ask her grandparents about. She hopes they can help with all this mage stuff. Looking around, she thinks it looks just like any other city, buildings and businesses. The Mages Ballroom, drinks and dancing. Vampire's Light, warm blood on tap. Shifter Wolves World, a howl of a time.

"Why does every business only allow a certain Fae species in?" she asks.

"Well, as we told you before, every species keeps to their kind. They don't interact in any way," Evie answers her.

"Why would they do that?"

"I'm not sure. That's just how it has always been. Even as a child, I can remember it being like this."

"How can it be that way, everyone lives among each other but never interacts?"

"It's just how it is. There is no hatred or dislike—we just don't mingle. If you noticed, that young wolf over there"—Evie points at a young, muscular man—"moved away when we came through the portal."

"I saw that, but I didn't think anything of it. We are a large group. I thought he was just moving aside for us, to be polite."

"Let's keep walking. I will show you more of the city as we walk to the council tower." Evie intertwines her arm with Aniya's and starts moving more into the city. As they come around the corner, there sits a corner store. The Cat's Meow Bar & Grill. Aniya covers her mouth with her hand and starts to giggle.

Rachel can't help but be in awe over all that she is seeing; she can hardly believe any of this is real, when she hears Aniya giggling. "What's so funny? What did I miss?" Rachel looks around.

Aniya points at the corner store.

"Where and how do they come up with these names?" Aniya giggles more, and Rachel joins in once she reads the sign.

"We do have a sense of humor, daughter. Look over there." The sign she points at reads "The Suckless Sucker," and the girls burst out into laughter. Evie can't help but join in.

They continue their walk toward the council tower. Along the way, there are many different stores. One store caught Aniya's attention. The store is dark, with one window busted out and a board in its place—Fire and Ice, Anything for All Seasons. Aniya walks toward the building and stops. "What happened?" Sadness is in each word.

"The dragons," Evie tells her.

"They are gone? Completely?"

"Yes, for hundreds of years now."

"So there is no hope of them coming back?"

Aniya can feel the deep loss, but why should she? The dragons have been gone for longer than she's been alive. She's never met a dragon, so why do tears fill her eyes at the thought of them being gone forever?

"Sadly, daughter, no." Evie hugs Aniya.

"Maybe that's the sadness I felt when we arrived."

"What sadness?" Mike had come up behind her along with everyone else.

"When I came through the portal, I felt this sadness, and then seeing this, it feels as if I have lost a part of me. It's not the same as what I feel for Broden and Brodrick. It's like when Mom died but deeper," she tries to explain.

"I wish I could take some of it away." Evie can see how truly hurt Aniya is. Hugging her again, she guides her away from the store toward the council tower once more.

Aniya lets Evie lead her away from the ruins that nature has started to overtake. When she next looks up, they are headed toward a tower that would have at one time been a magnificent structure. Now it has vines climbing up the wall, and the high double doors are covered in cracks and look broken. It's a dark gray tower that looks to be falling apart stone by stone, and strangely, there are no windows that can be seen.

"So if this is the council, how are they watching the realm? This is a building that has no windows." Aniya can't help but wonder, so she asks Evie and Mike.

"I don't know, but they always know what is happening." Evie shrugs.

Next to the huge broken doors is a whiskey barrel. Sitting on top is a hawk, and at the bottom lies a strange-looking but beautiful cat. Both are too thin, and their colors have faded. The hawk's feathers seem to bend in multiple different directions with bald spots in various areas, and the poor cat creature has matted fur that is also missing in areas. She moves to them, and when they flinch away from her, it breaks her heart.

"Hush now, you look so hungry." When Aniya bends to pet both of them, she can feel how scared they really are.

Iya, they are familiars.

Aniya turns to look at Sapphire, surprised to hear this.

You can tell that?

Yes, I can. We can talk to each other.

Who would mistreat their familiars like this, and why are they not with their mages?

Iya wants to know why you look like this, and where are your mages?

They leave us here, and we are told to not move.

Iya, they said they are told to stay and are left here alone.

"But they look like they haven't eaten in days!" Disbelief is in her voice.

We haven't.

They haven't, Iya.

"What? No, Who are their mages?" Aniya can barely speak through her anger.

We aren't supposed to say. They say only weak mages need familiars, they kick us and tell us to go away, the cat tells Sapphire.

Sapphire relays what they told her to Aniya.

Well, today, you are going to eat. That feeling of sadness overcomes her again, but this is one thing she can fix, she hopes. Praying this will work, she begins to pull on her magic and bring forth food to feed the poor creatures. The cat has four fish, and the hawk is given a slab of fresh meat.

Eat, and here's some water. She waves her hand so each has their own bowl of cool, fresh water.

The two animals are unsure if they should take what is being offered. What will this lady want from them if they do?

What does she want in return? Or will she hurt us when we go to eat and take the food away?

Iya, they want to know if you want anything in return for the food and water.

What? I only want them to eat and drink. I ask nothing in return.

She reaches to caress them, and they both flinch again.

She will hit us, then.

No! Iya would never hit you. She was going to pet you both. Let her, you will see. Iya, they thought you were going to hit them.

"No! I would never. You two just eat," Aniya tells them and watches as they reluctantly start to eat the food, still afraid they are going to be harmed.

Aniya turns toward her soul mates, and seeing the anger in their eyes, she knows Sapphire included them in their conversation.

"You heard. I can't believe someone, especially a mage, would do this."

"Even in the Fae realm, there are people who are cruel and uncaring," Broden says, trying to cool his temper.

"To ken a mage is mistreating their familiar, 'tis not something ye hear about. Their familiars make them stronger, nae weaken them," Brodrick says angrily.

Aniya's sadness flows like a river into him, and he is sure Broden can feel it too.

Brother, her sadness breaks my heart.

Aye, I ken it and feel it as weel.

"I could never do this to Sapphire." Aniya instinctively reaches for her. *I love you, Sapphire, never worry about that.*

I know, Iya.

"We need to go in now," Mike says, unaware of Aniya's inner turmoil.

"Okay," she quietly says.

The men walk to the door and push it open. Aniya goes through, and the lights inside automatically turn on, candlelight covering the small entryway with a glow that should have felt warm but instead it is cold and unwelcoming.

"Well, I had pictured this differently. I had expected there to be warmth and a feeling of welcome. Instead, I feel cold and the need to turn and run." Again she feels the heartbreaking sadness, and the tug she felt upon entering the city has become constant and unrelenting. Not knowing what else to do, she pushes it aside and continues. They move into the center of the room, where there are small green creatures inside, each standing next to a chain. Four in total, they bow to her, Broden, and Brodrick.

"How do we go up?"

"We take you, mistress," one of the green things says.

"And you are?"

"A goblin." A questioning look is on its face.

"No, I mean your names." Aniya smiles.

"We don't have names, just the chain Goblins."

"Well, that won't do. If you don't have names, I will have to give you one. Jon, Stan, Dan, and you will be Bill." She points at each goblin.

"Those are your names. Remember them. That will be what you are forever to be called." Each goblin looks at the others.

"We have names!" Dan says excitedly.

"I'm Jon."

"I'm Bill."

"And I'm Stan. Thank you, mistress," the goblin on her left says.

"You are most welcome. Now can you take us up, please?"

"Oh yes! Right away, mistress," Jon, the one to her right, answers.

"Please call me Aniya," she says, looking at them all.

"But we can't, we—" Bill says.

"I insist."

"So you want us to call you . . . Aniya?" Dan asks.

"Yes, please."

They all look at one another.

"Okay!" All four of them say at the same time, pulling on the chains with excitement. The ground under them starts to rise.

"Whoa!" Rachel comments.

"Oh wow!" Aniya echoes, realizing the strength of these little guys.

They ride higher and higher without anyone saying a word, until finally they stop in front of another set of huge double doors.

"Here you are, Miss . . . Aniya," Bill tells her.

"The Fae Council room, you may want to leave the tiger here. We promise to keep her safe."

"No, she goes where I go, but thank you for offering."

"They won't like it that she's in there," Dan warns.

"Sapphire stays with me."

"Sapphire? You named her too?" Stan asks.

"Yes, why wouldn't I name my familiar?"

"No reason. It's a beautiful name, Miss Aniya."

"I like your names too." She smiles at them.

"We do too," Jon says with a very crooked-toothed grin.

"Everyone ready?' Aniya asks them all.

"Peter and Rachel will have to stay here. The council room is only for Fae and humans going before the council to become soul mates," Evie says apologetically.

"I will not wait out here while my daughter goes in there alone." Peter crosses his arms over his chest, getting a little frustrated at the politics here in the Fae realm.

"I won't be there by myself."

"I don't like it, Aniya."

"Neither do I," Rachel pipes up.

"Really, guys." Aniya points at those who are going with her. "Stay here with our new friends," she says, waving her hand in the direction of the goblins. "This hopefully won't take too long."

"Aniya, I don't—"

"Dad, stop! I will be fine, I promise."

Evie moves to the doors and pushes them open. They walk into the huge room and stop in the center, where Evie starts giving the introductions.

Iya, I smell evil! It's not safe here! Sapphire warns the three of them.

Beastie, are ye sure?

"Familiars are not allowed in here. It needs to leave," Ada the mage council member says.

"Sapphire is mine, she goes where I go." Aniya steps forward.

Ada's eyes go wide; no one dares to stand up to her like that. "Who do you think you are? What makes you think you can speak to us in that tone?" Ada snaps at her.

"I don't care who you are. Sapphire is mine, she goes with me."

Iya, we need to leave now.

Sapphire cautiously steps backward toward the doors.

Mother, we need to leave NOW.

Son, we are fine.

No, we are nae. I'll explain once we leave this place.

Evie can hear the threat and uncertainty in Broden's tone.

Aniya feels as if a magical chain has been placed around her waist, and the pulling is almost painful, making it hard for her to catch her breath and ignore it any longer.

"It apparently is not a good time to stop by. We will come back in a few days." Aniya turns to leave.

"No, it's fine," she hears a male voice say when she turns back around to face them.

"Don't worry. I promise we will return. All of us!" she assures them, insinuating this isn't over just yet. She grabs both of her soul mates by the hand and walks through the doors, assuming everyone else will follow them out. Nothing felt right about the council room, from its black marble to the candlelit chandelier. It's all wrong, and Sapphire smelling evil? The council is made up of mated Fae. Love should be the epitome of the council, and that wasn't what she felt. At least now she knows who those poor familiars belong to. None of this is making any sense, Aniya thinks to herself.

"What the hell is going on?" yells Aniya in frustration.

Peter and Rachel look at them curiously once they are all on the platform again. "Wait, what happened?" Peter asks.

"Get us out of here, and I will tell you. Jon, Bill, Stan, and Dan, take us down, please?" Aniya tells them after the council room doors begin to close.

"Yes, Miss Aniya." They start releasing the chains, to take them down.

"She named them!" says a loud muffled voice from behind the closed doors.

"You bet your ass I did," Aniya mutters back at them.

Everyone is quiet as they descend the tower. Once they have reached the bottom, they move to the doors and open them. The bright sunlight is blinding, so Aniya takes the time to take a couple deep breaths while she waits for her eyes to adjust to the natural light.

Peter asks Aniya, "Now can you tell me what happened in there?" pointing up at the tower, and his face red with anger.

"Well, Dad, they ordered Sapphire out but not before she smelled evil. I told them that she stays with me and I didn't give a damn who they are, I wasn't going to change my mind. Oh, and I might have threatened them," she says, turning toward him.

"You threatened them! Aniya, what were you thinking?"

"I was thinking they pissed me off, ordering *my* familiar out. And let's not forget the evil Sapphire informed us of. There shouldn't be any evil—it's the council. All I said was that I promised them we will all be coming back. I will figure out what's happening in there, and that is not a threat—that is a promise. Nothing feels right about this place." Aniya turns away, looking at the familiars still sitting by the big broken doors.

They look a bit better. Their colors have a subtle change, looking a little brighter than when she had gone in.

"Well, you two look a little better," she tells them and begins caressing the bird and cat.

We feel better. The pains are gone.

Sapphire relays the message.

"Well, I'm glad." With a small smile, she moves away and starts walking.

The hawk takes to the air until he lands on Aniya's shoulder; the cat follows and falls in behind Sapphire.

No, come and walk next to us. Never will you be anything less than I am.

Sapphire tells the cat, who had stopped at the word *no.* Then slowly moves up next to her. *She is safe?*

Yes, Iya is safe.

"Well, hello! You two want to come with us?" Aniya looks up at the hawk, and he looks at Sapphire. *Is it okay to come?*

Iya, he said okay.

No, I didn't.

Do you want to go back?

No! They both send to Sapphire.

"Yes, you both can come with us." She tells them, feeling some satisfaction in taking the familiars from those two wretched people. "I am going to assume they never named you? So I will call you Cera and you will be Bolt, if that is okay with the two of you?" With a nod from both of the creatures, she decides to offer up opening a line of communication between them. "If you take my blood, we will be able to talk to each other." Reaching for the knife that Brodrick carries on his hip, she cuts her finger and offers it to both animals, who hesitate at first.

"Go ahead, before it heals." She watches Cera lick her finger and then lifts her finger to Bolt, who lowers his beak to the small cut, both taking a small amount of her blood.

You gave us food? Cera asks Aniya.

You were hungry.

You touched us with no pain, Bolt adds.

I promise I will never inflict pain on either of you, only love and kindness.

We don't feel connected to them anymore. Your blood is strong.

I would like for you both to take Broden and Brodrick's blood too so that they will be able to communicate with you.

"Broden, Brodrick, can you give these two a bit of your blood so we may all talk to each other." Once the guys do, they continue on their way.

Bolt, come sit on my shoulder, please? Broden waits for the bird to leave Aniya and climb onto his shoulder instead.

Thank you, Bolt, you are a big bird. You don't have to stay with us if you don't want to. You can fly instead.

You will let me fly?

Of course, ye be our eyes in the sky. Brodrick answers for all of them.

You both are part of our ever-growing little family now. You should have never lived in fear, but you will never have to fear us, Aniya promises.

Mike starts to lead them to their next stop. The sadness, though still present, is not as strong but the pull she keeps feeling is slightly painful and leading her in a different direction than the one Mike is trying to go.

"We need to go this way." Aniya stops walking to tell them.

"Your grandparents are this way though," Mike says, pointing in a direction opposite to where Aniya is being pulled.

"I get that, I do, but this pull I keep feeling is painful, and I can't ignore it any longer. We have to go this way."

"Why?"

"I don't know, but we are going this way." Aniya starts walking in the direction the pull is coming from.

"Aniya, there is nothing but an old mage village that way."

"Well, maybe that's why I need to go? They are my people, right? For whatever reason, I have to go this way. Now stop questioning me, please. I don't get it either."

"Okay, okay, we will go this way." Mike raises both hands up as a sign of surrender.

They all follow Aniya for a while, when the small village comes into view. It's run down as well, and nature has taken back most of the land, except for a few of the homes that still have occupants. "Are they all like this?" Aniya stops and looks around, surprised that a few mages remain in the village.

"Most are, yes," Mike answers.

"Where have they all gone?"

"Some have died. Many seem to have just up and left."

"What would make them all leave like this?"

"I wish I could answer that."

Aniya feels the pull again and starts moving. It looks as if they will be taking a walk in the woods, she thinks as she approaches the edge of the forest.

"Aniya?"

"Dad, don't. We are going." She puts her hand up to stop any argument from her father.

Continuing further into the woods, it isn't long before Aniya can smell smoke.

"Sapphire, Cera, do either of you smell anything?"

It's a fireplace, Iya.

Yes, I smell it too.

But not a fire?

No. They both answer.

Bolt, fly up and see if you see anything, please?

The hawk takes off into the sky.

It's a small house, just through those trees.

No danger? Aniya asks them all.

No danger.

Nope, no danger, Iya.

Now that she knows it is safe, she continues with caution through the next line of trees. There, tucked into a gathering of trees, is a small cottage. Smoke rises out of the chimney, and a young woman is standing with her hands on her hips. Her hair starts out a brownish red and then fades into brighter red; her eyes are almost clear-crystal color. Aniya is going to tower over this tiny woman. Her skin is golden toned and she has a cherub face; she is beautiful.

"Way to use your familiars," the woman says.

"Familiars?"

"You severed their bond from Edward and Ada when you offered your blood and they accepted it, making them yours now."

"Well, good. They don't deserve Cera and Bolt."

"I have been calling you since you arrived, Aniya. How is that you were able to ignore it? Nobody can ignore my pulls."

"Called me? I don't even know you. How did you call me?"

"You didn't feel it?

"I felt a pull."

"That was me calling you."

"How do you even know me? We have never met."

"How were you able to ignore my call?"

"I don't know. I just did, I pushed it aside,"

"How can you just push away my call? You shouldn't have been able to push it away. If I'm calling you, you're supposed to come to me, not ignore me. You're certainly not supposed to be able to just brush me aside. Considering who I am, that should have been impossible. I needed you to come to me before you went to the council."

"Who are you?" Aniya asks again, getting annoyed at the woman's refusal to answer her question; she pushes her persuasion at her this time.

"Do not use your gifts on me, young lady. I have every intention of telling you who I am. There's no need for that, now come. I've made tea." With that, the woman turns and walks into the small hut. The group moves toward the small home. Bolt and Cera stop at the door. When everyone else has gone in, including Sapphire, they still haven't moved to enter the cottage.

Cera, Bolt, come on, Broden sends to them.

We aren't allowed inside.

Who said?

They did.

You go where we go. Now, come on, Aniya tells them, waiting and watching as they slowly inch toward her.

If you are that worried, stay next to Broden, Brodrick, or me.

"Bolt, Cera, come in," the woman says encouragingly.

As the two familiars start to enter the house, Aniya crouches down to Cera's level and calls Bolt to her.

"Listen to me, okay?" she says out loud.

They nod.

"You are ours now. You will be loved, fed, cared for, and you will never be hurt again. I need you with me like I need Sapphire. They will never take you from us. I won't allow it. They will never hurt you again. I don't want you to fear us." Aniya hugs Cera and turns to do the same with Bolt, who opens his huge wings awkwardly and returns the hug.

"Now stay close, all three of you." Aniya stands and rejoins the others.

"I still don't know who you are." Aniya looks at the woman.

"I thought by now that might be obvious. I'm the seer, my dear, and yes, we do have much to discuss," she says, adding some final touches to the tea she has been preparing.

CHAPTER 11

"Yer the seer?"

"Yes, Brodrick."

"And ye ken who we are?"

"I do, Broden."

"You also know we are soul mates?"

"I've known that and have seen it as well, Aniya." The seer looks up at the three of them. "Why haven't you completed the bond?" It sounds more like a scolding accusation than a question. "You three need to be fully bonded before you go to stand in front of the council. That is why I kept pulling at you. This needs to be done!"

"That's really none of your business. What I do with my mates doesn't and shouldn't concern you."

"Yes, it does, it actually concerns the entire realm. You're in danger, and the only way to protect the three of you is to complete the bond."

"In danger? From what, and why is our bonding so important?" Aniya asks, getting frustrated with the seer.

"Aniya, she's the seer. You need to calm down," Evie scolds her.

"No, I'm tired of all the puzzles and riddles. Either give it to us straight or let us be on our way."

"I can't give you all the answers you seek. I can guide you, but the decisions you make will either save us or the Fae will die."

"What decisions?"

"Aniya, you are the mage, the one they've been searching for!" she explains pointing from one of the guys to the other.

"I did wonder about that. We thought we were drawn to her because she is our mate," Brodrick reveals.

"Yes, you were drawn to her for that reason but also because of who you all are meant to be, depending on the choices you make."

"What the hell does that mean?" Aniya demands.

"I will give you the prophecy, and you can come to your own conclusion." The seer moves to a wall that has a picture hanging, removing the picture as she waves her hand over the area and reveals a lock. Her back is turned, but they can see her left arm and a ding-a-ling can be heard; the click of a lock opens a small area in the wall. It takes her a few more minutes before she turns to them, holding a very old scroll.

"That took a lot of work to retrieve," Peter comments after seeing what she had to do to get into the hiding place.

"About 100 years ago or so, the prophecy was stolen, and once I got it back, I needed a better way to keep it hidden and protect it."

"Who would steal a prophecy that didn't belong to them?" Evie asks.

"Somebody who would gain a lot if the prophecy is not fulfilled."

"Who would gain from that?" Aniya asks.

"That I cannot tell you."

"But the council already knows the prophecy."

"No, they only have half of the prophecy. They are not supposed to know all of it." The seer hands the scroll to Aniya. "This is for the three of you."

Aniya takes it, unrolls the scroll, and begins reading.

In the twentieth century
a mage child will be
born
when a fall from the past meets
the future
the Fae may be saved.
In the light, darkness will show
depending on the mage's soul.

Once in pieces brought
together, this mage will bring us
back.
with this mage come many more
to make our halves become a whole.

"It says a mage born in the twentieth century—are you sure I am this mage?" Aniya studies the scroll as she asks the question.

"You were the only mage born in that century."

"What about my mother? Could she have been the mage?"

"Your mother was over a hundred years old, Aniya, she wasn't born in the twentieth century. She shouldn't have been able to even have a child."

"I know it's rare, but why shouldn't she have been able to have a child?"

"You weren't meant to be born, Aniya."

"But why?"

"You are far more valuable than you realize. Who you are is only the beginning of who you are meant to be."

"What does that even mean?"

Aniya shrugs her shoulders, looking at the seer, when she sees her eyes have gone solid white and a distant look shows on her face. Blue and purple lights circle her as if to shield her. Aniya watches the beautiful colors until they fade and the seer's eyes are once again crystal clear.

"The fates have decided, the Fae may be saved.

The choice has been made, the realm will not fade."

The seer collapses to the floor. Immediately, Aniya and Broden go to help her stand and move her to a chair close by.

"Seer, are you okay?"

"Sierra—my name is Sierra and I am fine. My visions take a lot of energy. Thank you for helping me. I generally end up lying in a heap on the floor for a time." She smiles at them both.

"Here, drink this." Rachel hands a cup of tea to Sierra.

"Thank you, Rachel, and just so you know, you have a place in all of this as well, in time, of course," she tells her.

"How do you know my name? Have we met before?"

"Many lifetimes ago, and how do I know any of your names, Rachel? I'm a seer," Sierra says, giving her a sly wink.

Rachel in turn shoots her a questioning look.

"In time. Now that was unexpected, but then again, my visions have a mind of their own. Is there anything else I can help you with?" Sierra directs the question to the group.

"Well, we were wondering, how is it that I am soul mate to both Broden and Brodrick? Can you help us understand that?"

"Well, I can tell you that it is all part of what is going to unfold the next time you go before the council. You will soon understand."

"Will deciphering the prophecy help us understand what decisions will need to be made to save the realm?"

"Not exactly, it's more of a guide to help you get to where you need to go. A direction, so to speak."

"So more questions than answers yet again. Great!" Aniya tosses her hands in the air, struggling with her emotions.

"The answers you seek will be revealed when you least expect it," Sierra tells Aniya.

"Well, that doesn't help us now."

"Follow your instincts. Now before you leave, there are a few things I can tell you. Brodrick, you are now part mage. Use your gifts along this path. If it feels natural, then just let your magic flow." Sierra turns to face Evie.

"When do you plan on bonding with your soul mate?"

"Oh, ummm, when the time is right. There are more important matters at hand, and those need to be settled first." Evie's eyes move to Peter; she sees the look of hurt on his face and aches to ease it.

Soon, she thinks to herself.

"Aniya?" Sierra rises from the chair and hugs her. "You need to keep the scroll close at all times. Do not, under any circumstances, let it out of your sight," she whispers to her.

"Off with all of you. There is much to be done. If you have any questions, all you need to do is call my name. I will hear you. Now go, your grandparents await."

"I will call the portal to their closest home, and from there, we can take a portal to the next house if they aren't there," Mike says.

"If we have a map, I am a finder and mage. Maybe I can use both to locate them," Brodrick offers.

"That could work and would save us a bit of time," Mike agrees.

"Here's a map." Sierra hands it over.

"Thank ye." Brodrick accepts the map and opens it. Remembering what Mike told Aniya, he pulls his magic forth and calls on his finder skills, searching with his eyes closed, hand hovering over the map, focusing. A picture forms, and he sends it to Aniya and Broden.

"Summer," all three say together.

"Nice job, Brodrick. Do you want to try to call the portal?" Mike asks.

"Aye, I'll try." Calling forth his magic again, he calls for the portal.

"Son, you did it." Evie claps in excitement.

"Let's go," Aniya says.

"Let's hope the house is close." Rachel heaves her bag up and onto her back.

They all move to the portal and, after saying their goodbyes to Sierra, go through one at a time. Once they are on the other side, a huge house stands before them.

"Nice job, Brodrick, it took me quite a while to be able to portal so close to my destination." Mike pats him on the back while walking up to the house.

"Aye! We are nae called the finders without reason." Brodrick grins.

Aniya has no words for what she sees laid out in front of her. The house is huge, at least three stories high, made of stone that sparkles in the sunlight. Its frame is made of wood as are the doors, with a wraparound stone porch that would give a breathless view from any angle, no matter where you would be standing. Beautiful vines creep up the walls with hundreds of red, pink, purple, and blue flowers. The lawn has a stream running around the property, with a small wooden bridge to cross over.

"This is beautiful." Aniya looks around, taking in the sight.

"It's like a fairy tale," Rachel chimes in.

Evie smiles at the awe she can see on both women's faces. Pride fills her as she takes in the view.

"The Fae realm is very beautiful, is it not?" she asked, looking up at Peter. When he looks back at Evie, he gets lost in her spectacular green eyes.

"My view is even more beautiful," Peter replies. Realizing he said his thoughts out loud, his face turns a bright red.

"Yes, yes, it is quite beautiful here!" Peter gets out as he clears his throat.

The most magnificent smile is shining back at Peter before Evie turns and asks the group, "Are we ready to go in? I'm not sure about the rest of you, but this has been a long day and I'm starving." Yeah and yes come from all of them. Aniya suddenly starts to feel a bit nervous. Knowing they are family and have been watching her over the years isn't helping much at the moment. Peter abruptly stops walking and grabs Aniya's forearm as she goes to walk by him.

"Hang on, guys. I need a minute with my daughter."

Aniya looks up at her father curiously and waves away Broden and Brodrick, signaling she needs a moment of privacy.

"What's wrong, Dad?"

"Nothing is wrong. I just wanted to make sure you were okay and let you know your grandparents' names. In all this commotion, neither Mike nor I thought to tell you."

"Oh well, yeah, that might be good to know. It might have been a little embarrassing going in there and not having that information ahead of time."

Peter gives her an apologetic look. "I'm sorry you feel we kept things from you. My only response is that I was only doing what I thought was right. I was wrong. I can't undo what has been done, but what I can do is, from this moment on, I promise to never keep things like that from you."

Before he continues, Aniya cuts him off, needing to say something as well.

"Dad, I'm sorry too. I know raising me after Mom died had to have been difficult. I know you were only trying to do what was right, and I should have thought about that before I flew off the handle. I am angry, but I can also understand and respect why you did what you did. Now we had best get in there. I'm not sure how much longer I will be able to stand."

Laughing, Peter hugs his daughter and with a relieved smile says, "Keyara and Maxwell—and you will love them! They are wonderful people who love you and loved your mother very much. This was very hard on them. Please try and understand that."

"I would never be cruel, but can also understand their fear. No worries, Dad." Aniya starts walking back toward the rest of the group.

"Is all weel, lass?" Broden steps forward and takes her hand.

"Oh yes, everything is fine." She takes his hand and reaches for Brodrick's hand as well. Aniya sends the conversation she had with her father to Brodrick and asks that he share it with Broden.

I can see why he would have worried. You have been on one hell of a journey with things thrown at ye at every turn, Brodrick sends to her.

Yes, well, such is life. Apparently a Fae's life is far more exciting than that of a human.

Gathering together, they all begin walking again toward the small bridge which is approximately twenty feet or so from the front doors. Once they approach the front of the house, Mike reaches for the knocker and with a rap, rap, rap, knocks on the doors. Aniya, who is feeling more anxious than before, begins to fidget. Brodrick puts one arm around her waist, and Broden squeezes her hand, stroking it with his thumb, calming her.

"Hush, lass, all will be fine," Broden whispers.

"Ye are nae alone in this." Brodrick follows up.

Everyone is standing behind Mike when one of the doors opens.

"Oh, Mike! What a surprise. Is everything okay with Aniya and her soul mates, is Sapphire okay?" The voice is not what Aniya expected. It's soft and doesn't crackle. And yes, her grandparents must be keeping up with her. Those details are quite new.

"Well, actually . . ." Mike says, stepping to the side, revealing their party.

"Oh my gosh, Max! Max, come quick, she's here! She's actually here!" Keyara is full of joy and excitement, walking up to Aniya, not sure if she should hug her or just say hello. Aniya takes the choice away when she steps forward and wraps the crying woman in her arms. If Aniya hadn't known her mother was dead, she would swear this woman was her, from the beautiful white-blonde hair to her blue eyes that match Aniya's, and even her height is how Aniya remembers her mother.

"You and Mom are identical," Aniya said once the hug was finished and she got a good look. Keyara doesn't look old enough to have a daughter, let alone a granddaughter. The Fae definitely do not age much.

"Yes, my Marriam did look like me, but to me, she was the most beautiful girl I had ever seen until I saw you." Keyara wipes at the tears that have begun running down her face. "I'm so glad you are here. Where is Sapphire?"

Sapphire comes out from behind Broden and Brodrick.

"How you've grown. Look at you!" Keyara bends down to Sapphire.

"Yes, thank you so much for Sapphire. I'm so sorry, I didn't think I'd be so emotional—nervous, yes, crying, no. Seeing you was like seeing Mom again." Aniya wipes at her own tears. Keyara looks up at Aniya from where she is bent down petting Sapphire, then rises.

"Yes, I can understand that. I see so much of Marriam in you as well." She hugs Aniya once more.

"Why don't you all come in? If you're hungry, I will have more plates set out for supper." Keyara stands aside to let everyone pass. As they enter the house, a man is standing there, watching.

"I wanted to give your grandmother a minute. Hello, Aniya, you do look so much like your mom." The man's blue eyes sparkle with pride. His brunette hair is almost the same color as Aniya's but a bit lighter. His sharp angled face is handsome and fits his large muscular figure.

"Hi, I know you both have watched over me my whole life, but I'm just meeting you that I can remember. So I'm not sure what to call you," Aniya says honestly.

"Well, my friends call me Max, but please, whatever you're comfortable with. I'd like to be Grandpa one day, when you're ready."

"And I've waited so long to hear you call me Grandma, but I understand as well, so Keyara is fine."

"For now, I'll call you both by your names. In time, I'm sure that will change. Is that okay?"

"Absolutely, darling."

"Yes, that's fine, granddaughter."

"Now let's move into the dining room—the food should be about ready." Keyara starts walking them into the next room.

Everyone follows Keyara and Max. Most of them have kept quiet, just observing, letting Aniya have this moment with her grandparents. However, once the word *food* was mentioned, they are all ready to move.

"Please have a seat. Wow, this is quite a group. Does everyone have a seat and plate?" Keyara takes a seat next to Aniya.

"Oh, yes! I'm sorry. Let me introduce everyone. Rachel, Broden, Brodrick, my soul mates, of course you know Mike and Dad, and over there is Evilyn, Evie for short—she is Broden and Brodrick's mother." Aniya points at each person as they are introduced.

"And that over there sitting on Broden's shoulder is Bolt and this here is Cera, our newest and most welcomed additions."

Thank you, both Cera and Bolt send to Aniya.

You both are as much a part of our group as Sapphire or anybody else.

"Wait! Evilyn? Amelia and Alfred's daughter?"

"Yes, you know my parents?"

"We do, but they are vampires. Does that mean . . . Wait, they are your sons, they're vampires?" Keyara's surprise is clear on her face.

"Yes, all three of us."

"And soul mates to our Aniya. Now that's something," Max says with a coy smile.

"So Bolt and Cera belong to whom then?"

"Us," Aniya tells them.

"Okay, um? Well, we can discuss all of this later. I'm sure you all are hungry. Please bring in the food," Keyara says to a smallish green goblin in a bright pink dress.

"You use goblins?" Aniya doesn't like the fact that her own grandparents might use and mistreat the creatures.

"We don't use them, Aniya. This is Sofie, and she is here because she chooses to be. We treat them well, each have their own room and things. We feed them and love them. We are not like some of those in the city or the few that sit on the council."

Aniya can see the fire of anger in Keyara eyes at the thought. That helps to calm her own temper.

Max sees and hears the conversation between his wife and Aniya. "Well, the apple doesn't fall far from this tree. Two women out to conquer unfairness in the realm." He smiles with pride.

During the short misunderstanding, the goblins have brought in tray after tray of food. Fruits, meats, and everything in between now sit on the table. Broden picks up what looks like a purple apple and cuts a piece of it to give to Aniya. She takes a bite, and it definitely isn't any apple she has ever tasted. The flavors explode in her mouth, a cross of a kiwi and pineapple. Some of the juice drips from her lips.

I will be more than happy to lick that up for you, sweetling.

Brodrick's flirtation catches Aniya off guard, causing her cheeks to turn bright red. She grabs her napkin and wipes off the juice, then she looks at Brodrick.

Maybe later.

While everyone is eating and filling her grandparents in on all that has been going on, Aniya takes in the simple but elegant dining room. Sheer curtains cover the two windows still letting in the late-evening sunlight. Pictures of land she has never seen before hang in frames on the wall.

"Your house is beautiful, Keyara."

"It's one of our favorites. We love our summer home." Keyara looks around the room.

"I can see why. The colors are so different here, some I've never seen before."

"Yes, Mike and Peter both have said the same. Our home is your home." Keyara sends a radiant smile to Aniya.

Once everyone seems to have had their fill of food and drink, Keyara stands and says, "Well, I'm sure you all are tired and might even want a hot shower after everything. Why don't we show you to your rooms? There will be time to talk tomorrow. I know you have questions."

"Yes, I do, but I think a bath and bed is what we all need right now. The answers will still be the same tomorrow," is Aniya's exhausted reply.

Brother, why do nae ye take Mother, Bolt, and Cera for a run and reintroduce the two to hunting. Make sure Mother and yerself feed as weel. I'll stay here with Sapphire and Aniya, then hunt when ye return.

Aye, I think we'll need our strength. Make sure Aniya takes a bath. I will feed her when I return. Och, aye, I weel.

Mother, Bolt, and Cera, let's go for a run. Brodrick sends to the three of them.

Yes, I need to feed.

We haven't hunted in a while.

I will help ye both.

Brodrick rises from the table and excuses himself. "I'm going out for a run. Bolt, Cera, come. Sapphire, stay."

"I will come with you. A walk sounds great." Evie rises as well.

"The woods behind the house are a good place for a stroll," Max tells them, knowing what it is that they need to do.

"Thank ye." Brodrick moves to the front door.

Aniya stands next.

"Can you show me to a room and bathroom, please, Keyara?" Broden rises to follow and looks at Sapphire.

Sapphire, come on.

I need to feed too, Broden.

Ye will, lovely, when they return. We'll go out and feed together.

Okay.

Aniya follows Keyara out of the dining room and down a hallway. Pictures cover almost every wall. She can see her mother growing in them, baby pictures all the way up to her parents' wedding. The last picture is of the three of them and was taken days before her mother's death. Aniya is sitting between her parents; they are on a couch and smiling.

"You can't tell they weren't soul mates. They were so happy." Aniya had stopped to look at the picture. "And we were happy for Marriam.

She never even thought about a soul mate. Her life was happy with you and Peter."

"This was taken a couple days before her murder. I remember it. They were tickling me."

"Let's keep walking." Keyara continues down the hall, pushing down the sob that was threatening to escape. Seeing more pictures, Aniya follows her grandmother. These are Aniya's life after her mother was gone: school photos, snapshots her father and Mike had taken. One from when she had a cast on her leg. Her first car, graduation from high school and college. Even one from when she had bought her house—she is standing in front of the door, holding the keys, with a huge smile on her face. Dad had taken that one.

"You really did watch over me."

"Yes, we love you, and after your mom died, you are all we have. Peter and Mike made sure to keep in contact, so even though we weren't there, we could still watch you grow up. Come on, we can talk more tomorrow. Here is your room. The bed should be big enough for all three of you, and there is a private bathroom." Keyara opens the door she had stopped in front of and moves inside.

"There is a door leading outside so the familiars can be let out. Though I still wonder why you have three. One for each of you, maybe?"

"Not exactly. I will explain it tomorrow. Thank you, the room is perfect." Aniya hugs her grandmother.

Broden and Sapphire have already entered the room when Broden turns and says, "Thank ye very much, Keyara."

"You're family, no need to thank me. I will show Brodrick to the room when he returns. Sleep well." With that, she closes the door.

Aniya looks around the room before her eyes fall on Broden. "Well, this has been an eventful day."

"Aye, it has. Let me run ye a bath, lass."

"That would be wonderful." Aniya moves to him and reaches up to give him a kiss. "Please, would you mind?"

Broden wraps his arms around Aniya. "Nay, lass, I would nae mind. I could use one myself." He kisses her before letting go and moving to the bathroom.

"Ye, me, and Brodrick could fit in this tub."

"What do you mean?" Aniya follows him into the bathroom.

"That's not a tub. That's a Jacuzzi on steroids!" The tub is round, built into one side of the room, which could easily be as big as her bedroom in her house. The bathtub itself could be the size of a walk-in closet. The faucet is more like a small waterfall and could fill the tub in minutes.

"What is steroids?" Broden isn't familiar with the word.

"Nothing, a figure of speech. It means something is oversized." Aniya didn't know how to describe her meaning.

"Okay, well, should I turn it on and fill the tub?"

"Yes! Please." Aniya tries not to sound too eager but fails miserably.

"Would ye like bubbles?"

"They have bubbles?"

"I think that's what is over there." Boden points to a shelf with bottles on the opposite wall.

Aniya practically runs to look at the labels, reading each one. "What is backleberry?"

"The wine Mother gave ye at the hotel was backleberry. It's a type of berry that would taste like a cross between the humans' blackberry and purple grapes." Broden isn't sure if that's the best description, but it was the closest description he could come up with.

"Oh . . . Wow! It smells as good as it tasted. Use this, please." Aniya hands over the small bottle.

Broden takes the bottle from her and tests the warmth of the water before adding a small amount into its stream.

"I think you are going to need more than that. It's a huge tub."

"Nay, lass, 'tis enough."

"Broden, I hones—Oh!" Aniya watches as bubbles start to fill the tub. "They're purple!"

"Aye."

"Whoa, it smells better than it did in the bottle." Aniya starts to remove her clothing.

Broden is still bent over the tub when she walks over, using him to balance herself, and gets into the water, onto steps right next to where he is kneeling.

He watches as one foot takes the first step then the next, his eyes following her beautiful legs and catching a full view of Aniya's round rear as she takes the last step into the tub.

"Lass, I intend on joining ye."

"Oh wow! I hope you do. This feels amazing." Broden groans softly.

"Did you say something?" Aniya asks, looking up at him.

"Aye, I said I'd be joining ye," he repeats, hoping she hadn't heard him groan a moment ago. He then begins to remove his clothing.

"You're going to smell all pretty." Aniya giggles.

"I will smell ye on me all night, then." Removing the last of his clothing, he enters the tub, setting himself behind Aniya, and reaches to turn off the faucet.

"Ye are right, this does feel very good. Come, let me rub your back." Aniya moves between Broden's legs and goes to lean against him.

"Nay, sit forward, loving, so I can wash yer lower back."

Aniya leans forward, bringing her legs up. Broden starts to massage her lower back, moving upward, making sure to hit every pressure point and muscle, working out every knot she has acquired from the last few days.

"Aww, mmm, oh."

"There ye go, lass." Broden begins working on her shoulders, causing Aniya to lower her legs and lean back against Broden's wide chest.

"Oh, Broden, that feels amazing," Aniya whispers.

He bends to kiss her neck. His hands work their way down to her breasts, moving over the mounds. He runs his fingers over her nipples, already taut little buds.

"Ohhh."

"That's it, lass. Enjoy it, feel me."

Broden continues his erotic torture with her nipples, slightly pinching them while kissing her neck, moving from one side and kissing his way to the other. His hands move lower, so Aniya rests her head back against him and relaxes into his touch. His hands work magic on her breasts, every motion sending electricity through her, causing tingles to erupt there. She feels his hands move lower over her stomach and navel and down even further. She can feel his cock pressed against her lower back.

"Oh, Broden!" His hands roam over her hips; one hand stretches between her legs, seeking out that one special place. Once he finds it, he begins to rub it gently, pressing and then circling her clit, causing her to jerk with his every rub. His other hand moves back up to her breasts, kneading them and slightly squeezing before he uses his thumb to caress her nipple, then repeating the actions on the other breast. With his other hand, he works at her clit before he inserts one finger and then another into her hot body, causing Aniya to whimper with pleasure.

"Broden!"

She can feel herself climbing higher and higher as Broden kisses her neck and continues his assault on her body, moving his fingers in and out of her, using his thumb on her clit to push her over the edge.

"OH GOD!" Aniya can't stop the scream any more than she could stop her hips from thrusting to meet his fingers when the world around her shatters into a million pieces, each with wave of pleasure.

Aniya gives one last cry of ecstasy.

"That's it, Aniya. Give in to it, ride it out," Broden says between the kisses he is pressing to her neck. Aniya settles back against him after what felt like hours; the last wave of pleasure had faded. When she moves to turn toward him, he stops her.

"Nay, lass, this eve was for ye. I wanted to help ye ease some tension."

"But—" Aniya gets cut off by Broden's next words.

"Nay, loving. We will bond but nae this night. Ye are exhausted, and I only wanted ye to relax. Brodrick will be returning soon, and I need to take Sapphire out hunting. When the time is right, we will but nae tonight. Let me hold you a bit longer before I get out," Broden insists.

A short while later, Aniya and Broden can hear the door open and shut.

"Ye both did weel," they hear Brodrick say.

Broden moves out from behind Aniya to get out of the tub.

"Stay, lass. Yer hair still needs to be washed," he says when he sees her begin to get out of the tub. He reaches for a towel to dry himself off and leaves the bathroom, wrapping the towel around his waist as he walks out.

"Time to hunt, Sapphire." Then Aniya hears Sapphire's paws hit the floor.

"She is in the tub," Broden tells Brodrick.

"I could use a bath."

"Enjoy, brother." Broden opens the door leading to the outside.

Which direction, lovely?

This way, Broden.

Sapphire takes off in a direction, and Broden follows.

Brodrick moves to the bathroom and sees Aniya lying back in the tub.

"Ye look relaxed."

"Oh, I am."

"Mind if I join ye? I could wash yer hair."

"I can't lift my arms, so by all means . . ." Aniya lazily sits up.

Brodrick strips and climbs in. "'Tis still hot too. Come to me, lass." Brodrick takes her in his arms.

"Did you feed?" Aniya asks.

"Aye, and ye need to as weel. I will make sure to help ye with that."

"I just ate dinner."

"Aye, but ye are part vampire and do need blood for your strength. Dinna ye worry, ye will feed from me tonight."

Brodrick lifts his wrist and then bites himself; he then offers his wrist to Aniya. "Drink, lass."

Aniya smells the blood, and some part of her craves the thick red liquid. She moves her mouth to his wrist, and instinct seems to take over. She latches onto Brodrick's wrist and drinks deep.

"That's it, sweetling." Brodrick bends to kiss the side of her neck.

Aniya takes her fill and then closes the wound on his wrist. A small surge of power seems to rush through her.

"Oh, that's different."

"Ye felt the surge?"

"Yes, through my whole body."

"I ken the feeling. Here, let me wash your hair."

When Brodrick finishes with Aniya's hair, he holds her and she falls asleep in his arms. Gently, he moves to get out of the tub and drain the water while making sure to keep one arm under Aniya's sleeping form so she doesn't slide. He lifts her in his arms and reaches for a towel. Aniya stirs and wakes with a jolt when cold air hits her.

"I fell asleep?"

"Aye, ye did."

"Put me down so I can dry off and dress, please."

Brodrick does as she asks because he needs to do the same.

"Are Broden and Sapphire back yet?"

"Nay, but they should be back any minute now." Aniya dresses and climbs onto the huge bed.

Come, Cera, Bolt. Are you settled?

I am.

Me too.

Aniya smiles and watches as Sapphire and Broden come back in from the outside. Sapphire jumps up on the bed and takes her usual spot on the end.

Cera, come up on the bed.

Can I?

Yes, it's our spots.

Cera doesn't hesitate and jumps up on the bed, lying down, her head next to Sapphire's. "Good girls." Aniya moves to caress them both.

And boy, she sends to Bolt before lying back down.

"Did she feed, brother?"

"Aye, she did."

Both brothers just watch the scene before them and then climb into bed, one on either side of Aniya.

CHAPTER 12

Aniya awakes the next morning with all three familiars still in the room with her. Broden and Brodrick must have beat her awake this morning.

They had us wait for you, Iya.

They said to tell you they went to the kitchen and will be there.

We are to escort you.

"Well, let me dress and we can go."

She moves out of the bed and to the bathroom. Once she comes out, she is dressed in a tank top and jean shorts with tennis shoes.

"Let's go, hopefully I didn't miss breakfast," she tells Sapphire, Cera, and Bolt before moving to the door. Bolt flies over and lands on Aniya's shoulder. She reaches up to caress his feathers and notices they have straightened out and are more plentiful. He has even gained some weight. "Bolt, you are looking more and more handsome every day," Aniya tells him.

She then looks down at Cera. "The missing fur patches have filled in some, but you can still see the areas somewhat. However, those will be gone soon. Your black spots and fur are looking healthier as well, and you have gained some weight too."

I just want to run around. I feel so good.

"I'm so happy Sapphire and you are full grown already," Aniya tells Cera before talking to Sapphire.

We grow faster.

"I know. It's just hard to believe is all."

Our family has grown too.

"Yes, it has."

She can hear the chatter coming from the dining room, and when she enters, "good morning" sounds from every direction.

"Good morning," she replies.

"How did you sleep, dear?"

"Great and quite hard."

Aniya moves to the empty seat between Brodrick and Broden, kissing them both once she sits down. "The food looks amazing. Is there a coffee?"

"Thank goodness they do, and if it's not, it tastes just like coffee," Rachel says, handing her a cup of the dark liquid.

"It's coffee!" Aniya says after taking a sip.

Everyone continues eating while Aniya takes a moment to enjoy her coffee and wake up. She then notices, off in the corner of the dining room, that an otter and a gray wolf are watching everyone. The otter is swimming around in a box-type thing, playing with a yellow ball, and the wolf is just standing there, observing everyone.

"Are those your familiars?"

"Yes, Dribbles and Asher." Both animals look up at their names.

"I was only introducing you both." The two animals nod and go back to what they were doing. "Why don't you and the boys follow us onto the porch so we can talk and the animals can play a bit in the yard while everyone else finishes up," Keyara suggests.

"That sounds good. It's always nice to have a minute to relax, and the animals do deserve it," Aniya answers.

Aniya rises from the table, grabs her coffee, and with the guys, she follows her grandparents onto the porch. Aniya sits on a loveseat with Broden on her right and Brodrick on her left, sitting on the arm of the sofa. Her grandparents both take the chairs that are across from them.

"We know you have a lot of questions. So before we get into that, we wanted you to know we do love you and are so proud of the woman you have become. We never meant to hurt you, but we had to protect you the best we could," Keyara explains, saddened by the events that have brought them to this point. Max then grabs her hand and lightly kisses it, giving her some of his strength.

"I have so many questions. I'm not sure where to begin."

"Well, how much of the Fae world have you been told about—more specifically, the mages?" Keyara looks at Aniya.

She relays all that Mike told her. Aniya goes over where their magic comes from and how to use it.

She breezes over what he has said about soul mates and how a mage knows they have one. "I did have a bonding question. Is it normal for a mage light to throw their mate across the room?" Aniya blushes slightly when she asks the question.

"Wh— um. It, uh, did what? You say it threw him across the room? That isn't supposed to happen," Keyara mumbles.

"But if you are who we believe you are, it's possible."

"Aniya, um, a mage's light is only so strong. The fact that you have two soul mates should actually make you weaker. You share your light with both men, and when they receive it, it should only have been . . . well, crap!" Keyara stands and begins pacing behind her chair.

"It should have been a little light and so weak it would have barely been able to enter them." The words rush out.

"That can't be right. Brodrick flew so hard he broke my wall." Aniya looks up at him while explaining what had happened to Keyara.

Max reaches up behind him for Keyara's hand as she makes another round of pacing. He brings her hand to his chest; she naturally brings her other hand over to do the same when he gently starts rubbing the backs of both beautifully manicured hands that Aniya can see have bright red nail polish. She can actually feel the love they have for each other. Calming, Keyara looks back at Aniya, and asks, "Can you explain exactly what happened?"

Aniya's face turns bright red, and her eyes look as if they are about to pop out.

Keyara laughs. "Not what got you to that point, silly girl. Only what happened once your light withdrew from you." She laughs a bit more.

"OH! Yeah, well, I can do that." The relief is apparent on Aniya's face, and Keyara can't help but laugh again.

Aniya goes on to explain how the light rose out of her, the lights splitting into three different pieces, one of which went into Brodrick and the other two retracting back into her. She explains how the light never dulled even after one piece had entered Brodrick. She makes sure to give even the smallest of details from when her light withdrew to when it reentered her.

"Brodrick, when you received the light, how did it feel to you?" Max asked curiously.

"That shite hurt! Felt like I was hit by a ten-ton bus. It caused me to fly clear across the room." Brodrick rubs his chest, remembering how it felt.

"Really? When our mage lights combined and then split into two entering us again, it just flowed back into us and felt similar to butterflies. There was no pain," Max explains.

"We don't want to give you false information. It could be a few different reasons why your light would do that. One of those is you may be that strong, another is the fact that there are three of you, and the last could be that they are vampires and you're mage. Maybe it has to do with the blood exchange and you receiving vampire gifts, which also could make you stronger. Did that happen with Broden as well?"

"Well, I haven't bonded with Broden yet, just Brodrick. Remember when I told you my light split in three? Two went back into me. I think the second light was looking for Broden, but when it couldn't find him, it retreated."

"Oh, I thought you were fully bonded. There might still be some things that still haven't been revealed yet." Keyara sounds surprised.

"I'm not understanding any of this. I'm not sure what's going on, and there are so many questions and no answers because this has never happened so nobody knows what should or shouldn't be going on. Every time I think I have an answer to something, another question comes up. It's just so much, and we haven't even touched on Mom or why she was in the human realm or why after she died, I didn't have any relationship with either of you. That doesn't even include me finding out I'm mage and learning about a realm I knew nothing of two weeks ago!" Aniya says in an exasperated tone.

"Honey, we'll do our best to help. Let's start with something we can answer for you." Max looks up at Keyara then offers her a seat next to him again.

"Let's start with Mom. Why was she in the human realm?"

"Well, Mike told you that soul mates have been hard to find. That's been happening for a few centuries now. We were the last mages to become soul mates, and that was a long time ago. Marriam was 150 years old when she left to go to the human realm and still hadn't found her soul mate and we had noticed how hard it was for her. By this time, many mages had started to disappear. Literally here one day, gone the next. A mated pair here, single one there. We honestly thought they were just leaving," Keyara starts explaining.

"I had noticed there seem to be only a few. We saw a mage village, and there were only three mages that I saw. The houses look to have been empty for a while," Aniya confirms.

"There were only a few more during this time frame. Well, we were all talking one day and had mentioned that we noticed mages just disappearing to Marriam. She, being the beautiful girl she was, offered to go to the human realm to search for the mages and maybe even find her soul mate. She thought that if he wasn't here, maybe he would be in the human realm. So of course, we had to agree, hoping she would find her soul mate. Off she went. She was quite excited. She thought of it as an adventure, and this was going to be the first one she'd ever been on. Your mother loved adventures." Keyara pauses, smiling at the memory before continuing.

"The next time she came home, she told us she had met Peter and said he was a good man. She also told us she hadn't found her soul mate or any mages. We then told her that more had gone missing and we still didn't know why. She assured us that she would continue looking and went back to the human realm. It was shortly after Marriam went back that Sierra came to us with a warning."

"A warning? That woman talks in riddles. How can you decipher anything she says?" Aniya asks.

"Well, yes, but there was no riddle with what she told us. The warning was that something big was going to happen and that we needed to distance ourselves from everyone, including the council and the center city. She said that it was actually safer for Marriam in the human realm. This confused us, and when we asked what was happening, all Sierra said was to heed her warning. Of course, for our daughter, we did. Marriam came back, and this time, she brought Peter. She told us that she was happy with Peter and had agreed to marry him in the human way. She also told us that she had explained everything to him, from who and what she was to soul mates and how that all worked. He had told her that if her soul mate ever did appear, he would understand the pull she would have toward them and could love her enough to let her go. The pull between soul mates would be too strong for Marriam to ignore and Peter would have to let her go, but they loved each other so much that they didn't want to waste what time they did have. So your parents married, and when we learned your mother was pregnant with you, we were overjoyed. To have a grandchild was something we thought would never happen because it's so rare for an unmated couple to conceive and you were the first mage child born in years. Once you were born, Marriam and Peter would visit as much as possible. We adored you and still do, but our happiness at your arrival was cut short when again Sierra came to see us after one of our visits. She told us that things were getting worse and you needed to be protected at all costs and it was of the utmost importance that you not keep coming to the Fae realm because you were in danger, and when we were told that, it broke our hearts. Next to Marriam, you were our everything, and we weren't going to be able to watch you grow or learn about who you were. But of course, we listened and then sent Mike to watch over and protect you. When we next saw you, we told Marriam and Peter that we thought it best if they didn't come visit anymore because it wasn't safe and they raised you in the human realm, away from the Fae. We also explained that we had somebody there watching and protecting you, but would keep their distance until it became necessary to move in closer, just in case something was to happen and you needed help. They agreed even though it didn't seem right that you wouldn't know us, but they promised to keep in contact as much as possible. That was the last time we saw you before yesterday, other than pictures. The next time we saw Peter was when he told us Marriam had been shot and had passed away. Mike had showed up but couldn't do anything. Marriam had made him promise to protect you, and from that day on, he was Uncle Mike, which made it easier for him to stay close to you," Keyara finishes.

"Well, I can't call him Uncle Mike anymore. It's too weird. He looks my age."

"Yet he is much older than you are, my dear."

"Yes but still weird."

"Does that help you understand why we kept our distance and maybe answer a few of your questions?" Max asks.

"Where Mom is concerned, yes, but now there is still this prophecy Sierra gave me and why I have two soul mates. Not that it's a bad thing." Aniya smiles up at Broden and Brodrick.

"And why somebody wants me dead. I have come to terms with the fact that my accidents were not just accidents. With everything I have learned since arriving in the Fae realm and if I'm the mage they have been searching for or whoever you"—pointing at her grandpa—"think I am, why kill me? I'm meant to save us, but how can I if I'm dead? Wouldn't that mean the Fae would die too? Why would somebody want that?"

"Sierra gave you a prophecy? May we see it?" Keyara looks at Aniya.

"Sierra told me to keep it on me at all times and not show it to anyone, but you have already done and gone through so much to protect me, I feel like I can trust you." Aniya reaches in her back pocket and withdraws the scroll, handing it to Max. He unrolls it, and Keyara bends over his shoulder to read the words.

Aniya looks over the yard and sees all the familiars still playing in and around the stream. She can't help but smile at the picture in front of her.

"Well, this doesn't make much sense, now does it?"

"To me either. Sorry, Aniya, we can't help with this," Keyara says as Max hands the scroll back to Aniya, who puts it back in her pocket.

"I didn't think so."

"Can you tell us what abilities you had before your mage light came on?"

"I noticed that at a young age, I could persuade people. I try to use that ability to help only. I can also look inside someone and see their souls and injuries. When my mage light came on, I got the ability to heal myself. Since Brodrick and I bonded, I haven't really used any of my gifts because I haven't needed to, so if anything is different, I don't know," Aniya explains to her grandparents.

"Persuasion is a rare gift, and I have never met another mage who can see the souls of others. Do you just look at them and see it?"

"No, I have to touch them and focus on it. It's the same with seeing injuries. I would have to touch you."

"Oh, okay, I kind of wondered what our souls look like." Keyara laughs a bit.

"I can, I mean, if you want me to." Aniya goes to reach for Keyara's hands but then pulls back.

"If you want." Keyara reaches for Aniya's hand and holds it.

Aniya focuses on her grandmother, the picture forms, and she can see her grandmother's soul is white and bright. The picture soon looks to expand and then indigo blends with the light and glows outward into green. Aniya releases her hand.

"Well, that was a bit different."

"What? Is something wrong?"

"Oh, no, your soul is bright white, but there were other colors, something I have never seen before."

"Other colors?"

"Yes, indigo and green seem to flow from your light. That's not ever happened before. I haven't touched anyone since Rachel, which was before I bonded with Brodrick."

"That sounds like my aura, Aniya, and you have never seen that before me?"

"No, maybe that's because I did bond with Brodrick, but then what happens when I am bonded to them both?"

"It could be. Your bonding is so different because there are three of you. This makes it so much harder, and because it's never happened, we are kind of lost on how to help you. But we will do what we can." Keyara smiles.

"I know and appreciate that. I know familiars are meant to be protectors, companions, and to feed us energy if we need it, but Sapphire told me something both times I have been attacked. She said she smelled evil, and then when we went to the council, she said she smelled evil there as well. How is it possible that evil could be among the council? Isn't everyone that sits on the council soul-mated? I mean, that's why they're sitting in those spots. And how come you and Max aren't on it?" Aniya asks the question with a raised eyebrow.

"Our familiars are an extension of us, and yes, they can help protect us. If Sapphire said she smelled evil, she most certainly did, but why she smelled evil in the council tower I can't say. I believe her, and I know you all plan to go back there, so I'm going to ask that you keep the guys and your familiars close. Under no circumstances do you separate from them," Keyara states, with fear in her voice.

"They wouldn't leave me, especially if there is any sign of danger."

Max chooses this moment to chime in. "Sapphire is a tiger so her ability to smell evil would naturally be strong, just not sure why she would smell it with the council. The council are our leaders, they guide us, set laws and taxes. They are our voices, kind of similar to what the human realm has with their human politics, just with much less control."

Aniya shrugs her shoulders. "I thought maybe with the council being built by soul-mated couples with love, it would be more welcoming, but it just didn't feel right."

"We haven't been to see the council in years. There has been no need for us to go. Now if something were to happen to Edward and Ada, we would take their spot, but because they are older and stronger than us, they represent all of us mages," Max explains.

"Sierra mentioned Edward and Ada. What do they have to do with you and sitting on the council?"

"Ada is my aunt and Edward is her husband. She is much older and more powerful than I am, and that's why she and Edward sit on the council," Keyara tells Aniya.

"I'm related to those two! She has an attitude problem and he is just rude, not to mention they mistreated their familiars—they treated them like they were nothing. Cera and Bolt were dirty, starving, and terrified. I'm happy I took them from those two!"

"Do you mean those two were Ada and Edward's familiars?" Keyara sounds surprised.

"Keyword *was*. I fed them and severed the bond, with my blood. Serves them right for mistreating those two."

"You severed a familiar's bond?" Max asks.

"Yes, I did and I don't regret it." Aniya sits a little straighter on the loveseat, proud of herself, and then she continues, "Now some things are starting to make sense, but a lot of it still doesn't help me to understand why I felt the way I did or why Sapphire smelled evil among the council. Again more questions than answers. It's becoming very frustrating. I think I'm going to go for a walk. I need to process all of this and see if maybe I can put at least some of this together." Aniya rises from where she has been sitting.

"I need to go alone. Could you keep watch over the animals?" She directs the question to the guys.

"Lass, if you think we would let ye go by yourself, no. I will come with ye. Brother, can ye go to the council tower and mayhap do a little looking around? See if something comes up. Can ye take the familiars with ye and have Mother and Mike go as well? I ken it's much to ask, but we will meet ye as soon as we can and ye need only to call us if ye have need," Broden requests.

"Aye, brother. Max, Keyara, 'tis okay if Peter and Rachel stay with ye? They are nae Fae, and it is probably safer for them if they stay here."

"Absolutely, we can catch up with Peter and get to know Rachel."

Aniya kisses Brodrick and moves to step off the porch with Broden. She begins walking in no particular direction, when Sapphire rises to follow.

No, beautiful girl, go with Brodrick. Broden will go with me.

But, Iya—

No buts. Please.

I don't like it, Iya.

Neither do I.

Nor I.

Thank you all. Do not worry. I'm just going on a little walk.

Aniya and Broden continue walking, headed for the woods. He is giving her some space and can see she is really trying to sort through all the information she has been given over the last two weeks. Aniya looks around, not really seeing any of the beauty around her. Her thoughts are going in many different directions, trying to find any connection. She can hear water rushing by somewhere in the distance but just keeps walking. The next time she comes out of her thoughts long enough to actually see where she is, there, just about thirty feet away, is a huge tree. The tree stretches, reaching high into the sky at least fifty feet and looks very similar to the human realm's weeping willows, but the trunk is bigger and the branches go off in various directions, with little white buds of some sort of flower on them. Aniya moves to the tree and looks up between the branches and leaves. It's massive.

"This tree is absolutely beautiful, Broden."

"Nay, Aniya, ye are beautiful. The tree is no comparison to ye," Broden whispers in a soft tone. Aniya smiles and moves to Broden. She wraps her arms around his neck and stands on tiptoes to kiss him. His arms move around her and pull her to him, deepening the kiss. Their tongues dance. Aniya pushes into Broden, and when his mouth moves to her neck, Aniya's eyes open and she can see the tree branches growing. Instead of the branches going in different directions, they have begun to move and stretch toward the ground. It's as if a curtain is forming. As the darkness engulfs them, the little buds on the tree begin to glow, giving the area a low-light candlelit space. It's not very bright, and the romantic glow casts a shadow of Broden and Aniya, showing them as one and giving them enough light that they can see each other. A few feet from where they are standing, a rock rises out of the ground. The rock's top starts to cover itself in a green moss. By the time the rock has stopped rising, it's about four feet off the ground, layered with luscious green moss and could easily be a place for Aniya and Broden to lie. In the distance, Aniya can still hear the rushing water. It's almost soothing to her. Broden nips at Aniya's neck, causing her attention to fall back to him.

"Broden, look," she whispers.

Lifting his head, Broden looks around them. The tree branches have stopped growing and sway gently, even with no breeze, causing the buds on each branch to look as if they are flickering. The thick curtain the branches have created give Broden and Aniya more privacy than the room at her grandparents'. The curtain circles around, with the trunk of the tree being in the center of the 20 by 20 foot area. The moss-covered rock is placed right by the tree trunk without a scratch to the bark and is slightly angled downward, making it easy to lie upon without slipping down the flat surface on top of the rock.

"We have been given a room, loving." Broden moves Aniya toward the rock, and Aniya lets him guide her backward. She pulls his shirt up and helps pull it over his head. She kicks her shoes off and reaches for her shorts, unbuttoning them before pushing them down her legs and stepping out of them. Broden removes his jeans and boots, kicking both aside. He looks at Aniya, eyes moving from the top of her head, over her loose brunette hair, her blue eyes sparkling in the low light and looking like she has stars in them, moving over her ample breasts with her rosy nipples, hard and begging for his touch, down her slightly rounded tummy and navel to the hair he can see resting between her legs, her curls glistening with dampness. He continues down her long legs all the way to her toes. Every inch of her is perfect.

"Ye are so gorgeous, Aniya."

She gives him a seductive smile. "I want you, Broden." He wastes no time in granting her request. Taking her in his arms, he lifts her, which causes her to wrap her legs around his narrow waist, and when he lays her on the rock, which isn't hard but soft and feels more like a cloud, she runs her hands over his flat chest, down his taut stomach, and reaches for his cock. Broden gasps when he feels her hand wrap his shaft and move her fingers up and down his length and over the sensitive head.

"Aye, lass."

Relieving her of his cock, he bends down to kiss her lips, taking his fill of her mouth. He moves down to her breasts. With one hand, he kneads the soft flesh while he nips and sucks his way over the other one. Aniya's hands are in his black hair, urging his mouth to continue. Broden moves over to her other breast, making sure to give each breast his full attention before his kisses move over her stomach and further down. Settling his head between Aniya's legs, he kisses her inner thighs and moves to the button of nerves hidden in her folds.

"Broden."

"Ye taste of honeyed wine. I could drink from ye forever." He rises long enough to say the words before moving back and uses his tongue and fingers to give her even more pleasure, suckling her like the sweetest nectar. Broden then moves his fingers to her entrance, and with two fingers, he thrusts inside her, matching his fingers to the same rhythm as his tongue works her clit.

"Oh god."

Aniya's hips matching his fingers, she is reaching for the stars as Broden's tongue and fingers work together to bring her closer to the edge. When she tumbles over, pleasure surges through her. Broden can feel the moment her orgasm rocks through her. Her inner walls contract and release his fingers and still he continues.

"OOHH, AWW!"

Aniya feels every surge of her climax, and when Broden doesn't lift his head from between her legs, she moves off the rock to grab him. She turns him around and gives him a gentle push toward the rock. She moves and rises up to kiss him, running her hands over every inch of him that she can reach before kneeling in front of him. She moves in, kissing the tip of his erection before taking his cock into her mouth and sucking.

"Aniya!" Broden braces himself on the rock. His ass sits on the mossy top; he uses his hands to hold his weight so he can watch as Aniya takes him deep into her mouth and down her throat before withdrawing and dropping her mouth over him again. Every nerve in Broden's body is on fire with pleasure. Aniya takes his shaft once more down her throat, enjoying the taste of him but needing to feel him inside her. She stands up and pushes Broden down so he is lying on his back. Straddling him, she reaches for his cock and positions it at her entrance and slowly eases herself down and onto him, taking each and every beautiful inch of him, all the way to the base, before raising herself and then coming back down. Aniya moans and Broden releases his own groan. She rides him hard for a few more minutes before Broden rises, with his cock still buried inside Aniya, and turns her so she is lying down on her back. He thrusts into her, bending to kiss her neck and breast. His teeth lengthening, he sinks them deep into her, right over her left breast. She is hot and tastes of the finest wine. Aniya moans when she feels his teeth sink into her breast. No pain, just pure pleasure. She can feel her own teeth lengthen, and once he has taken his fill of her, he continues his slow sensual thrusts in and out of her. Aniya pushes herself up and kisses Broden's chest over his heart, where she can feel it pounding, and sinks her teeth in. He groans out his pleasure when he feels her drink him, and when she is finished, she closes the wound. She thrusts her hips to meet his. Aniya can feel her light start to rise out of her. She and Broden watch as the light rises into the air and splits in two.

Broden keeps thrusting in and out of her while she matches him thrust for thrust.

"Broden, watch out!" Aniya manages to say between moans.

"Lass, I ken it but cannae stop!" Broden gasps out between his thrusting.

"Do not stop. Ohh!" Aniya moans and throws her head back.

"Nay, never!"

Their moans mingle together. Aniya can feel she is close to her release. Broden feels Aniya's vaginal walls start to contract. He thrusts faster.

"Broden!"

"Aniya!"

They both climax. There are orgasms simultaneous to each other. Wave after intense wave rock their bodies. The lights floating above them move together, one aiming for Broden's chest, throwing him backward. But he doesn't hit the ground; branches catch him in midair.

"What the—" Broden's words are cut off as he looks at Aniya. She is raised into the air, her light surrounding her. The light that entered him rises again, and both seem to explode. Waves of blinding light coming from every angle shoot outward through the tree branches, and all Broden can see is endless light.

"What the hell is happening?" His eyes move to Aniya, who is still floating in the bright light.

CHAPTER 13

Brodrick has just entered the council tower and is moving toward the council room. Once he gets in and before he can say anything, he feels a strange rising in his chest. He watches as his light from Aniya rises out of him and causes his steps to halt.

"Brodrick, what's happening?" Mike looks at him, stopping next to Brodrick.

"Son, are you all right?" Evie asks with a worried tone.

"I dinna know, and yes, I'm fine, Moth—"

Before he can finish his sentence, the light has risen above him and it starts to shoot out stream after stream of light in all directions.

The lights start hitting the walls of the council room, disintegrating the marble before falling in bits and pieces of reds, blues, greens, yellows, and purples, any color you could think of. The light rays hit the council seats, lowering them, and in the middle of the far wall directly in front of Brodrick, Evie, and Mike, they can see three high-backed stone chairs, each connected to the other, rise above the council seats. As the light continues to shoot rays at the black marble, blasting it with magic, which then spreads over the marble as the magic passes over every inch of the room, pristine white stone with gray-and-gold marble replaces the black. Where the light hit the walls just seconds ago form openings that circle the room, and glass appears where stone had been.

"Those are windows!" someone exclaims.

"How is this happening?" says another voice.

"Is that a throne? For three?" says somebody else.

Once the light has made its way around the room and retracted to the ball above Brodrick, it shoots back into him, knocking him back a few feet.

"Again! Was nae once enough?" Brodrick regains his footing and rubs his chest.

"At least it didn't throw you across the room again," Mike points out with a grin.

"Oh, shut it, Mike!" Brodrick shoots back at him.

Mike tries his best not to laugh out loud at Brodrick, but he cannot help himself and loses it to a loud round of laughter.

Everyone looks around the new council room. Windows circle the walls. Each view is of one of the seasons. What was once black marble is now white; the throne has vines climbing it, with flowers that have bloomed all along them. It's no longer lit by one chandelier but by natural light and small candle fixtures hanging from the ceiling in multiple spots.

"Brodrick, go get Broden and Aniya. They have to see this," Evie whispers.

Broden watches as his and Aniya's lights rise into the air and seem to explode; streams of light seem to go in all directions. There is a shift somewhere in the realm that he can feel. The branches are still holding him, while Aniya is raised above the rock, arms out, and she is surrounded by a bright glow. Her arms are out, with balls of light in every color you could imagine circling her, starting off slow and then moving faster and faster. The balls form lines of light, looking like a rainbow that's moving continuously around Aniya. Broden can see that they are starting to slow and Aniya is slowly being lowered back to the rock. As he watches, he can see their lights recede back to their original form and shoot back into them. If the branches didn't have hold of Broden, the force of the magic entering his body would have knocked him off his feet again. He can feel the branches untwine themselves from his body, and as soon as he is released, he runs to Aniya.

"Loving! Are ye all right?"

"Yes, but what was that?" Aniya sits up from where she had gently been laid.

"I dinna know, but we should dress and meet Brodrick and the others."

"Yes, I'd say after that, we probably need to get back." Both move to gather their clothes and begin dressing.

Brother, I can feel ye and Aniya. I have need of ye—both. I am coming to ye now.

Aye, brother, we are coming.

"Brodrick just—" Broden is cut off by Aniya.

"I heard him and you."

"Ye heard us?"

"Yes, that's new." She had stopped dressing when she heard the mental conversation between Broden and Brodrick.

"Let's finish dressing," Aniya says.

Once they are fully dressed again, the branches on the tree lift, and they start to run in the direction they had come from. Aniya seems to know exactly how far from her grandparents they are and where they need to go. It isn't long after they have begun running when Brodrick appears with Sapphire, Bolt, and Cera.

Before any of them can start talking, Sapphire is mentally shouting a warning at them. *Danger!*

An arrow lands between the three of them. Screams come from the trees that surround them. All the familiars close around them in a protective stance.

"Get them!"

"Attack!"

A small army of different Fae comes out of the trees, running at them. An orc comes at Aniya as she starts shouting orders.

"Broden, Brodrick, call on your magic, picture what you want and push it through you!" Aniya yells and suddenly has a shield and sword made of lightning in her hands.

"Do it! Sapphire, watch your back! Bolt, fly! Cera, cover the guys!" Aniya blocks a minotaur that has come at her with a gavel. She raises her shield, blocking the hit with a sounding boom of thunder from the hit. Aniya is so concentrated on the Fae in front of her she doesn't see the one at her back, and a loud roar comes from behind her. She turns and sees a black tiger with white stripes has just taken down the thing that was going to attack her from behind. Its eyes meet hers and it nods. She nods back and returns to the fight. Bolts of light are coming from above. Aniya looks up, and she can see that it's Bolt.

"Where the hell did that come from?"

I don't know. It just happened. Bolt answers before sending another strike of lightning at a creature coming at Aniya from the side.

"Where are they coming from?" Broden shouts as he strikes down another creature with the sword he had conjured. The black tiger jumps in front of him, bringing down a vampire that has come at Broden, before biting him quickly on his shoulder then licking the wound. "Ah, what the hell?"

Sorry, had to.

Broden hears the unfamiliar voice in his head. "Huh?"

Fight now! Explain later!

Broden turns and takes down some other creature.

"Brother, behind ye!" Broden warns, but the black tiger takes that one down too and then bites Brodrick on the side of his right leg and licks the wound just as fast as he had done with Broden.

"Ouch, ye beast! Really? Now?" Brodrick curses.

Need to communicate.

"Aniya, to your right!" She turns, and the black tiger is there and bites her abdomen and quickly licks the wound, healing it after taking down that creature.

Duck!

Aniya does, and the tiger jumps over her, taking out the creatures.

"Thanks," she says, thrusting her sword into a creature to her left. She has about had enough. Aniya is back to back with Broden and Brodrick. The familiars are backing toward them. Aniya straightens from her fighting stance and calls on every ounce of her magic.

"THAT'S ENOUGH!" Holding her sword in one hand and her other balled into a fist around the handle of her shield, she flings her arms out, sending a circle of white light out from her in a huge wave.

It's so strong everyone in the vicinity is knocked over, and all fighting stops. Her eyes have gone crystal blue, and she glows white as her magic surrounds her. After a moment, Broden stands and moves to Aniya's right, and Brodrick takes up her left.

"Lass, calm," Broden whispers.

"Aniya, bring it back." Brodrick uses a calm voice.

Iya, a warning next time you do that, please. Sapphire stands and shakes off the dirt and grass that she was covered in when she was knocked over by Aniya's burst of magic.

I'll try, sorry, beautiful girl.

Aniya takes a deep breath and calls back her magic. The white lights recede and enter back into her. "Now," she says walking to a creature that is sitting on the ground. It has a pig nose with small tusks protruding from its mouth. Aniya stands over it, looking down.

"Who are you and why would you attack us?" she asks.

"I am Nork. I didn't have a choice. They have my family. We are from an orc village in the spring season," Nork replies.

Aniya moves to the next being. "And you?"

"I'm a wolf shifter. They told me you were here to destroy us all and our homes."

"And you, in the back! Come here. Why did you attack us?"

"I'm vampire, Trance from the winter season. They came and took my sister then told me that they would kill her if I didn't do as they said," Trance explains.

"So all of ye were forced or coerced in some way to attack us. Then what?" Broden asks, his arms folded over his broad chest.

"We were told to kill the girl or kidnap the two of you," someone in the back says.

Aniya approaches one of the many beings.

"Who are 'they'?" she asks. When no one answers, she lays her hand on Trance, saying, "I don't want to kill any of you, but"—Aniya sends a shock through her arm and into Trance, who winces—"if you do not answer me, you will make that choice for me."

"I cannot. They will kill my sister," Trance says and gasps in pain when Aniya sends another shock through him.

"And what will happen to your sister if you do not return?"

"Laddie, if ye want to help yer sister, ye had better answer—truthfully," Brodrick says, hoping to give him a minute to think on it.

"So I'll ask you one more time. Who are 'they'?" Aniya puts persuasion into her words and sends a stronger shock through the vampire.

"AHH! It's . . . Edward and Ada! From the council!" Trance finally gives the names.

"My aunt and uncle! But why?"

"Ye better not be lying, lad!" Broden steps forward.

"I'm not!"

"It is them who took my family," Nork says.

"They also told me you were here to destroy us." The wolf stands.

"They, along with the rest of the council, were the ones who sent Evie to search for my soul mates. Why would they do that if they wanted me dead?" Aniya asks.

"Your soul mates!" a voice from the back shouts.

"Yes, they"—she points from Broden to Brodrick—"are my soul mates."

"The legend is true!"

"No, it was just a story!"

Gasps and talking erupt around Aniya and her group, every one of them standing.

"Enough. What legend? Someone explain this," Aniya says after everyone quiets back down and looks at her.

"The tale of the queen and two kings," Nork answers Aniya.

"How do you not know the tale?" a voice asks.

"I was not raised in the Fae realm. Somebody will need to tell me this legend."

"I will," Trance offers.

"Then continue," Aniya tells him.

"The legend says that many hundreds of years ago, a queen and two kings ruled the Fae realm. Many species did not agree with the realm being ruled by just the queen and kings. Some thought it wasn't right that a woman had two soul mates, and they didn't care how strong it made them. At this time, the realm flourished, but the Fae decided they wanted a council instead of rulers and fought to overturn the queen and kings. It is said they just disappeared. Once they were gone, the throne disappeared as well. All that was left was a piece of parchment that read, 'When a fall from the past meets the future, the Fae may be saved.' Nobody understood the phrase but went on to build the council. That's all the legend tells. I pledge allegiance, my queen and kings." Trance finishes and kneels before the three of them.

Before any of them could say more, the small army left standing also kneels. Aniya and her guys watch in awe as every Fae before them bows and kneels.

"Your Majesties."

"Highnesses."

"Queen, kings."

The voices come from all over. It seems even the trees, flowers, and animals all follow suit.

"The prophecy," Aniya whispers, thinking out loud.

"The prophecy, my queen? No, it was legend," Trance says, still kneeling.

"All of you, please rise. I know, but Sierra gave me a prophecy."

"Oh. The seer? We know nothing of a prophecy."

"You wouldn't. The council kept it quiet. We need to go see my grandparents," Aniya tells Broden and Brodrick.

As they start to walk, those in their way move to the other side of Aniya and the guys, then form two lines, following them as they walk.

"You all may go back to your homes now. We will make sure this is dealt with and your loved ones return to you. You will be safe."

"My queen, we pledged our allegiance to you and the new kings. We follow you now, and we will help defend and protect you and the realm," Nork replies.

"You do what you feel is right."

"Standing with you is what's right. I am called Frasier, Your Highness," the wolf shifter informs her.

"I am Aniya. They are Broden and Brodrick."

"Yes, Queen Aniya."

"What about you?" Aniya directs her question to the black tiger.

I am Onyx.

"Onyx?"

I'm black—it made sense.

And you just happen to know you would be needed? The question comes from Brodrick.

No, I have been drawn to the two of you since you first came to the Fae realm. I've followed you since, though it never made sense until today.

Today? Why? This time, the question comes from Broden.

You both are now half mage. I'm your familiar.

"Loving?"

"I heard and he's right."

I see three other familiars as well.

Yes, Sapphire was given to me once my light was turned on. We sort of adopted Cera and Bolt.

You mean you cut their ties to their mages.

Accidentally. But they chose to come with us.

Enough said.

Broden is listening to Onyx and Aniya's mental conversation, when a picture forms in his head. He, Aniya, and Brodrick look like they are underground, with cages everywhere. Then the cages open, and people and animals slowly and with caution begin emerging. That's where it stops. Broden doesn't understand the picture and, for now, decides to keep it to himself and continues to walk.

They emerge out of the woods about fifty yards from her grandparents' home. Aniya can see both anxiously watching the edge of the woods and, when they see her, begin coming toward her.

"Oh, Aniya! Thank the Goddess," Keyara says.

"Keyara, wait! Look!" Max approaches his wife just as the small army behind Aniya, Broden, and Brodrick comes into sight. "What in the realm?"

"Keyara, I'll explain once we are in the house. All of you please wait for us in the field over in that direction." Aniya points to her right, where an empty grass field sits.

"Keyara, Max, we need to speak to you." Aniya comes to stand in front of them both.

"Okay, but did you see the light that shot through the realm? It's changed something. Though we could feel it, we weren't sure what *it* was," Keyara explains as they walk to the house and onto the porch.

"That was Broden and I."

"'Tis me as well, sweetling," Brodrick tells her.

"Your light as well?"

"Aye, in the council room. I was coming to get you both when—" Brodrick stops talking.

"When what? That was your light? That means you and Broden . . ." Keyara guesses.

"Yes, and all hell broke loose after that." Aniya doesn't even blush, knowing that it seems the entire Fae realm knows she had just had sex.

"What do you mean?" Max asks.

Aniya gives a quick rundown of what happened and the battle.

"They attacked you!" Keyara says in surprise.

"Yes, every one of them was forced in some way to do Edward and Ada's dirty work." Aniya can feel her anger flare again.

"Edward and Ada? Isn't Edward the one who sent Evie to find Broden and Brodrick?"

"Nae him per se. The council sent Mother, he just issued the order," Brodrick corrects her.

"So they have been trying to kill you your entire life?" The thought causes Keyara's heart to break.

"It would seem so. They used humans when I was in the human realm, and when I was a child, they tried to make it look like an accident. I'm beginning to wonder if that mugger who shot Mom wasn't an attempt as well. She pushed me behind her and took the bullet that might have been meant for me." Aniya's anger is close to boiling over; she can feel her magic coming forward.

"But if you are meant to save the Fae, killing you would doom us all, and not just the Fae realm but the human realm as well. It makes no sense to kill you," Max says.

"Unless they don't want to save us. I intend to find out when we go to the council. I'm going to confront them," Aniya says, before adding, "Do either of you know the legend of the queen and two kings?"

"Yes, but it's more of a children's story than a legend, Aniya. How do you know of it?" Keyara is twisting her hands in front of her.

"I was told the legend after I ended the battle. Do you remember the parchment that was left behind and what it said?" Aniya reaches into her pocket for the prophecy.

"Well, yes, it said, 'When a fall from the past—'" Keyara's hands move to her mouth as she gasps and looks at Max, who has made the same connection as she has.

"The prophecy!" they both say together.

Aniya unrolls the scroll and starts reciting it one line at a time. "'In the twentieth century a mage child is born'—that's me, if I truly am the only mage born in that century. 'A fall from the past'—that could be one of them, or it could also be referring to the fall of the queen and two kings, 'meets the future' meaning me again. They are the past and I am the future. 'The Fae may be saved'—that's us together could save the Fae. 'In the light, darkness will show, depending on the mage's soul.' I'm guessing that is our bonding, meaning we all have to be bonded to complete our souls—you know, kind of like one whole soul, which makes all three complete. That's the first half of the prophecy. I haven't figured out the second half yet." Aniya rolls the scroll up again and places it back in her pocket.

"Aniya, if this is all true, you and they are the queen and two kings."

Brodrick steps forward. "'Tis true and the reason I told ye I needed to talk to ye both. When I was in the council room, my light rose from me and shot rays of light throughout the council room, hitting and knocking out walls. The black marble turned white, and a throne with three seats rose up and shifted the council seats so the throne set above them. Windows replaced walls so those who sat on the throne can see the whole realm. I was coming to tell you both when we were attacked," Brodrick explains.

"We need to get to the council now!" Aniya exclaims.

"Granddaughter, you are not going to the council dressed like that," Keyara tells Aniya, who looks down. Her shirt is ripped and scorched in several places, her shorts might as well be completely gone, and she has recently healed skin in multiple places.

"I better go and change."

"I have just the outfit for you! It was your mother's. Come, let's get you dressed so you can properly address the council." Keyara grabs Aniya's hand and moves to enter the house.

Once inside, she leaves Aniya in the guest room she shared with Brodrick and Broden.

"Wait here. I'll be right back."

Aniya wonders what outfit her grandmother had that was her mother's, and would it even fit her? Every picture she had seen of Marriam showed she was smaller than Aniya. She couldn't possibly fit into something that belonged to her mother, Aniya thinks to herself. Keyara reenters the room and Aniya can see the outfit she carries.

"Uhhh, no! No way! That will not fit me!" Aniya denies, looking at the outfit.

"Aniya, it's magic. I promise you, it will. Just try it on."

"But, Keyara, its skintight, and that's even if I can squeeze into it."

"Aniya, trust me."

Aniya sighs, taking the outfit from her grandmother if only to prove Keyara wrong. She removes what's left of her tank top and jean shorts and begins to put on the outfit.

"I forgot the boots. I'll go get them." Keyara leaves the room, and Aniya finishes dressing.

When Keyara returns to Aniya, she is carrying a pair of black boots. Once she sees Aniya, pride overtakes her, and her eyes glisten with tears.

"See, I told you it would fit," she says, handing the boots to Aniya.

"It was weird. When I put it on, it seemed to conform to me, and when I move, it moves with me." Aniya sits on the end of the bed to put on the boots.

"It's magic, my dear, so are those." Keyara points at Aniya's feet. "Now you're ready. Time to properly introduce you to the council." Keyara hugs Aniya.

"Yes, and some housecleaning as well." Aniya hugs her back. "Let's go!"

CHAPTER 14

Brodrick and Broden are talking with Max when they hear the door to the house open and close. Brodrick looks up first and stops midsentence once he sees Aniya.

"Brother." Brodrick nudges Broden's arm, attempting to get his attention. "Brother," he says again, eyes still on his soul mate. "Broden!"

"What is it, what is wrong?" Broden looks up at Brodrick and can see he is looking wide-eyed at something. Following the direction of his brother's eyes, his land on Aniya. At once, they stand as Aniya is walking toward them, dressed in all-black leather, carrying what looks like a jacket. The black corset conforms to her breasts, pushing them upward. Aniya lifts the jacket and inserts one arm then the other, tying the thigh-length overcoat at her waist, covering those beautiful breasts. Her shapely legs seem to move easily in the leather pants that show off her toned curves, and the look is topped off with black boots that add about two inches to Aniya's 5'8" height. She looks at them and smirks seductively.

"You look like you've never seen a girl in leather."

Once she is standing in front of them, Aniya, who still has to stand on her tiptoes, kisses them both.

"Sweetling, ye look stunning."

"Loving, absolutely beautiful."

"Thank you. It was my mom's," Aniya tells them.

Both men look at Max, who just shrugs. "Marriam was her own person. But we never understood why she had the outfit made." Max moves over to Keyara and places his arm around her waist.

"You look gorgeous, granddaughter," Max tells Aniya.

"Thank you, Max." She smiles.

"Is there anything else before we leave?" Aniya asks her guys, who still seem in awe over her outfit.

Broden, Brodrick, we need you back at the council. Ada and Edward have just arrived. Evie sounds frantic even in their minds.

"Aniya, we—"

"Yes, I heard her through our connection. Let's move." Aniya's demeanor that was just seconds ago flirty and teasing turns into that of a queen ready to defend her kingdom.

"She is amazing," Broden and Brodrick both say in unison as they watch their soul mate move.

"Keyara, Max, please stay with my dad and Rachel. If anything—" Keyara cuts Aniya off.

"Shh, shh, nothing will happen, Aniya." Keyara holds up her hands as she talks to Aniya.

"If something is to happen to us, make sure they are safe and no retaliation falls back on them."

"Okay, we promise, but you will come back to us." Max walks over to Aniya and hugs her. Keyara does the same as tears fill her eyes.

"You had better stay safe and come back to us. We have only just got you back into our lives. I cannot lose you again."

"I will do my best. Broden, Brodrick, let's go."

Aniya moves off the porch and toward the army that's been waiting for orders. She with Brodrick on her left and Broden on her right stand before their people. All eyes are on them.

"We move to the council tower. Once there, I want all of you to circle it and wait for further orders. As much as you all want to stand behind us, the council room will not fit us all. Trance, Nork, and Frazier." She waits for them to approach.

"You will go up with us and cover Evie and Mike if needed."

"Yes, my queen," all three say together and bow.

"Sapphire, Onyx, Cera, and Bolt, fall in."

Sapphire stands between Aniya and Broden. Onyx is between Aniya and Brodrick. Bolt perches himself on Brodrick's shoulder, and Cera is on the other side of Broden.

Time to kick some ass! Sapphire sends to everyone.

Where did she learn that language? Onyx sends to Broden, Brodrick, and Aniya.

"From us," all three say together proudly.

Aniya calls a portal, but unlike before, this one is big enough for all of them to enter together. They all walk through, and they can see the city laid out in front of them. Aniya can feel the second their group has come through the portal.

"Close," is all she says.

It seems word travels fast even in the Fae realm. Everyone that can see them approaching moves out of the way, bowing to them as they pass. Aniya and the guys acknowledge everyone with nods but continue walking. Gasps come from different directions as their small army moves past them. So many different Fae in a large group parading through the city isn't something many Fae have ever seen. Aniya can see that their combined light has even made changes in the city itself. Bright flowers can be seen; the buildings, though in good condition before, look newer and brighter now. Aniya wants to keep looking but turns her eyes back to their destination and keeps walking.

"The council isn't going to like this," Brodrick hears.

"She is beautiful!" says another voice.

Brodrick keeps walking. As they continue into the city, he begins to hear hushed whispers. One is louder than the others.

Don't go in there, it's too dangerous. They will kill you!

Brodrick breaks from their group and moves to a small group standing to watch. "Which of ye gave us that warning?"

"None of us said anything," a wood elf informs him, looking scared.

He lays a hand on the elf's shoulder. "We are not here to hurt ye," Brodrick tells him, recognizing the voice of the elf that he now knows was the one who shouted the warning, when he hears, *Could he hear me?*

Strangely, it doesn't come from the elf's mouth.

Brodrick releases the elf.

"Thank ye for the warning." He zaps back to the front of their group and takes his position next to Aniya.

"Is all weel, brother?" Broden leans forward to look at Brodrick.

"Aye," is all he says.

They make their way through the city and are in front of the council tower when Aniya turns to the Fae who had lined up behind them.

"Remember your orders. No one leaves the tower until we say otherwise." She turns and sees that the wooden door looks new and the cracks are gone as well. The doors open for her and the guys, and when they enter, they see that there are no goblins. Broden and Brodrick, Nork and Trance all move to the chains.

"There is no need, just call on your magic."

Aniya and the guys all pull on their magic, becoming one large ball of white light. After only seconds of using their magic, they begin to move the chains and start climbing the tower.

Brodrick can hear the whispering again, dulled this time, which he guesses is because it is coming from inside the council room. "Can ye hear the whispers?"

"Whispers, brother? Nay."

Once they have stopped in front of the large double doors leading into the council room, Aniya looks at the doors.

"Open," is all she says. When the doors do as she has asked, she and her group begin to enter.

Evie and Mike look at her. Evie smiles with pride, while Mike looks completely shocked.

"This can't be. It's only a legend!" Aniya hears a very shocked Ada say.

"Oh, I promise you it sure as hell can be," Aniya answers her aunt as she walks to the center of the room to face her aunt and uncle. "And the two of you are going to answer a few questions."

"Who are you to demand anything of us? You traitors do not belong here, you need to get out!" Edward shouts.

"Take those filthy cats with you when you do!" Ada adds.

"You no longer have control over them, and you know this. As I said when we first met, they go where we go." Aniya sneers back at them.

"How is it you have severed the bonds of our familiars?" Ada asks.

"That, Aunt, is none of your concern and neither is the Fae realm anymore."

"AUNT! I am not your aunt. I don't even know who you are."

"You don't recognize me? Oh, wait, how would you, when you send others to do your dirty work? Let me introduce you to my soul mates. This here is Broden, and that is Brodrick." Both her guys step up next to her with their arms folded over their identical broad chests.

"Have you already forgotten that you forced Trance, Nork, and Frasier"—each man steps forward to stand with Aniya and the guys when their names are called—"along with the small army downstairs that you sent to attack and kill me but are now waiting for my orders? Maybe your ages are finally catching up with you both," Aniya says, resting her hands on her hips.

Edward steps forward, arms out as if to hug her. "Aniya, is that you? Wow!" He tries to sound excited and caring, but Aniya can sense the lies dripping from his every word.

"Don't come any closer, Edward. I'd hate to have to kill you before I get any of my questions answered."

Aniya can see the anger flash across Edward's face before he masks it. "Why would you want to kill me? I am your uncle, we are family. I'd be happy to answer any questions you have." Edward continues the charade of the loving uncle, having no knowledge that Aniya can see his true nature.

"Drop the act. I know you're lying." Aniya calls him out, and his facial expression changes from the soft and caring uncle to that of hate and disdain.

"There it is, there is the real Edward. Now about those questions—"

"We do not owe you anything. Leave here. We have council business to attend to, and you are not part of that," Edward spits out.

"Council business? Oh, but I am council business, didn't you send for me?" Aniya asks them both.

"Why would we send for you? You're nobody," Ada remarks, looking down at Aniya.

"You did send for the Finder, didn't you?"

"How do you know that?"

"Well, I'm glad you asked, so why send them to find me if you were just going to kill me?"

"We sent them to find the mage, not a child."

"Haven't you figured it out yet? I am the mage, the one you have been looking for. I am also part vampire too." Aniya smiles at the shock that runs across Ada and Edward's faces.

"How can that be?" Edward demands. "Fae races can't be soul mates to any species but their own."

"That is where you're wrong. We are most definitely soul mates, and I am the mage. Who knew I would also be the finder's soul mate as well? Which brings me to my next question. Why send them out to find the mage a.k.a. me, if you had no intention of trying to save the Fae?"

"They were supposed to bring the mage to us when they found them. We had a plan," Edward answers Aniya.

"I am here. What do you intend to do? What's the plan, then?"

"You don't need to know the plan."

"Actually, I do. You never had any intention to save the Fae realm, did you?"

Edward and Ada look at one another. She is the mage. They know there is nothing they can do now that she is bonded. Why didn't they bring her to them before they bonded? That way they could have killed her and been done with it like they had planned.

"According to the prophecy that seer gave us, the mage was going to help save the realm. It wasn't until we stole the other half of the prophecy that we discovered when the mage would be born. Once we heard of your birth, that's when we knew it was you and set out to destroy you. Had they done what they were told and brought you to us, we would have had you. We could have done what we wanted with you. They weren't supposed to become your soul mates!" Edward shouts at them, finally dropping the act.

"Oh, you mean this prophecy? Maybe I should read it so the rest of the council knows what it says." Aniya holds up the rolled-up scroll and begins to open it.

"NO! They do not need to hear it!" Ada shouts, holding up her hand.

"But they do." Aniya goes on to read the prophecy out loud to the council. Once she is finished, she rolls up the scroll and places it back in her jacket.

Gasps come from the council members.

"WHY?"

"The realm would die."

"We knew you were evil, but this!"

"Oh my Goddess, they wanted to kill us all." Everyone is talking at once.

"All of you shut up!" Edward shouts, but the talking continues.

"Please calm yourselves!" Aniya raises her voice only a bit, and the council room goes quiet.

Anger is clear for all to see on Edward and Ada's faces once more.

"We have poisoned you, hit you with a car, run you off the road, had you shot, and even killed your mother with the bullet meant for you. How are you still living? One of any of those things would have killed any other being." Edward's voice is full of hatred.

"I have to give you credit. The poison almost got me. I was near death, but fortunately, Mike figured out what you poisoned me with and was able to find an antidote. My mother saved me. Had she not stepped in front of that bullet, I would have been killed. My soul mates realized someone was trying to kill me before I did. I honestly thought I was just clumsy." Aniya looks at the twins and sends them both a loving look before turning to look at the council members, catching every change in detail that has been made. I'm impressed, she thinks to herself as she addresses the council.

"You had to have known what they were doing. Can you all sit on your now not-so-high chairs and tell me you didn't know?"

"Pfft, none of them would dare to cross us." Edward's voice challenges all of them.

"We didn't have a choice, my queen and kings. They have my family," says the wood elf council member.

"They used them against us, tortured them in front of us." The orc member stands.

"We had no idea all this was happening. We have only been on the council a short time." This comes from the leprechaun council member.

"There are so many of you and only two of them. You could have stood up to them and saved your families," Aniya points out.

"We don't know where they keep them. When we have seen them, they are brought to us. We have never been to where Edward and Ada have them held," answers a shifter member.

"With the strength of all of you, you could have forced them to tell you. Excuses are not going to work," Aniya explains.

"My queen, until today, I wasn't even aware they held so many members in their grasp."

"We feared for our lives and those of our family. We may be Fae but we can be killed. I personally didn't want anyone else sitting in my spot and having to deal with those two."

"So you thought that by staying and letting them control you, you were saving somebody else. I can understand that concept, but why even let it get that far?" Aniya confronts all the members.

"Fear is a powerful thing, and seeing our loved ones in chains, beaten and abused, is a good way to keep someone in check."

Aniya looks back at Edward and Ada. Really concentrating, she thinks, *I need to see their souls.*

Through her command, Aniya can now see Edward and Ada along with their souls, black all the way through to their hearts.

"You should have never been allowed to sit on the council. You have no love. You both are black to the core, as are your hearts." Aniya's disgust can be heard in her every word.

"Oh, now that's where you are wrong. We have love—love of power, fear, torment, and pain. We thrive on it." Ada gives them a sickening, cruel smile.

"What of the Fae ye have killed? The mages?" Broden asks.

"We couldn't have allowed ourselves to be replaced, now could we?" she answers with a snicker.

"What about the other races? Aye, the mages have suffered greatly, but how many different species have or are gone as weel?" Brodrick asks.

"Mages get boring. We needed to mix it up a bit." Ada shrugs. *Besides, who said they are dead?* Brodrick hears the thought she meant to keep silent.

"You are monsters!" Aniya tells them.

"We far surpassed monsters long ago." Edward smiles sadistically.

"The core of the Fae realm is magic and love. It wasn't meant to be ruled by a council. From the moment the queen and kings disappeared, it started to crumble and divide the Fae. You all have only sped up its destruction! Have none of you figured that out?" Aniya looks around the room again. "You all are the problem, and we vow, once we sit on that throne," Aniya points at the wall where the three chairs sit above the others, "the balance will return and the realm will be restored."

"You think a legend is real? You really are just a child!" Edward takes a step toward Aniya.

"Have you really not figured out who we are?" Aniya looks at Edward, who stops at the question.

"You only think you are somebody. You may be the mage, but without the council, the realm will fall. The queen and two kings is a child's story, a fairy tale."

"As I have recently learned, there is always some truth to every tale. Did you not see and feel the shift just hours ago? Look out the windows that appeared from our lights, look all around. Even the city has changed. It's already begun. Have you seriously not realized yet who we are and why that throne just appeared?" Aniya can't see how anyone couldn't know what has occurred.

"When a fall from the past meets the future, the Fae may be saved. Is that not the same line that was written on a piece of parchment when the prior queen and kings disappeared? They left it, and it is in the prophecy as well. That should tell you something." Aniya is getting frustrated.

"Why do you think we tried to kill you, stupid girl?" Ada spits back.

"Why did you try to kill me? You've been trying my entire life, so explain that to me."

"At first we didn't want to kill the mage, we only wanted to capture and use them. We wanted to know what made this mage so different from myself or Edward. We thought if we could keep the mage locked up and maybe even turn them to our side and teach them our ways, we could continue running the realm and be even more powerful because we would have had everything. That is, until we got the other part of that damned prophecy. We knew then that we would have to kill the mage and that you were who those two"—Ada points toward Broden and Brodrick—"had been looking for, when you were the only mage born in the twentieth century. We realized you would become stronger than us even if you were never bonded, and if the prophecy was correct, you and your soul mates would be damn near unstoppable, so we sought to kill you before that could happen. They should have brought you to us the minute they even had a thought you could be the mage." Ada finishes, looking at Broden and Brodrick as though her possible demise is their fault.

"And what of the realm? It couldn't have been saved without me. What would have happened had you succeeded in killing me?"

"We would have found a way to save the realm, but not because we care what happens to the Fae," Edward informs her.

"Ye admit it, then, in front of all here?" Brodrick looks at the two mages.

Aniya notices a black fog that sinks into the white marble floor, and veins start to spread in various directions.

"Why deny it? We wanted the power, and as long as she lives, it is threatened. So yes, we sought to remove the obstacle in our path and would have if you had done the job you were made for and not bonded with her." Ada raises her voice.

"I can't say I'm sorry for ruining your plans, because I'm not." Aniya shrugs.

Aniya turns her attention back to the other council members. "You all now know the truth. Do you follow them or us?" she asks, looking at every member.

"You."

"You, my queen and kings."

"We stand with you."

Iya, look out!

At the warning from Sapphire, Aniya turns to face Edward and Ada when a dark ball of magic hits her in the abdomen. Looking down, she sees the leather is scorched through and a hole shows in her flesh.

"Aniya!" Evie screams.

Gasps come from all in the room.

Iya, no!

"That really fucking hurt, you son of a bitch!" Aniya looks Edward in the eye and stands straight up. The wound has already started closing, flesh coming back together as internal organs regrow and become whole again. Aniya watches as the smile on Edward's face fades and it is replaced with fear for the first time.

"What—" Alfred, Evie's father, says.

"How is that possible?" This comes from Amelia.

"It went right through her!" another voice screams.

"It wasn't meant to hurt, it was supposed to kill you!" Ada yells.

The council stands at once and moves behind Aniya and the group, realizing the danger they could be in.

"Aniya?" Broden calls out.

She turns to look and she can see the black veins are working their way toward them all. Aniya shoots a ball of white energy at them and watches as the veins quickly burst into flames. Behind the fire are more black veins moving in their direction, and Broden throws his magic at them. Ada decides to attack Aniya again and moves to raise her hands, but all four familiars move at the same time, jumping at Ada and Edward. Growls erupt as claws and teeth bite at whatever they can reach on the two mages. Aniya is fighting off more of the black veins when she hears an animal cry out. Turning, she sees Sapphire thrown across the room and runs over to her.

"Sapphire, no!" Aniya kneels down next to her and frantically looks inside Sapphire for any injuries. "Sapphire?" Aniya asks as the holes in

Sapphire begin to close and the tiger stands, shakes out her white-and-black striped fur.

Iya! I can heal? That's new!

"Beautiful girl, you scared me!"

I'm fine. Watch out! Sapphire pushes Aniya over just as a blast of dark magic hits the wall where she had been. Aniya stands and turns, walking toward Ada and Edward just as a bolt of lightning hits Edward in the leg. The familiars move aside to let her pass.

"Dinna get too close, loving."

"Aye, sweetling, they dinna fight fair."

"I never thought they would, loves," Aniya answers them both.

She bends down to where Edward and Ada are crouched after their fight with the familiars.

"You want to try that again?" Aniya asks.

"We will kill you!" Edward wipes his lips and spits out blood while working to stand. Ada moves to her feet as well.

"You shot a ball of energy right through me, and I'm still standing." Aniya backs away from them.

"This isn't over!" Ada screams and throws balls of black energy at those who are trapped in the veins. One hits Brodrick. As the veins begin to climb his body, Aniya shoots her own magic at the black things, stopping their movement, giving Brodrick time to send his own magic, setting them on fire. It isn't long before more veins are coming at them again. Aniya brings up her sword of lightning and cuts at the veins. Broden and Brodrick do the same. They are not fast enough to stop the veins from entrapping them. Aniya turns her glare back to Ada and Edward.

"I'm going to give the both of you an opportunity to live. We can stop fighting and I will take your magic but you will live—as mortals. Release them," Aniya demands.

"We just want to destroy you. We don't care if all others die in the process as long as you are among them!" Edward snarls at her and sends another burst of magic but aims for the twins.

"That was a big mistake!" Aniya extends her arms, eyes turning crystal-clear blue, and she begins to glow in the center of her chest.

Broden stills and looks at the others in the room, knowing what's coming.

"Mother, get out!" Brodrick yells to Evie.

"Mike, ye go as well," Broden calls out.

Edward and Ada continue to throw balls of magic at Aniya. Broden and Brodrick call on their magic to form walls of stone in front of Aniya and those who are trapped in the veins, attempting to protect everyone. Brodrick has formed a dagger and tries to cut at the black veins wrapped around his wrists and abdomen. Evie didn't hesitate or question them; she grabs her parents and moves out of the council room, Mike following her.

Aniya continues calling on her magic, causing her to glow a bright white. Broden and Brodrick send their magic to her, attempting to aid her. Lightning shoots out of them and into Aniya; she then calls on the familiars to lend her their energy as well. Everyone in the council room is watching as the familiars step toward Aniya and push whatever energy they can at her. Streams of white lights now connect Aniya to her familiars, Broden, and Brodrick.

"I am going to give you one last opportunity to save yourselves. I will take your immortality and magic but allow you to stay in the realm, or we can end this here and now," Aniya offers again.

"Or we can end you, then nothing changes!" Edward gathers all his magic, as does Ada, and aims it at Aniya's heart. It shoots through the air and hits an invisible wall, which causes the magic to bounce back at them, knocking them both to the ground.

"You have made your choice, then." Aniya shoots a blue ball of magic at them,

"You killed my mother!" A ball of white light hits Edward and Ada.

"You have killed Fae!" Another magic ball hits them.

"You have had us attacked. You tried and failed to kill me throughout my life. Your hearts are black, your souls do not have even the slightest bit of light, and you have attempted to kill my soul mates and familiars!" Aniya gathers all the magic she has into a huge ball of white-and-blue lightning, which has collected between her hands, and raises them above her head.

"No longer will your black stain of evil be seen." Aniya releases the ball of magic and watches as the ball strikes her aunt and uncle. She is still being fed magic by Broden, Brodrick, and the familiars as she walks over to Edward and Ada. She begins to pull their magic from them, the black mist collecting between her hands as she rolls it into a ball.

"Now you are done." Aniya uses her white magic to absorb and disintegrates the tarlike substance that was their life force. She can see the minute their magic is destroyed and their souls are gone. Ada and Edward's bodies collapse to the floor, one on top of the other. Small white balls of light rise out of their bodies; there must be hundreds of them, all circling frantically before disappearing out the council room door and through the walls and windows. The black veins that held everyone dissolve, releasing them all at once.

"Loving?" Broden carefully approaches on Aniya's left.

"Sweetling, are ye weel?" Brodrick comes up on her right.

Aniya turns to them both, and they can see the tears streaming down her face as she moves to bury herself in their warmth.

"I gave them the opportunity. I gave them a choice. Why choose death? They wouldn't have had their magic, but they would still be alive." Aniya's strength falters, and remorse sets in as she realizes she just took the lives of two people.

Broden and Brodrick wrap their arms around her, shielding Aniya from anyone who might see her at her most vulnerable moment.

"I'm supposed to save lives, yet I just took two. No, I'm not well. I didn't enjoy that."

"Ye took only two, loving. They have taken many. Nobody thinks ye did anything wrong. Ye just saved the realm." Broden works to calm her tears and reassure her that everything will be fine.

"Ye did what any queen in the same position would have done. I think some of those Fae we thought dead may still be living." Brodrick kisses the top of Aniya's head.

"What?" She looks up at him, wiping at her tears.

"Brother, how do ye ken that?"

"I heard Ada's thoughts."

"You heard what?"

"I heard her thoughts. Her thoughts make me believe at least some are still alive. 'Who said they are dead?' was the thought I heard."

"When did ye start hearing thoughts, brother?"

"In the city, I heard whispers and a warning from one of those elves on our way here."

"That mayhap could explain my vision in the woods after the battle."

"Wait, you had a vision, and you are hearing thoughts? I thought we agreed no more hiding things from me." Aniya cuts in on their conversation.

"We just fought a hard battle, loving."

"I thought I could use it as an advantage, sweetling."

"Ugh, fine but never again. What was your vision, Broden?"

CHAPTER 15

"We were in a dungeon with the iron doors all closed. When they opened, many different Fae emerged. 'Tis all I saw," Broden explains to them both.

Trance approaches them at that moment to ask, "What do you want done with them, my queen, kings?" He is pointing to Edward and Ada.

"Take them out and burn them, to show everyone what happens to the traitors of our realm," Broden answers.

"Let's go find this dungeon and release those who are imprisoned there," Aniya says, being the strong and confident queen again.

"Do any of ye ken of a dungeon? Someplace Edward and Ada might have kept prisoners?" Brodrick asks, looking at the council members.

"They never mentioned any such place if they had one."

"Would you have done anything, had you known?" Aniya glares at the one who spoke.

"You are right to assume the worst of us, my queen, but please try to understand, they had all the control."

"It should have never gotten to that. You are the council—none of you should have been above the others. We will rebuild the council, and you all will prove to us that you belong in those seats. No longer will it be just because you are soul mates. It will be earned. We will deal with that once we return from freeing those who have been trapped for the Goddess only knows how long." Aniya moves to the door.

Before they can step through, Evie has her arms around them in a group hug.

"Why did you have me leave? I could have helped. Are you really the new queen and kings?" she asks, releasing them. "I didn't even think about the legend when the boys told me they had the same soul mate. Had I remembered, this all might have made more sense."

"Weel, the last time Aniya called on her magic like that, she knocked us on our arses, and this time, she was drawing from us as weel. We were concerned the blast might cause harm or destroy the tower. And aye, we are," Broden answers.

"If you think about all that's happened, it fits. I had wondered why I felt like I was a small piece to an even bigger puzzle, and once I met them, it felt like this puzzle had started to come together. As for what just happened, it took a lot of concentration to call on all my magic and even more to center it on Edward and Ada. I'm surprised I was able to. I took magic from both of you and the familiars to do what I did and end them. I hope we don't have to do that again." Remorse is in Aniya's voice once more.

"I apparently missed a lot," Evie comments.

"We will tell you about it, but first we need to find that dungeon."

Aniya, we can show you, Cera sends to her.

They took us there only a few times, but we remember, Bolt adds.

You're sure you can find it? Aniya asks them.

Yes.

Yes.

Then let's go. Sapphire, come.

Onyx, ye too.

They all move to the platform and use their magic to take them down. Once outside, they can see the small army is now quite large.

"My queen and kings, what can I do to help?" A centaur bows to them.

"Can you help Trance?" Aniya asks.

"Trance?"

"Yes, he is the vampire in the council room. He may need some help removing a couple of bodies."

"Yes, my queen." The centaur sends a look to Broden and Brodrick. They grin and nod.

"Is there anything I may do, Your Majesties?" asks a fire elf.

"Can you have a bonfire made up?"

"Bonfire, my queen?"

"A big fire, big enough to lay to rest a couple of mages. Please?"

"Oh yes! I will."

"Thank you." Aniya watches as the centaur and Trance emerge from the tower, one with Edward, one with Ada.

They move past the army, and they can see the fire elf is building the fire.

"Take them over there, please." Aniya points to the fire.

The wood elves have built a place to put Edward and Ada as they burn and their bodies are set side by side. It's more than they deserve but it's a burial, Aniya thinks to herself.

"Let this be a lesson to all. We do not want any more lives lost, but if ye choose to try overthrowing us, this will be yer fate as well. We vow to protect the realm and bring back the balance that once was. We only ask that ye stand with us?" Brodrick turns and speaks to those who have gathered.

"We stand with the queen and two kings!" shouts a Fae toward the back of the army and then all others roar their acceptance.

"Now 'tis safe for ye all to return to yer homes. We have learned that Edward and Ada locked away many Fae. We go now to free them," Broden announces.

"Those of you who might have loved ones there, please come with us. The best thing for them will be to see a familiar face. Let's go." Aniya starts to follow Cera with Bolt resting on her shoulder.

"Aniya, I can go get your grandparents and let them know you are safe. I will bring them, Peter, and Rachel back and meet you in the throne room," Mike offers.

"Yes, please, and Mike, thank you." She walks to him and kisses his cheek before he calls the portal.

"Always," he says and moves through the portal.

Cera and Bolt direct them to the dungeon. They get most of the way there before there is some confusion on which direction to go in next.

It's this way, Bolt.

No, Cera, it's the other way.

Okay, both of ye settle. Give me a minute. Brodrick concentrates on the voices he hears, low in sound but desperate.

I want to go home.

I miss my brother.

We need food.

Brodrick listens to see if he can tell which direction they are coming from.

"'Tis this way!" He points and starts walking.

Aniya has paid close attention to where they were going, and she isn't surprised to see that Ada and Edward liked to keep their prisoners close; they can still see the tower from where they are.

"They liked to work close to home, I see. I can feel their sadness," Aniya says.

"Aye, they didn't seem afraid that this place would be discovered," Broden points out.

"Nay, they ken that they had all the advantages and no one would come looking, knowing they or their family would be punished," Brodrick adds.

Soon, they come to the opening of a cave with an iron door. Aniya feels the sadness and now their fear. She uses her magic to blast the door open. Cries can be heard from inside the cave by all those there. Everyone begins to rush in all at once.

"NO! Wait, we need to make sure it's safe. Let us enter first. I know you are anxious to see your loved ones. We only ask for a few more minutes to make sure Edward and Ada didn't set any traps." Aniya stops those who tried to pass them and proceeds inside the cave.

Iya, I can feel familiars.

We do as well.

As do I.

"I can feel everything. We will help them."

The sadness is almost unbearable. This must be what she felt in the tower the day they arrived, Aniya thinks to herself.

Broden looks around the cave, seeing it again but not in his mind's eye like before. It looks much worse. A rock with blood and a gavel lying on the ground next to it is off to the left. Chains hang from the walls. Aniya doesn't want to think about what those were used for. There are barrels everywhere with stagnant water and bugs in them. On the right wall, there is a trough with moldy bread and rotten vegetables piled high. The stench is overwhelming.

"This is what I saw," Broden confirms.

Aniya steps forward and pulls on her magic, waving her hand. Clicks sound all around the cave, and doors swing open. Slowly and one by one, Fae and animals emerge from the open cells, eyes on Aniya and the guys.

"Our names are Broden and Brodrick, and this is Aniya. We are the kings and queen of the Fae realm. We are sorry this has been done to ye, and those responsible are gone. We are going to call in the others in just a moment and hope yer families are among them." Broden tries to send comfort in his words.

"Sweetling, can we at least clean and dress them?"

The state of those that were trapped is almost worse than the condition of the cave they have been held in. The clothes, if you can call them that, are ripped and torn, dirty, and probably what they had been wearing when they were imprisoned. The fur and feathers of the animals have no distinguishing colors. You can see where some have dried blood mixed with dirt and grime, and some haven't healed from their most recent encounter with Ada and Edward.

"Yes, and we will, just call on your magic." The three of them bring forth their magic, wave their hands, sending waves of white light over everyone in the cave. It extends outward, lighting the cave and washing away the dirt and cleaning every person and animal. Their hair is washed and put up if needed. Each Fae is now clean, with new clothing, and the animals' colors can finally be seen. "We can't fix what has been done, but we do promise you will be taken care of. Please, find your familiar if you have one, while we go and bring your families in," Aniya tells them before turning and moving to the mouth of this disgusting cave.

We are going to destroy this place before we leave here. The Fae realm will not have a place like this.

I agree.

As do I.

Upon exiting the cave, the queen and two kings face their people.

"Please follow us inside." Aniya moves back to the cave. Before entering, she takes a deep breath of the fresh air. Once again entering the cave, hopefully for the last time, she can see that there is some happiness from those who have been reunited with their familiars, but all goes quiet again when they see Aniya and the twins.

"Please find your families." Aniya watches from between Brodrick and Broden, who have their arms around her, as those from outside meet those from the inside. Cries of happiness can be heard as they all find their friends and family. It's a sight to behold; their people are saved at last.

Trance finds his sister.

Nork is reunited with his family.

Aniya, Brodrick, and Broden smile as they watch the cave begin to clear out; those who have been trapped now leave their prison with their loved ones, thanking Aniya and her guys.

"My queen and kings."

"Lords and lady."

"Thank you kindly."

Familiars jump around in excitement as they leave the cave and walk into open air for the first time in a long time. Some go off in different directions, to hunt, most likely. Others stay close to their mages. Birds of different types take flight, stretching their wings.

Look, Iya, they are so happy!

That's how I felt too.

Flying felt amazing.

Aniya smiles down at their familiars. When she looks up, she can see that there are a few Fae standing at the entrance of the cave. Among them are two children, a boy about fourteen and the prettiest little girl, who looks about five. Broden and Brodrick see them as well.

"Do ye know who yer families are?" Broden asks those remaining.

"Mine were killed, my king."

"Same with mine."

"I've been here for so long my family are most likely dead or they thought me gone."

"And the two of you? Do you have family?" Aniya asks the two children.

"I've been locked up here for as long as I can remember. They said their tricks and poison did not work to rid her body of us as they had done many times before and said she was my responsibility now. I call her Angelica. She is who kept me alive, and they"—he points to those who still remain—"helped me survive before Angelica."

"Are 'they' Edward and Ada?" Aniya feels she knows the answer when the two children flinch.

"Weel, they are gone forever, we promise ye."

"But what about us?"

"You will come and be with us. Never again will you see their evil or this place. Is that okay with you?" Aniya asks them.

"Will we be safe?" Angelica asked in a quiet voice while holding her brother's hand.

"Always, and that's a promise. Do you have a name?" Aniya's last question is directed to the boy.

He shakes his head.

"We can give ye one if ye like," Brodrick lays his hand softly on the boy's shoulder.

"A name?"

"Aye, a strong name like Tristan," Broden suggests. "It was our father's name."

"I like Tristan."

"Then that will be your name. Come, let's leave this place." Aniya smiles at them.

Iya, our family has grown a lot.

Yes, it has.

"The rest of you can come with us. We will make sure you have places to go, or if you like, you can stay with us."

"Thank you, my queen."

"Before we leave here, I want to collapse this cave. Broden and Brodrick, help me take it down."

"Ye all stand behind us, please."

Together, Aniya and her guys use their magic to take down the cave and level the ground where it was. The cave will never be used again.

"All right, much better. Let's return to the throne room." They all move together, Aniya holding hands with the twins, while they watch the children take in the realm.

Once they have returned to the tower, Aniya's grandparents run to her and embrace her before hugging each of the twins as well.

"We are so happy you are okay. Mike told us what happened," Keyara says.

"Granddaughter, we are extremely proud of you." Max beams a smile at her.

"I did what I had to."

"Aniya! Don't ever leave like that without telling me. I was scared out of my mind," Peter tells her.

"Dad, we are fine, and we want to introduce you to a couple people. Dad, Keyara, Max, this is Tristan and this is Angelica. They will be living with us now." Aniya signals to the two children.

"Hello, I'm Keyara, this is my husband Max. We are Aniya's grandparents, and Peter right there is Aniya's father."

The children look a bit scared, but time will help to ease their fears.

"Hi," Angelica's sweet voice says.

"Hello," Tristan says shyly.

"Let's move up to the throne room. There is one thing left to do," Aniya tells them.

They all move up to the throne room, where most of the council still sit, but they stand when Aniya, Broden, and Brodrick enter and move to the three chairs at the back of the throne room and turn to face the council.

"Today marks a new beginning. The realm has begun to heal, the wicked are gone, and no longer will the council be in charge. They are to help us, but any decisions to be made we will make together. The Fae are no longer divided, and we work together as one to rebuild and bring back the balance that has been forgotten. We are the queen and two kings." Aniya sits in the middle chair as Broden sits to her left and Brodrick to her right. The children move to the left side of the throne, not really sure what to do, Peter and Evie are next to them as Max and Keyara stand on the right side of the throne, showing support to their queen and kings. Sapphire sits at Aniya's feet, Cera is at Brodrick's feet, Onyx at Broden's, and Bolt perches himself on one of the thrones' armrests.

"The Fae Realm is once again ruled by a queen and two kings." Before anyone can say more, bright colorful lights flash in the middle of the room, blinding everyone for a second, and when the lights dim, standing before them are a woman and identical twin men. The woman has pointed ears; she is taller than Aniya, slender, with long white hair and crystal-clear blue eyes. She smiles at Aniya. The men look to be the same height as Broden and Brodrick; they have blond hair that goes just past their shoulders, with green eyes, and look more like Vikings, with their broad shoulders and muscular physiques. They are dressed in clothing made of white leather. The woman's top covers all but her midriff, and her leggings cover her legs all the way down to her bare feet. The twins look to be wearing the same except no shirts.

"Aniya, Broden, and Brodrick,"—the woman's voice echoes through the room—"we knew this day would come. We are pleased that the queen and kings have returned."

"Are you the prior queen and kings?"

"Yes," says the deep voice of one of the twins.

"Why did you disappear? The realm—"

The prior queen holds up a hand, politely cutting Aniya off. "We were going to be overthrown, we chose to disappear. The Fae of the realm needed to see what it would be like without us. They all needed to learn the reason we existed. We lived out our lives in peace, though we could feel the evil spreading once Edward and Ada were placed on the council. We did mean to return, but by that time, we had been trapped by the evil. I am part seer and I knew you would come. That was why we left the piece of parchment. We worried that you wouldn't make it in time. But here you are, and we can now rest, knowing the realm will flourish again and the balance has already begun to return. We are pleased. You all are strong, and though there will still be troubles, we know you and the kings can handle it. We go now and leave the realm in your hands. Take care, my queen and kings."

"Rest well." Aniya bids them goodbye as they disappear and the lights fade.

"That was short and sweet, not very informative, but they had gorgeous covered, for sure!" Rachel's words break the silence that followed the prior queen and kings' departure.

"Always so blunt, are ye not, Rachel?" Brodrick smiles.

"Would you have it any other way?"

"No, absolutely not. Never change." Aniya stands and walks over to Rachel and hugs her.

"Never. Can I stay?"

"Yes, of course!"

Both women start laughing, and those around them do the same.

EPILOGUE

Fae Realm, Five Months Later

It is a day before the wedding. Camille, Aniya's friend from college, arrived about a week prior, and they have spent their time catching up. Aniya and Rachel have shown her around their home. Camille is a rock climber and very much into outdoorsy stuff. She plans on hiking the terrain in the Fae realm as soon as the wedding is over, really needing some time alone to think things over. Aniya is so happy her friend will be staying around for a while. They are sitting around and finishing up some last-minute wedding details before tomorrow's ceremony.

"Aniya, I can't believe you're getting married tomorrow!" Camille smiles.

"I've been so busy with this queen stuff I thought we would never get to this day. So much has been happening."

"It's about time!" Rachel exclaims.

"Well, it won't be long now."

"How are the children?"

"They are adjusting. They went through a lot. Angelica is doing extremely well. She doesn't seem to remember as much about that awful place. Tristan is coming around. He's more at ease with Broden and Brodrick, and they both have begun to call me Mom, so that's something."

"Wow, that's great!" Camille says.

"It's a step in the right direction. I want them to be comfortable. The guys have started to involve Tristan in training, and Angelica is usually with me or my grandparents. They love the fact that there are children around again."

"How's Peter, and Mike?"

"Both are doing well. When we returned to the human realm a few months back, Dad stayed behind to sell my house and finish a few things. He now lives here with us. Evie seems to be doing well too. I know she has found her soul mate, but she hasn't told me who it is yet."

"Well, it's late, and you have a big day tomorrow, time to go to bed." Rachel has taken it upon herself to make sure Aniya is not overdoing herself.

"Yeah, I am tired." Aniya yawns.

She makes her way toward her and the boys' room, looking around the castle the Fae helped build. It's a beautiful home and a place she is proud of. The tower still stands, and it is where the council, she, and the guys deal with realm matters. She wanted to keep the council so that everything doesn't fall on just her, Broden, and Brodrick. The Fae have all become more accepting of each other, and though they have had a few who tried to keep the old ways, they quickly deal with them.

Everything is running much smoother. There is still a lot of healing to do, but they take it one day at a time and they will continue to do it that way.

It's the day of the wedding, and Aniya is in a tent set in the courtyard, getting ready. Her bright red dress flows over her, and the train is almost out the tent flap.

"You look beautiful, Aniya," Camille tells her.

"The dress is the perfect color for you." Rachel finishes up the buttons on the back. A voice on the other side of the flap draws Aniya's attention.

"Come in!"

Peter enters the tent. "You look beautiful, sweetie."

"Thanks, Dad. I wish Mom was here."

"She is, granddaughter, even if you can't see her." Keyara enters with Max, behind Peter.

"Hello, Grandma and Grandpa," Aniya says.

Both Keyara and Max stop at the words she just said. They have waited a long time to hear those words.

"Oh, Aniya, thank you so much!" Keyara runs to hug her.

"That means so much to us." Max walks over and kisses Aniya's cheek.

"Are you ready, daughter?" Evie asks.

"I think so."

They all leave the tent and move to the aisle they had created between the chairs. Aniya can see all the chairs are filled and the courtyard is almost bursting with Fae. They invited the entire realm, and she shouldn't be surprised to see so many of their people. Some are even sitting on the roof of the castle to get a good look at the wedding. Before they continue the short walk to Broden and Brodrick, the train of the dress is picked up by Jon, Dan, Stan, and Bill. Sofie runs up in a little white dress to hand Aniya a bouquet of purple, blue, and gold flowers wrapped in lace at the stems. "Thank you, Sofie."

"Welcome, Aniya."

Oh, Iya, you're the beautiful girl now!

Yes, the most beautiful.

Cera and Sapphire move in front of her as escort while Peter and Max both take her arms.

"Thank you." Aniya smiles.

The reception that follows the wedding has every Fae in the realm dancing, laughing, and eating together. Aniya, Broden, and Brodrick are sitting at the head of a table in the courtyard. One of the guys hands her a glass of wine.

"No, thank you. We can't have any of that." She smiles.

"What do ye mean, lass?" Broden asks. "'Tis wine."

"We?" Brodrick lifts his brow.

"Yes, we can't have that right now." Aniya takes hold of one of their hands each and places it over her abdomen.

"Nay!"

"Truly, loving?"

"A babe?"

"A bairn?"

"Yes!" She nods her head.

"How long?"

"Three and a half months."

They both take turns kissing her, grins wide.

"Daughter, may I have but a moment with you?" Evie asks, not realizing she has interrupted a special moment between the three of them.

"Oh, sure. Is everything all right?" Aniya asks as she rises from her seat and begins walking with Evie.

"Yes, everything is fine. I know you know I have a soul mate. I told you when the time is right, I'd tell you who it is."

"Yeah, so who is it? Mike?" She smiles at Evie.

"No, daughter. Mike was not with us at the hospital after you were shot."

Aniya thinks a minute. Her father was the only other person with them. Realization hits Aniya. "It's Dad!" She gasps.

"Yes, it is Peter."

"Why didn't you tell me? I'm so happy." Aniya hugs Evie.

"Well, there was so much going on, and I wanted to make sure you all were okay first." Evie hugs her back, smiling.

"We get to plan another wedding!"

"I'm so glad you're happy."

"I'm beyond happy, and your grandchild will love you both so much."

Peter walks up behind Evie at that second. "Grandchild?"

"Our grandchild? Aniya, are you—"

"Yes! Three and a half months."

"What a wonderful day!"

"Hey, what did I miss this time?" Rachel walks up to them.

"What's happening?" Camille asks.

"Aniya's pregnant!" Evie shouts.

"Really?"

"Oh, Aniya, what great news." They all hug her at once.

Brodrick is watching his soul mate as he listens to her tell them the news of the babe and can't help but smile. He scans the courtyard and sees a wolf shifter watching Rachel.

"Ye are the one we saw in the winter season, are ye not?" He walks up and asks.

"I am."

"And yer name?"

"I'm Christian, alpha to the winter season wolf pack." He holds out his hand to Brodrick. "My king." He bows.

"Ye watch Rachel like prey." Brodrick shakes the shifter's hand.

"Not prey, she is my soul mate," Christian explains.

"Yer her soul mate? Ye are sure?"

"Yes."

"Ye will have yer work cut out for ye where that lass is concerned. Do try to talk and get to ken her first. She is special—ye will need to understand her background. So take yer time. We will be watching ye as weel," Brodrick tells him and walks back toward his brother and their soul mate. This is about to get even more interesting than it has been, Brodrick thinks to himself.

CPSIA information can be obtained
at www.ICGtesting.com
Printed in the USA
BVHW030319181120
593598BV00004BA/46